MASS
EFFECT
REVELATION

MASS EFFECT™
REVELATION

DREW KARPYSHYN

orbit

www.orbitbooks.net

ORBIT

First published in the United States in 2007 by Del Rey Books,
an imprint of The Random House Publishing Group
First published in Great Britain in 2007 by Orbit
Reprinted 2007, 2008, 2009 (twice), 2010, 2011

A CIP catalogue record for this book
is available from the British Library.

ISBN 978-1-84149-675-7

Printed in the UK by CPI Mackays, Chatham ME5 8TD

Papers used by Orbit are natural, renewable and
recyclable products sourced from well-managed forests and certified
in accordance with the rules of the Forest Stewardship Council.

Mixed Sources
Product group from well-managed
forests and other controlled sources
www.fsc.org Cert no. SGS-COC-004081
© 1996 Forest Stewardship Council

Orbit
An imprint of
Little, Brown Book Group
100 Victoria Embankment
London EC4Y 0DY

An Hachette UK Company
www.hachette.co.uk

www.orbitbooks.net

To my wife, Jennifer

While I'm in the throes of creative madness, you never nag me to do my laundry. You never get upset when I forget to wash the dishes, or get mad when I forget to help out around the house. You're always there to read and review everything I write, and you always listen as I rant about all my crazy hopes and fears, even when I wake you up in the middle of the night to do it.

It's all these things you do to help and support me that make you so special. And that's why I love you.

ACKNOWLEDGMENTS

Creating an intellectual property with the depth and scope of Mass Effect is an enormous undertaking that simply would not have been possible without the efforts of all my friends and coworkers at BioWare.

In particular I'd like to thank Casey Hudson and Preston Watamaniuk for helping to shape the overall vision of Mass Effect, and I'd like to make a special mention of all the writers at BioWare who have worked on the project: Chris L'Etoile (our resident technical expert and science guru), Luke Kristjansen, Mac Walters, Patrick Weekes, and Mike Laidlaw.

I also want to thank Keith Clayton, my editor at Del Rey, for all he's done to help make my novel the best it could possibly be in the face of some rather tight deadlines.

This book could not have happened without these contributions, and I appreciate everything that you all have done.

PROLOGUE

"Approaching Arcturus. Disengaging FTL drive core."

Rear Admiral Jon Grissom of the Alliance, the most famous man on Earth and its three fledgling interstellar colonies, glanced up briefly as the voice of the SSV *New Delhi*'s helmsman came over the shipboard intercom. A second later he felt the unmistakable deceleration surge as the vessel's mass effect field generators wound down and the *New Delhi* dropped from faster-than-light travel into speeds more acceptable to an Einsteinian universe.

The ghostly illumination of the familiar red-shifted universe spilled in through the cabin's tiny viewport, gradually cooling to more normal hues as they decelerated. Grissom hated the viewports; Alliance ships were purely instrument driven—they required no visual references of any kind. But all vessels were designed with several tiny ports and at least one main viewing window, typically on the bridge, as a concession to antiquated romantic ideals of space travel.

The Alliance worked hard to maintain these romantic ideals—they were good for recruitment. To people back on Earth, the unexplored vastness of space was still a wonder. Humanity's expansion across the stars was a glorious adventure of discovery, and the mysteries of the galaxy were just waiting to be revealed.

Grissom knew the truth was much more complex. He had seen firsthand just how beautifully cold the galaxy could be. It was both magnificent and terrifying, and he knew there were some things humanity was not yet ready to face. The classified transmission he had received that morning from the base at Shanxi was proof of that.

In many ways humanity was like a child: naïve and sheltered. Not that this was surprising. In the whole of humanity's long history it was only in the last two centuries that they had broken the bonds of Earth and ventured into the cold vacuum of space beyond. And true interstellar travel—the ability to journey to destinations beyond their own solar system—had only been made possible in the last decade. Less than a decade, in fact.

It was in 2148, a mere nine years ago, that the mining team on Mars had unearthed the remains of a long-abandoned alien research station deep beneath the planet's surface. It was heralded as the most significant discovery in human history, a singular event that changed everything forever.

For the first time, humanity was faced with indisputable, incontrovertible proof that they were not alone in the universe. Every media outlet across the world had jumped on the story. Who were these mysterious aliens? Where were they now? Were they extinct? Would they return? What impact did they have on humanity's past evolution? What impact would they have on humanity's future? In those first few months, philosophers, scientists, and self-appointed experts endlessly debated the significance of the discovery on the news vids and across the info nets, vehemently and sometimes even violently.

Every major religion on Earth was rocked to its core. Dozens of new belief systems sprang up overnight, most of them based on the tenets of the Interventionary Evolutionists, who zealously proclaimed the discovery as proof that all human history had been directed and controlled by alien forces. Many existing faiths tried to incorporate the reality of alien species into their existing mythologies, others scrambled to rewrite their history, creeds, and beliefs in light of the new discovery. A stubborn few refused to acknowledge the truth, proclaiming the Mars bunker a secular hoax intended to deceive and mislead believers from the true path. Even now, nearly a decade later, most religions were still trying to reassemble the pieces.

The intercom crackled again, interrupting Grissom's thoughts and drawing his focus away from the offending viewport and back to the shipboard speaker in the ceiling. "We are cleared for docking at Arcturus. ETA approximately twelve minutes."

It had taken them nearly six hours to travel from Earth to Arcturus, the largest Alliance base outside humanity's own solar system. Grissom had spent most of that time hunched over a data screen, looking through status reports and reviewing personnel files.

The journey had been planned months ago as a public relations event. The Alliance wanted Grissom to address the first class of recruits to graduate from the Academy at Arcturus, a symbolic passing of the torch from a legend of the past to the leaders of the future. But a few hours before they were about to depart, the message from Shanxi had radically altered the primary purpose of his trip.

The last decade had been a golden age for humanity, like some glorious dream. Now he was about to bring a grim reality crashing down on them.

The *New Delhi* was almost at its destination; it was time for him to leave the peace and solitude of the private cabin. He transferred the personnel files from the data terminal to a tiny optical storage disk, which he slipped into the breast pocket of his Alliance uniform. Then he logged off, pushing himself away from his chair and stiffly standing up.

His quarters were small and cramped, and the data station he'd been working at was far from comfortable. Space on Alliance vessels was limited, private cabins were typically reserved exclusively for the commanding officer of the ship. On most missions even VIPs were expected to use the common mess or the communal sleeping pods. But Grissom was a living legend, and for him exceptions could be made. In this case the captain had generously offered his own quarters for the relatively short trip to Arcturus.

Grissom stretched, trying to work the knots out of his neck and shoulders. The admiral rolled his head from side to side until he was rewarded with a satisfying crack of the vertebrae. He made a quick check of his uniform in the mirror—keeping up appearances was one of the burdens of fame—before stepping out the door to make his way to the bridge in the bow of the starship.

Various members of the crew paused in their duties to stand at attention and salute as he marched past their stations. He responded in kind, barely aware that he was doing so. In the eight years since he had become a hero of the human race, he'd developed an instinctive ability to acknowledge the gestures of respect and admiration without any conscious awareness.

Grissom's mind was still distracted with thoughts of how much everything had changed with the discovery of the alien bunker on Mars . . . a line of thinking that was not surprising given the unsettling reports from Shanxi.

The revelation that humanity was not alone in the universe hadn't just impacted Earth's religions, it had far-reaching effects across the political spectrum as well. But where religion had descended into the chaos of schisms and extremist splinter groups, politically the discovery had actually drawn humanity closer together. It had fundamentally united the inhabitants of Earth, the swift and sudden culmination of the pan-global cultural identity that had been slowly but steadily developing over the last century.

Within a year the charter for the human Systems Alliance—the first all-encompassing global coalition—had been written and ratified by Earth's eighteen largest nation-states. For the first time in recorded history the inhabitants of Earth began to see themselves as a single, collective group: human as opposed to alien.

The Systems Alliance Military—a force dedicated to the protection and defense of Earth and its citizens against non-Terran threats—was formed soon after, drawing resources, soldiers, and officers from nearly every military organization on the planet.

There were some who insisted the sudden unification of Earth's various governments into a single political entity had happened a little too quickly and conveniently. The info nets were swarming with theories claiming the Mars bunker had actually been discovered long before it was publicly announced; the report of the mining team unearthing it was just a well-timed cover story. The formation of the Alliance, they asserted, was in fact the final stage of a long and complicated series of secret international treaties and clandestine backroom deals that had taken years or even decades to negotiate.

Public opinion generally dismissed such talk as conspiracy theory paranoia. Most people preferred the idealistic notion that the revelation was a catalyst that energized the governments and citizens of the world, driving them boldly forward into a brave new age of cooperation and mutual respect.

Grissom was too jaded to fully buy into that fantasy. Privately, he couldn't help but wonder if the politicians had known more than they publicly admitted. Even now he wondered if the communications drone carrying the distress call from Shanxi had caught them by surprise. Or had they been expecting something like this even before the Alliance was formed?

As he neared the bridge, he pushed all thoughts of alien research stations and shady conspiracies from his head. He was a practical man. The details behind the discovery of the bunker and the formation of the Alliance didn't really matter to him. The Alliance was sworn to protect and defend humanity throughout the stars, and everyone, including Grissom, had to play their part.

Captain Eisennhorn, commanding officer of the *New Delhi*, gazed out through the large viewport built into the foredeck of the ship. What he saw there sent a shiver of wonder down his spine.

Outside the window, the massive Arcturus space station grew steadily larger as the *New Delhi* approached. The Alliance fleet—nearly two hundred vessels ranging from twenty-man destroyers to dreadnoughts with crews of several hundred—stretched out from it in all directions, surrounding the station like an ocean of steel. The entire scene was illuminated by the orange glow emanating from the type-K red giant far in the distance: Arcturus, the system's sun for which the base had been named. The ships reflected the star's fiery glow, gleaming as if they burned with the flames of truth and triumph.

Though Eisennhorn had been witness to this grand spectacle dozens of times, it never ceased to amaze him—a dazzling reminder of how far they had come in such a short time. The discovery on Mars had elevated humanity, binding them together with a new sense of singular purpose as top experts from every field had united their resources in one glorious project—an attempt to unravel the technological mysteries stored inside the alien bunker.

Almost immediately it had become apparent that the Protheans—the name given to the unknown alien species—had been far more technologically advanced than humanity . . . and that they had vanished long,

long ago. Most estimates placed the find at nearly fifty thousand years old, predating the evolution of modern man. However, the Protheans had built the station from materials unlike anything found naturally on Earth, and even the passing of fifty millennia had done little to damage the valuable treasures inside.

Most remarkable were the data files the Protheans had left behind: millions of tetrabytes worth of knowledge—still viable, though compiled in a strange and unfamiliar language. Deciphering the contents of those data files became the holy grail of virtually every scientist on Earth. It took months of round-the-clock study, but eventually the code of the Prothean language was broken and the pieces began to fall into place.

For conspiracy theorists this was seen as fuel for their fire. It should have taken years, they argued, for anything useful to come out of the bunker. But their negativity went unheard or unheeded by most, left behind in the wake of spectacular scientific advances.

It was as if a dam had ruptured and a cascade of knowledge and discovery had been unleashed to flood the human psyche. Research that previously took decades to achieve results now seemed to require mere months. Through the adaptation of Prothean technology humanity was able to develop mass effect fields, enabling faster-than-light travel; no longer were vessels bound by the harsh and unforgiving limits of the space-time continuum. Similar leaps followed in other areas: clean and efficient new energy sources; ecological and environmental advances; terraforming.

Within a year the inhabitants of Earth began a rapid spread throughout the solar system. Ready access to resources from the other planets, moons, and asteroids allowed colonies to be established on orbiting space stations. Massive terraforming projects began to transform the lifeless surface of Earth's own moon into a habitable environment. And Eisennhorn, like most people, didn't care to listen to those who stubbornly claimed humanity's new Golden Age was a carefully orchestrated sham that had actually begun decades earlier.

"Officer on deck!" one of the crewmen barked out.

The sound of the entire bridge staff standing to salute the new arrival told Captain Eisennhorn who it was even before he turned around. Admiral Jon Grissom was a man who commanded respect. Serious and stern, there was a gravity about him, an undeniable *significance* in his mere presence.

"I'm surprised you're here," Eisennhorn said under his breath, turning back to gaze once more at the scene outside the window as Grissom crossed the bridge and took up position beside him. They'd known each other for nearly twenty years, having met as raw recruits during basic training with the U.S. Marine Corps before the Alliance even existed. "Aren't you the one who's always saying the viewports are a tactical weakness on Alliance ships?" Eisennhorn added.

"Have to do my part for the morale of the crew," Grissom whispered back. "Figured I could help reinforce the glory of the Alliance if I came up here and stared out at the fleet all wistful and misty-eyed like you."

"Tact is the art of making a point without making an enemy," Eisennhorn admonished him. "Sir Isaac Newton said that."

"I don't have any enemies," Grissom muttered. "I'm a goddamned hero, remember?"

Eisennhorn considered Grissom a friend, but that didn't change the fact that he was a difficult man to like. Professionally the admiral projected the perfect image for an Alliance officer: smart, tough, and demanding. On duty, he carried himself with an air of fierce purpose, unshakable confidence, and absolute authority that inspired loyalty and devotion in his troops. On a personal level, however, he could be moody and sullen. Things had only gotten worse once he'd been so visibly thrust into the public eye as an icon representing the entire Alliance. Years of being in the spotlight had seemingly transformed his harsh pragmatism into cynical pessimism.

Eisennhorn had expected him to be sour on this trip—the admiral was never a fan of these kinds of public performances. But Grissom's mood had been particularly dark even for him, and the captain was beginning to wonder if there was something more going on.

"You're not just here to speak to the graduating class, are you?" Eisennhorn asked, keeping his voice low.

"Need to know basis," Grissom said curtly, just loud enough for the captain to hear. "You don't need to know." After a second he added, "You don't want to know."

The two officers shared a minute of silence, simply staring out the viewport at the approaching station.

"Admit it," Eisennhorn said, hoping to dispel the other man's bleak humor. "Seeing Arcturus surrounded by the entire Alliance fleet . . . it's an impressive sight."

"The fleet won't look so impressive once it's spread out across a few dozen star systems," Grissom countered. "Our numbers are too small, and the galaxy's too damn big."

Eisennhorn had to admit that Grissom was probably more aware of that than anyone.

The technology of the Protheans had catapulted human society forward hundreds of years and allowed them to conquer the solar system. But it had required an even more amazing discovery to open up the vastness of space beyond their own sun.

In 2149 a research team exploring the farthest fringes of human expansion realized that Charon, a small satellite orbiting Pluto, wasn't really a moon at all. It was actually an enormous piece of dormant Prothean technology. A *mass relay*. Floating for tens of thousands of years in the cold depths of space, it had become encased in a shell of ice and frozen debris several hundred kilometers thick.

The experts back on Earth weren't completely unprepared for this particular revelation; the existence and purpose of mass relays had been mentioned in the data archives recovered from the Mars bunker. In simplest terms, the mass relays were a network of linked gates that could transport a ship from one relay to the next, instantaneously traversing thousands of light-years. The underlying scientific theory behind the creation of mass relays was still beyond the scope of humanity's top experts. But even though they couldn't construct one themselves, scientists were able to reactivate the dormant relay they had stumbled across.

The mass relay was a door that could open up the entire galaxy . . . or lead right into the heart of a burning star or black hole. Exploratory probes sent through immediately dropped out of contact—not unexpectedly, considering the notion that they were being instantly transported thousands of light-years away. In the end, the only way to truly know what was on the other side was to send somebody through; someone willing to brave the great unknown and face whatever dangers and challenges waited on the other side.

The Alliance handpicked a crew of brave men and women: soldiers willing to risk their own lives, individuals ready to make the ultimate sacrifice in the name of discovery and progress. And to lead this crew they chose a man of unique character and unquestioned strength, one they knew would not falter in the face of untold adversity. A man named Jon Grissom.

Upon their successful return through the mass relay, the entire crew had been hailed as heroes. But the media had chosen Grissom—the imposing, solemn commander of the mission—to become the flagbearer of the Alliance as humanity forged ahead into a new age of unparalleled discovery and expansion.

"Whatever's happened," Eisennhorn said, still hoping he could pull Grissom from his dark state of mind, "you have to believe we can deal with it. You and I never could have imagined that we could accomplish all this in such a short time!"

Grissom gave a snort of derision. "We couldn't have done a damn thing if it wasn't for the Protheans."

Eisennhorn shook his head. While it had been the discovery and adaptation of Prothean technology that had opened up these great possibilities, it was the actions of people like Grissom that had transformed possibility into reality.

"If I have seen farther, it is by standing on the shoulders of giants," Eisennhorn countered. "Sir Isaac Newton said that, too."

"Why the obsession with Newton? He a relative or something?"

"Actually, my grandfather was tracing our family's genealogy and he—"

"I didn't really want to know," Grissom growled, cutting him off.

They were almost at their destination. The Arcturus space station dominated the entire window now, blocking out everything else. The docking bay loomed before them, a gaping hole in the gleaming hull of the station's exterior.

"I should go," Grissom said with a weary sigh. "They'll want to see me come marching down the gangway as soon as we touch down."

"Take it easy on those recruits," Eisennhorn suggested, only half joking. "Remember, they're barely more than kids."

"I didn't come here to meet with a bunch of kids," Grissom replied. "I came here looking for soldiers."

The first thing Grissom did when he arrived was request a private room. He was scheduled to address the entire graduating class at 14:00. In the four hours between then and now he planned to conduct private interviews with a handful of the recruits.

The brass at Arcturus weren't expecting his request, but they did their best to accommodate it. They set him up in a small room furnished with a desk, computer workstation, and a single chair. Grissom was sitting behind the desk reviewing the personnel files on the monitor one last time. Competition to be accepted into the N7 specialist training program at Arcturus was fierce. Every recruit on the station had been handpicked from the best young men and women the Alliance had to offer. Yet the handful of names on Grissom's list had distinguished themselves from the rest of the elite; even here they stood out from the crowd.

There was a knock at the door—two quick, firm raps.

"Come in," the admiral called out.

The door slid open and Second Lieutenant David Edward Anderson, the first name on Grissom's list, walked in. Fresh out of training, he had already been marked for the ranks of junior officers, and looking at his file it was easy to see why. Grissom's list was arranged alphabetically, but based on Anderson's marks at the Academy and the evaluations of his training officers, his name would probably have been right at the top regardless.

The lieutenant was a tall man, six foot three according to his file. At twenty years old he was just starting to fill out his large frame, still growing into his broad chest and wide, square shoulders. His skin was dark brown, his black hair cut high and tight in accordance with Alliance regulations. His features, like most citizens in the multicultural society of the late twenty-second century, were a mix of several different racial characteristics. Predominantly African, but Grissom thought he could see lingering traces of Central European and Native American ancestry as well.

Anderson marched smartly across the floor and stopped directly in front of the desk, standing at attention as he snapped off a formal salute.

"At ease, Lieutenant," Grissom ordered, instinctively returning the salute.

The young man did as he was told, relaxing his stance so that he stood with his arms clasped behind his back and his legs spread wide.

"Sir?" he asked. "If I may?" Even though he was a junior officer making a request of a rear admiral he spoke with confidence; there was no hesitation in his voice.

Grissom scowled before nodding at him to continue. The file showed Anderson had been born and raised in London, but he had almost no discernible regional accent. His generic dialect was likely the product of cross-cultural exposure through e-schooling and the info nets combined with a steady barrage of pan-global entertainment vids and music.

"I just want to tell you what an honor it is meeting you in person, Admiral," the young man informed him. He wasn't gushing or fawning, for which Grissom was grateful; he simply stated it as a matter of fact. "I remember seeing you on the news after the Charon expedition when I was only twelve. That's when I decided I wanted to join the Alliance."

"Are you trying to make me feel old, son?"

Anderson started to smile, thinking it was a joke. But the smile withered under Grissom's glare.

"No, sir," he replied, his voice still sure and strong. "I only meant you're an inspiration to us all."

He'd expected the lieutenant to stutter and stammer out some kind of apology, but Anderson wasn't so easily rattled. Grissom made a quick note in his file.

"I see it says here you're married, Lieutenant."

"Yes, sir. She's a civilian. Lives back on Earth."

"I was married to a civilian," Grissom told him. "We had a daughter. I haven't seen her in twelve years."

Anderson was momentarily thrown off balance by the unexpected personal disclosure. "I . . . I'm sorry, sir."

"It's hell keeping a marriage together when you're in the service," Grissom warned him. "You don't think worrying about a wife back on Earth is going to make it harder when you're out on a six-month tour?"

"Might make it easier, sir," Anderson countered. "It's nice to know I've got someone back home waiting for me."

There was no hint of anger in the young man's voice, but it was clear he wasn't going to be intimidated, even when speaking to a rear admiral. Grissom nodded and made another note in the file.

"Do you know why I scheduled this meeting, Lieutenant?" he asked.

After a moment of serious consideration Anderson simply shook his head. "No, sir."

"Twelve days ago an expedition fleet left our outpost at Shanxi. They were heading through the Shanxi-Theta mass relay into an uncharted region of space: two cargo vessels and three frigates.

"They made contact with an alien species out there. Some kind of patrol fleet, we think. Only one of our frigates made it back."

Grissom had just dropped a bombshell in the young man's lap, but Anderson's expression barely changed. His only reaction was a momentary widening of his eyes.

"Protheans, sir?" he asked, driving right to the heart of the matter.

"We don't think so," Grissom told him. "Technologically, they seem to be on about the same level as us."

"How do we know that, sir?"

"Because the ships Shanxi sent out to engage them the next day had enough firepower to wipe out their whole patrol."

Anderson gasped, then took a deep breath to collect himself. Grissom didn't blame him; so far he'd been impressed with how well the lieutenant had handled the whole situation.

"Any further retaliation from the aliens, sir?"

The kid was smart. His mind worked quickly, analyzing the situation and moving forward to the relevant questions after only a few seconds.

"They sent reinforcements," Grissom informed him. "They captured Shanxi. We don't have any other details yet. Comm satellites are down; we only got word because someone got off a message drone just before Shanxi fell."

Anderson nodded to show he understood, but he didn't say anything right away. Grissom was glad to see the young man had the patience to give himself time to process the information. It was a lot to wrap one's head around.

"You're sending us into action, aren't you, sir?"

"Alliance Command makes that decision," Grissom said. "All I can do is advise them. That's why I'm here."

"I'm afraid I don't understand, Admiral."

"Every military engagement has only three options, Lieutenant: engage, retreat, or surrender."

"We can't just turn our backs on Shanxi! We have to engage!" Anderson exclaimed. "With all due respect, sir," he added a second later, remembering who he was talking to.

"It's not that simple," Grissom explained. "This is completely unprecedented; we've never faced an enemy like this before. We know nothing about them.

"If we escalate this into a war against an alien species, we have no way to predict how it will end. They could have a fleet a thousand times the size of ours.

"We could be on the verge of starting a war that will culminate in the total annihilation of the human race." Grissom paused for emphasis, letting his words sink in. "Do you honestly think we should take that risk, Lieutenant Anderson?"

"You're asking me, sir?"

"Alliance Command wants my advice before they make their decision. But I'm not going to be on the front lines fighting the war, Lieutenant. You were a squad leader during your N7 training. I want to know what you think. Do you believe our troops are ready for this?"

Anderson frowned, thinking long and hard before he offered his answer.

"Sir, I don't think we have any other choice," he said, choosing his words carefully. "Retreat isn't an option. Now that the aliens know about us they aren't just going to sit at Shanxi and do nothing. Eventually we'll have to either engage or surrender."

"And you don't think surrender is an option?"

"I don't think humanity could survive being subjugated under alien rule," Anderson replied. "Freedom is worth fighting for."

"Even if we lose?" Grissom pressed. "This isn't just about what *you're* willing to sacrifice, soldier. We provoke them and this war could make its way to Earth. Think about your wife. Are you willing to risk *her* life for the sake of freedom?"

"I don't know, sir" was Anderson's solemn reply. "Are you willing to condemn your daughter to the life of a slave?"

"That's the answer I was looking for," Grissom said with a sharp nod. "With enough soldiers like you, Anderson, humanity just might be ready for this after all."

ONE

Eight Years Later

Staff Lieutenant David Anderson, executive officer on the SSV *Hastings*, rolled out of his bunk at the first sound of the alarm. His body moved instinctively, conditioned by years of active service aboard Systems Alliance Space Vessels. By the time his feet hit the floor he was already awake and alert, his mind evaluating the situation.

The alarm rang again, echoing off the hull to rebound throughout the ship. Two short blasts, repeating over and over. A general call to stations. At least they weren't under immediate attack.

As he pulled his uniform on, Anderson ran through the possible scenarios. The *Hastings* was a patrol vessel in the Skyllian Verge, an isolated region on the farthest fringes of Alliance space. Their primary purpose was to protect the dozens of human colonies and research outposts scattered across the sector. A general call to stations probably meant they'd spotted an unauthorized vessel in Alliance territory. Either that or they were responding to a distress call. Anderson hoped it was the former.

It wasn't easy getting dressed in the tight confines of the sleeping quarters he shared with two other crewmen, but he'd had lots of practice. In less than a minute he had his uniform on, his boots secured, and was moving quickly through the narrow corridors toward the bridge, where Captain Belliard would be waiting for him. As the executive officer it fell to Anderson to relay the captain's orders to the enlisted crew . . . and to make sure those orders were properly carried out.

Space was the most precious resource on any military vessel, and Anderson was constantly reminded of this as he encountered other crewmen heading in the opposite direction as they rushed to their assigned posts. Invariably, they would press themselves against the corridor walls in an effort to let Anderson by, snapping off awkward salutes to their superior as he squeezed past them. But despite the cramped conditions, the entire process was carried out with an efficiency and crisp precision that was the hallmark of every crew in the Alliance fleet.

Anderson was almost at his destination. He was passing navigation, where he noticed a pair of junior officers making rapid calculations and applying them to a three-dimensional star chart projected above their consoles. They each gave their XO a curt but respectful nod as he passed, too engrossed in their duties to be encumbered by the formality of a true salute. Anderson responded with a grim tilt of his head. He could see they were plotting a route through the nearest mass relay. That meant the *Hastings* was responding to a distress call. And the brutal truth was that more often than not their response came too late.

In the years following the First Contact War, humanity had spread out too far and too fast; they didn't have enough ships to properly patrol a region the size of the Verge. Settlers who lived out here knew the threat of attacks and raids was all too real, and too often the *Hastings* touched down on a world only to find a small but thriving colony reduced to corpses, burned-out buildings, and a handful of shell-shocked survivors.

Anderson still hadn't found a good way to cope with being a firsthand witness to that kind of death and destruction. He'd seen action during the war, but this was different. That had been primarily ship-to-ship warfare, killing enemy combatants from tens of thousands of kilometers away. It wasn't the same as picking through the charred rubble and blackened bodies of civilians.

The First Contact War, despite its name, had been a short and relatively bloodless campaign. It began an Alliance patrol inadvertently trespassed on the territory of the Turian Empire. For humanity it had been their first encounter with another intelligent species; for the turians it was an invasion by an aggressive and previously unknown race. Misunderstanding and overreaction on both sides had led to several intense battles between patrols and scout fleets. But the conflict never erupted into full-scale planetary war. The escalating hostilities and sudden deployment of turian fleets had drawn the attention of the greater galactic community. Luckily for humanity.

It turned out the turians were only one species among a dozen, each independent but voluntarily united beneath the rule of a governing body known as the Citadel Council. Eager to prevent interstellar war with the newly emerged humans, the Council had intervened, revealing itself to the Alliance and brokering a peaceful resolution between them and the turians. Less than two months after it had begun, the First Contact War was officially over.

Six hundred and twenty-three human lives had been lost. Most of the casualties were sustained in the first encounter and during the turian attack on Shanxi. Turian losses were slightly higher; the Alliance fleet sent to liberate the captured outpost had been ruthless, brutal, and very thorough. But on a galactic scale, the losses to both sides were minor. Humanity had been pulled back from the brink of a potentially devastating war, and instead became the newest member of a vast interstellar, pan-species society.

Anderson climbed the three steps separating the forward deck of the bridge from the main level of the ship. Captain Belliard was hunched over a small viewscreen, studying a stream of incoming transmissions. He stood up straight as Anderson approached, and returned his executive officer's salute with one of his own.

"We've got trouble, Lieutenant. We picked up a distress call when we linked up to the com relays," the captain explained by way of greeting.

"I was afraid of that, sir."

"It came from Sidon."

"Sidon?" Anderson recognized the name. "Don't we have a research base there?"

Belliard nodded. "A small one. Fifteen security personnel, twelve researchers, six support staff."

Anderson frowned. This was no ordinary attack. Raiders preferred to hit defenseless settlements and bug out before Alliance reinforcements arrived on the scene. A well-defended base like Sidon wasn't their typical target. It felt more like an act of war.

The turians were allies of the Human Systems Alliance now, at least officially. And the Skyllian Verge was too far removed from turian territory for them to get involved in any conflicts out here. But there were other species vying with humanity for control of the region. The Alliance was in direct competition with the batarian government to establish a presence in the Verge, but so far the two rival species had managed to avoid any real violence in their confrontations. Anderson doubted they'd start with something like this.

Still, there were plenty of other groups out there with the means and motive to hit an Alliance stronghold. Some of them were even made up of humans: nonaffiliated terrorist organizations and multispecies guerrilla factions eager to strike a blow against the powers-that-be; illegal paramilitary troops looking to stock up on high-grade weapons; independent mercenary bands hoping for one big score.

"Might be helpful to know what Sidon was working on, Captain," Anderson suggested.

"They're a top-security-clearance facility," the captain replied with a shake of his head. "I can't even get schematics for the base, never mind get anyone to tell me what they were working on."

Anderson frowned. Without schematics his team would be going in blind, giving up any tactical advantage they might have had from knowing the layout of the battleground. This mission just kept getting better and better.

"What's our ETA, sir?"

"Forty-six minutes."

Finally some good news. The *Hastings* followed random patrol routes; it was pure chance they happened to be this close to the source of the distress call. With luck they could still get there in time.

"I'll have the ground team ready, Captain."

"You always do, Lieutenant."

Anderson turned to go, acknowledging his commanding officer's compliment with a simple, "Aye-aye, sir!"

In the black void of space the *Hastings* was all but invisible to the naked eye. Surrounded by a self-generated mass effect field and traveling nearly fifty times faster than the speed of light, it was little more than a flickering blur, a slight wavering in the fabric of the space-time continuum.

The vessel altered its flight path as the helmsman made a quick course correction, a minor adjustment to the trajectory that sent the ship hurtling toward the nearest mass relay, nearly five billion kilometers away. At a speed of nearly fifteen million kilometers per second it didn't take long before their destination was in range.

Ten thousand kilometers out from their target, the helmsman took the element-zero drive core off-line, disengaging the mass effect fields. Blue-shifted energy waves radiated off the ship as it dropped out of FTL, igniting the darkness of space like a flare. The illumination of the blazing ship reflected off the mass relay growing steadily larger on the horizon. Although completely alien in design, the construction closely resembled an enormous gyroscope. At its center was a sphere made up of two concentric rings spinning around a single axis. Each ring was nearly five kilometers across, and two fifteen-kilometer arms protruded out from one end of the constantly rotating middle. The entire structure sparkled and flashed with white bursts of crackling energy.

At a signal from the Alliance vessel the mass relay began to move. It turned ponderously on its axis, orienting itself with a linked relay hundreds of light-years away. The *Hastings* picked up speed as it headed straight for the center of the enormous alien construct on a precalculated approach vector. The rings at the relay's heart began to spin faster, accelerating until they were nothing but a whirling blur. The sporadic bursts of energy emanating from its core became a solid, pulsing glow, growing in strength and intensity until it was almost impossible to look at.

The *Hastings* was less than five hundred kilometers away when the relay fired. A discharge of dark energy swept out from the spinning rings like a wave, engulfing the ship. It shimmered momentarily, then disappeared as if snuffed out of existence. Instantaneously it winked back into reality a thousand light-years from its previous location, emerging from apparent nothingness with a bright blue flash in the vicinity of a completely different mass relay.

The drive core of the *Hastings* roared to life and it jumped to FTL, vanishing into the darkness with a red-shifted burst of heat and radiation. Rapidly left behind, the receiving relay began to power down, the rings at its center already decelerating.

"We've cleared the mass relay. Engaging drive core. ETA to Sidon twenty-six minutes."

Huddled in the cargo hold with the other four members of the ground team, it was almost impossible to hear the sound of the voice coming over the shipboard intercom above the roaring of the engines. Not that Anderson needed to hear the updates to know what was happening. His stomach was still churning from the jump through the mass relay.

Scientifically, he knew the motion sickness shouldn't happen. Travel between relays—the jump from an originating, or transmitting, relay to the destination, or receiving, relay—was an instantaneous event. It took no time to occur; therefore, it couldn't possibly have any physical effect on his body. But while he acknowledged this theoretical fact, Anderson knew from firsthand experience that it wasn't true in practice.

Maybe this time the tightness in his gut was just a bad feeling about what they'd find when they reached the Sidon facility. Whoever had attacked the research base had been willing to take on fifteen Alliance marines. Even using the element of surprise to their advantage, they must have been a formidable force. The Alliance should be sending a troop transport in as reinforcements, not a patrol frigate that could only assemble a five-person ground team.

But nobody else was close enough to answer the distress call in time, and most Alliance vessels were too big to go planet side anyway. The *Hastings* was small enough to enter a world's atmosphere and touch down on its surface, and still be able to take off again. Anything bigger than a frigate would have to ferry troops down using shuttles or drop ships, and they didn't have time for that.

At least they were going in heavy. Every member of the ground team was wearing body armor equipped with fully charged kinetic shield generators, as well as three-quarters visored headgear. They each carried half a dozen grenades and the Alliance's standard issue Hahne-Kedar G-912 assault rifle. The ammo clip on each weapon held over four thousand rounds; miniature pellets smaller than grains of sand. When fired at sufficient velocity, the nearly microscopic projectiles were capable of inflicting massive damage.

That was the real problem. No matter how advanced defensive technology got, it was always a step behind. The Alliance spared no expense when it came to protecting its soldiers: their body armor was top of the line and their kinetic shields were the latest military prototype. But it still wasn't enough to withstand a direct hit from close range with heavy weapons.

If they were going to survive this mission, it wasn't going to be because of their equipment. It always came down to two things: training and leadership. Their lives were in Anderson's hands now, and he could sense their unease. Alliance marines were well trained to deal with the mental and physical stress of the human body's natural fight-or-flight instincts. But this was more than the normal adrenaline rush of impending combat.

He'd been careful not to expose his own doubts; he'd projected an image of absolute confidence and composure. But the members of his team were smart enough to figure things out on their own. They could put the pieces together, just as he had. Like the lieutenant, they knew ordinary raiders wouldn't attack a heavily defended Alliance base.

Anderson didn't believe in giving motivational speeches; they were all professionals here. But even for Alliance soldiers, those last nervous minutes before a mission were harder to endure in total silence. Besides, there was no sense hiding from the truth.

"Everyone stay sharp," he said, knowing the rest of the team could hear him clearly over the rumbling of the engines through the radios inside their helmets. "I get the feeling this wasn't just some slavers pulling a quick grab and run."

"Batarians, sir?"

The question came from Gunnery Chief Jill Dah. A year older than Anderson, she'd already been an Alliance marine on active duty back when he was still taking N7 training at Arcturus. They'd served in the same unit during the First Contact War. She stood just over six foot three, making her taller than most of the men she served with. She was stronger than a lot of them, too, judging by her wide shoulders, the well-defined muscles of her arms, and her generally large but not ill-proportioned frame. Some of the other soldiers in the unit had called her "Amy," short for Amazon . . . but never to her face. And when the fighting started they were all glad to have her on their side.

Anderson liked Dah, but she had a habit of rubbing people the wrong way. She didn't believe in diplomacy. If she had an opinion she let everybody know it, which probably explained why she was still a noncommissioned officer. Still, the lieutenant realized that if she asked a question it meant most of the others were probably wondering the exact same thing.

"Let's not jump to any conclusions, Chief."

"Any idea what they were working on over at Sidon?" This time it was Corporal Ahmed O'Reilly, technicians expert, asking the question.

"Classified. That's all I know. So be ready for anything."

The other two members of the team, Private Second Class Indigo Lee and PFC Dan Shay, didn't bother to comment, and the team lapsed once more into an uneasy silence. Nobody felt good about this mission, but Anderson knew they'd follow his lead. He'd brought them through the fire enough times to earn their trust.

"Approaching Sidon," the intercom crackled. "No response on any frequencies."

That was grim news. If any Alliance personnel were still alive inside the base, they should have answered the *Hastings*'s call. Anderson slammed his visor down to shield his face, and the rest of the crew followed suit. A minute later they felt the turbulence as the ship entered the tiny planet's atmosphere. At a nod from Anderson his team made a final weapons, com, and shields check.

"We have a visual of the base," the intercom crackled. "No ships on the ground and we're not picking up any non-Alliance vessels in the vicinity."

"Damn cowards already cut and ran," Anderson heard Dah mutter over the radio in his helmet.

With the *Hastings*'s quick response time, Anderson had been hoping they'd arrive to catch the enemy in the act, but he wasn't really surprised there were no other ships in the area. A raid against a target as well defended as Sidon would have required at least three vessels working together. The two larger ships would land on the surface and unload assault teams while a small scout vessel would stay in orbit, monitoring the nearby mass relay for any signs of activity.

The scout must have seen it spring to life as the *Hastings* approached the connecting relay on the far side of the region and radioed the ships on the ground. The advance warning would have given them just enough time to lift off, clear the planet's atmosphere, and engage their FTL drives before the *Hastings* arrived. The ships involved in the attack on the base were long gone . . . but in their hurried escape they might have been forced to leave some of their troops behind.

A few seconds later there was a heavy thump as the ship touched down at the landing port of the Sidon Research Facility; the interminable waiting was over. The pressure door of the *Hastings*'s cargo hold hissed open and the gangway ramp descended.

"Ground team," came Captain Belliard's voice over the intercom, "you are cleared for go."

TWO

Gunnery Chief Dah and Lee, the two marines on point, scuttled down the gangway. Weapons drawn, they scanned the area for a possible ambush while Anderson, O'Reilly, and Shay covered them from the hold above.

"Landing zone secured," Dah reported across the radio frequency.

Once the entire team was on the ground Anderson took stock of the situation. The landing port was small—room for three frigates, or maybe a pair of cargo ships. It was located a few hundred meters from a pair of heavy blast doors that led into the structure of the base itself: a rectangular single-story building that barely looked large enough to house the thirty-three people assigned to the project, let alone any kind of labs for research.

The exterior looked eerily normal; there was no hint that anything was out of the ordinary other than a half dozen large crates near one of the other landing pads.

That's how the attack began, Anderson thought to himself. Equipment and supplies coming in would have been ferried by hand from arriving ships on cargo sleds up to the doors. Sidon must have been expecting a shipment. When the raiders touched down they would have begun unloading the crates. Someone inside would have opened the blast doors and two or three of Sidon's security detail would have come out to help with the cargo . . . and been gunned down by enemy troops hiding inside the holds of the ships.

"Strange there are no bodies out here," Dah noted, echoing Anderson's own thoughts.

"Must have dragged them away after they secured the landing port," Anderson said, not certain why anyone would want to do that.

Using hand signals he motioned his team across the deserted landing port and up to the entrance of the base. The sliding blast doors were featureless and smooth—they were controlled by a simple security panel on the wall. But the fact that the doors were closed didn't sit well with the lieutenant.

Anderson was at the head of the team; they all stopped short when he crouched down and held up a raised fist. He held up two fingers, signaling for O'Reilly. Hunched over, the corporal moved to the head of the line and fell in beside his leader, resting on one knee.

"Any reason those doors should be closed?" the lieutenant asked him in a sharp whisper.

"Seems a little weird," he admitted. "If someone wanted to wipe out the base, why bother sealing the doors when you leave?"

"Check it out," Anderson told his tech expert. "Take it slow and careful."

O'Reilly hit a button on his assault rifle, causing

the handle, stock, and barrel to fold in on themselves until the gun was a compact rectangle half its normal length. He slapped the collapsed weapon into the locking holster on his hip. From a pocket on his other leg he pulled out an omnitool and crept forward, using it to scan the area for faint signals that would indicate the presence of any unusual electronics.

"Nice catch, LT," he muttered after checking the results. "Proximity mine wired to the door."

The corporal made a few adjustments to the omnitool, emitting a short energy pulse to jam the sensors on the mine so he could creep forward close enough to disarm it. The entire process took less than a minute. Anderson held his breath the whole time, only releasing it when O'Reilly turned and gave him the thumbs-up to indicate that the trap had been rendered harmless.

A nod from Anderson sent the rest of the team rushing forward to breach the door, taking up their preassigned positions. Anderson and Shay moved to either side of the entrance, backs pressed against the exterior wall of the building. Chief Dah crouched low in line with the door, a few meters away. Behind her and slightly off to the side Lee had his assault rifle raised and pointed at the entrance, providing Dah's cover.

O'Reilly, crouched down beside Anderson, reached up and punched in the access code on the panel. As the doors slid open, Dah tossed a flash-bang grenade from her belt into the foyer beyond, then dove to the side and rolled for cover. Lee did the same as the grenade detonated with a blinding flash of light and a fog of thin, wispy smoke.

An instant after the blast Anderson and Shay spun in through the door, rifles raised and ready to gun down any enemies inside. It was a classic flash-and-clear maneuver, executed with flawless precision. But the room beyond the door was empty, save for a few splatters of blood on the floor and walls.

"All clear," Anderson said, and the rest of the team came in to join him. The entry was a plain room with a single hallway leading off the back wall deeper into the base. There was a small table flipped in the corner and several overturned chairs. A monitor on the wall showed an image of the landing port outside.

"Guard post," Dah said, the evidence confirming for her what Anderson had suspected earlier. "Probably four of them stationed here to keep an eye on the space port. Must've opened the blast doors when the ships landed and went out to help them unload their cargo."

"I've got blood smears heading down this hallway, Lieutenant," Private Indigo called out. "Looks like the bodies were dragged out of this room and back into the facility."

Anderson still couldn't figure out why anyone would drag the bodies away like this, but at least it gave them a clear trail. The ground team slowly made their way deeper into the base, following the smears of blood. The trail took them through to the cafeteria, where they saw more overturned tables and chairs, as well as holes in the walls and ceiling—clear indication that the room had recently been witness to a brief but intense firefight.

Further in they passed two separate dormitory wings. The door to each individual room had been kicked open and the interiors, like the cafeteria, were riddled with bullet holes. A picture formed in Anderson's mind: the attackers, once inside, systematically going from room to room, massacring everyone in a hail of gunfire . . . and then dragging the bodies away with them.

By the time they reached the back of the building they had yet to see any sign that enemy troops were still here. They did, however, make a separate discovery that none of them had been expecting. At the very rear of the facility was a single large elevator going straight down into the earth below.

"No wonder this base looks so small," O'Reilly exclaimed. "All the good stuff is buried underground!

"Damn, I wish we knew what they were working on," he muttered a moment later in a more somber tone. "God knows what we're about to walk into."

Anderson agreed, but he was concerned with a more immediate detail. According to the panel on the side of the wall, the elevator was down at the bottom level. If someone had gone into the lower floors of the base only to flee when they got word the *Hastings* was coming, the elevator should have been on the top floor.

"Something wrong, LT?" Dah asked.

"Somebody took that elevator down," he said, tilting his head in the direction of the panel. "But they never took it back up."

"You think they're still down there?" the gunnery chief asked, her tone making it clear she hoped they were.

The lieutenant nodded, the hint of a grim smile on his lips.

"So what happened to their ships?" Private Shay asked, still not piecing it all together.

"Whoever attacked this base came for something," Anderson explained. "Whatever they were looking for wasn't up here. They must have sent a team down to the lower levels to finish up the job. Probably only left a few men up here to keep an eye on things.

"But they weren't counting on an Alliance patrol ship being close enough to respond to the distress call so quickly. When their scout ship sent word someone was coming through the mass relay they knew they had about twenty minutes to pick up and clear out. I bet they never even bothered to tell their buddies down below."

"What? Why not? Why wouldn't they tell them?"

"These elevators might go down two full kilometers," Corporal O'Reilly chimed in, helping to spell it out for the inexperienced private. "Looks like the com panel to the lower level was destroyed in the gunfire. No chance of getting a radio message to anyone down below through that much rock and ore. And it could take ten minutes for the elevator to make the trip one way.

"If they wanted to alert their friends in the basement, it'd take half an hour: ten minutes to call the elevator up from the lower floor, ten minutes to send someone from the top down to warn them, then ten more minutes back up again," he continued. "By then it'd be too late. Easier just to bug out and leave the others behind."

Shay's eyes were wide with disbelief. "They just abandoned their friends?"

"That's what separates mercenaries from soldiers,"

Anderson told him before turning his focus back to the mission. "This changes things. We've got an enemy unit down there, and they have no idea an Alliance squad is up above waiting for them."

"We can set up an ambush," Dah said. "As soon as those elevator doors open we start firing and rip those sons-of-bitches to ribbons!" She was speaking quickly, a wicked gleam in her eye. "They won't stand a chance!"

Anderson thought for a second, then shook his head. "It's obvious this is a seek-and-destroy mission: they aren't planning on leaving any survivors. There could still be Alliance personnel alive on the lower levels. If there's any chance we can still save them we have to try."

"Could be dangerous, sir," O'Reilly warned. "We're assuming they don't know we're here. If they somehow do, then we'll be the ones walking into an ambush."

"That's a risk we have to take," Anderson said, slamming his fist against the wall panel to call the elevator back up to the surface. "We're going in after them."

The rest of the group, including O'Reilly, responded with a sharp, "Sir, yes, sir!"

The long, slow elevator descent was even more agonizing than the wait in the ship's hull at the start of the mission. Minute by minute the tension grew as they sank deeper and deeper beneath the planet's surface.

The lieutenant could hear the faint hum of the elevator winch, a dull drone boring into the back of his skull that grew steadily fainter but never entirely disappeared as they dropped ever farther down the shaft. The air became heavy, warm, and moist. He felt his ears pop, and he noticed a strange smell in the air, an unfamiliar stench he imagined was a mixture of sulfurous gases mingling with alien molds and subterranean fungi.

Anderson was sweating profusely beneath his body armor, and he kept having to reach up with a free hand to wipe away the fog condensing on his visor. He did his best not to think about what would happen if the doors opened and the enemy was ready and waiting for them on the other side.

When they finally reached the bottom of the shaft the enemy *was* waiting for them, but they sure as hell weren't ready. The elevator opened into a large antechamber—a natural cave filled with stalagmites, stalactites, and thick limestone columns. The artificial lights strung across the ceiling illuminated the entire chamber, reflecting off thick veins of glistening metallic ore in the cavern's countless natural rock formations. At the far end was a passage that served as the cave's only other exit, a long tunnel that wound around a corner and out of sight.

The enemy forces, close to a dozen armed and armored mercenaries, were coming toward them from the far side of the chamber. They were laughing and joking, weapons at their sides as they headed for the elevator that would bring them back to the planet's surface.

It only took Anderson a fraction of a second to decide they looked like murdering raiders and not Alliance personnel, and he gave the order to fire. His team had been poised and ready as the elevator doors opened and they reacted almost instantaneously to his command, charging forward from the elevator with a barrage of gunfire. The first wave of their attack ripped into the pack of unsuspecting mercs. The fight would have ended right then if it wasn't for their body armor and kinetic shields.

Three of the enemy combatants dropped to the floor, but enough of the deadly projectiles were deflected or absorbed so that the rest of them were able to fall back and dive for cover behind the boulders and stalagmites that littered the cavern's floor.

The next few seconds of the battle were utter chaos. Anderson's team pushed forward, scrambling to use the cave's rock formations for cover. They had to fan out quickly, before enemy crossfire could pin the entire group down in a single location. The cavern echoed with the staccato recoil of assault rifles and the sharp *zip-zip-zip* of bullets ricocheting off the rock formations and walls, and the incandescent tracer bullets that made up every fifth round ignited the room with a ghostly luminescence.

Sprinting to a nearby large stalagmite, Anderson felt an all too familiar shudder as his kinetic shields repulsed several shots that would have otherwise found their mark. He hit the ground and rolled as a line of bullets struck the floor just in front of him, disintegrating the stone and sending tiny showers of water and dust up under his visor and into his face.

He came to his feet spitting out the foul grit, instinctively checking the remaining power on his shields. He was down to twenty percent—not nearly enough to give him a fighting chance if he had to make another run through direct enemy fire.

"Shield status!" Anderson shouted into his radio. The numbers came back at him rapid fire: "Twenty!" "Twenty-five!" "Twenty!" "Ten!"

His team was still at full strength, but their shields had taken a beating. They had lost their initial advantage of surprise, and they were now facing an enemy squad nearly double their number. But Alliance soldiers were trained to work as a team, to cover each other and watch one another's back. They trusted their teammates, and they trusted their leader. He figured that would give them the edge they needed over any band of mercs.

"Dah, Lee—move up on the right!" he barked. "Try to flank them!"

The lieutenant rolled to his right, emerging from behind the stalagmite shielding him from view and firing a quick covering burst in the direction of the enemy. He wasn't trying to hit anything; even with the smart-targeting technology built into all personal firearms it was almost impossible to hit a human-sized target without taking at least a half second to steady and aim. But inflicting damage was not his goal; all he wanted to do was disrupt the enemy so they wouldn't have time to line up Lee or Dah while they alternately advanced, darting in and out of cover.

After a two-second burst he rolled back behind his own cover; it wasn't good to stay out in view in one place for too long. Even as he did so, Shay popped out from behind a large boulder to lay down another covering burst for his squad-mates on the move, and as he ducked back to safety O'Reilly filled in.

As soon as the corporal pulled back, Anderson

poked his head out and fired again. This time he emerged from the left side of the stalagmite; jumping out from behind cover in the same position twice in a row was a sure way to catch an enemy round in the teeth.

He ducked back in and heard Dah over his radio saying, "In position. Laying down cover fire!"

Now it was his turn to move. "I'm on the go!" he shouted just before he scrambled out into the open, crouched low and running hard for another nearby piece of the cave's natural architecture that was large enough to protect him from enemy bullets.

Skidding to a stop behind a thick column, he had just enough time to catch his breath and lay down covering fire as he ordered Shay and O'Reilly to make their runs.

Again and again they repeated the process; Anderson sending one person on the move while the others laid down covering fire to keep the enemy on the defensive. He varied who would go each time; the key was to keep the team moving and keep their opponents off balance. Staying in one place would let their enemies focus on them and bring multiple shooters to bear or, even worse, start lobbing grenades in their direction. But there had to be purpose and direction to the movement; they had to follow a plan.

For all the mayhem and random confusion of battle, the lieutenant had been trained to approach firefights like a game of chess. It was all about tactics and strategy, protecting and defending your pieces as you maneuvered them one by one to develop a stronger overall position. Working as a single unit, the Alliance squad was pushing its advantage one soldier at a time, slowly maneuvering themselves to where they could flank the enemy, drive them from their cover, and catch them in the crossfire.

The mercs could feel it happening, too. They were pinned down by the coordinated efforts of Anderson and his crew, trapped, virtually helpless. It was only a matter of time before they launched a suicidal counter-assault or broke ranks in a desperate retreat. In this case, they chose the latter.

It seemed to happen all at once; the mercs burst from their cover, backpedaling toward the passage be-hind them as they fired wild bursts in the vague direc-tion of the Alliance soldiers. Exactly what Anderson and his team had been waiting for.

As the mercs fell back Anderson stood up from be-hind the boulder he was using for cover. He was ex-posing his head and shoulders, but someone running backwards while shooting an assault rifle would be lucky to hit the broadside of a battleship, let alone a target half the size of a human torso. He braced his weapon on the top of the boulder to steady it, took careful aim at one of the mercs, let his weapon's auto-targeting systems get a hard lock, then slowly squeezed the trigger. The merc did a short, stuttering dance as a steady stream of bullets depleted his shields, shred-ded his armor, and ripped through his flesh.

The whole sequence took maybe four seconds from start to finish—an eternity if they had been worried about someone on the other side calmly lining them up in their sights. But with that threat now gone, An-derson had more than enough time to guarantee his aim was lethally accurate. He even had a chance to line up a second merc and take her down, too.

And he wasn't the only one taking advantage of the situation. All told his team dropped seven of the mercs during their desperate retreat. Only two managed to escape with their lives, making it to the safety of the passage and disappearing around the corner.

THREE

Anderson didn't immediately send his crew chasing after the fleeing mercs. As soon as they lost visual contact with their enemy, pursuing them turned into a fool's game. Every corner, turn, or branching hallway they'd come across would represent a chance for a potential ambush.

Instead, Dah, O'Reilly, and Lee took up defensive positions guarding the passage in case the mercs came back, possibly with reinforcements. With the only point of insurgence covered, Anderson and Shay were free to examine the bodies.

They'd killed ten mercs in the battle. Now they were picking through their corpses—a ghoulish but necessary denouement to every engagement. Step one was to identify any wounded survivors who could pose a potential threat. Anderson was relieved to find all of the downed figures were already dead. It wasn't Alliance policy to execute helpless foes, but taking prisoners would have introduced a whole new set of logistical problems to a mission that was already complicated enough.

The next step was to try and identify who they were working for. Five of the dead were batarians, three were humans, and two were turians: eight males, two females. Their equipment was a hodge-podge of military and commercial arms from a wide variety of manufacturers. Officially recognized military units tended to be made up of a single species and carried only one brand of weapons and armor; the inevitable result of corporations signing exclusive supply contracts with the overseeing governments.

These were most likely soldiers of fortune, members of one of the Verge's many freelance mercenary bands that hired themselves out to the highest bidders. Most mercs had tattoos or brands burned into their flesh proclaiming their allegiance to one group or another; usually prominently displayed on the arms, neck, and face. But the only markings Anderson found on the fallen were indistinct splotches of raw, scabby skin.

He was disappointed, but not surprised. For jobs where secrecy was important crews often had their markings removed with an exfoliating acid wash, then reapplied after the mission: a simple but painful procedure that was charged back to whoever had hired them. Obviously the group hired to attack Sidon had feared Alliance retaliation and done their best to remove anything that might expose them if something went wrong.

There had still been no counterattack from the enemy by the time Anderson and Shay finished stripping the bodies of grenades, medigel, and anything else useful and small enough to easily carry.

"Looks like they're not coming out again," Dah grumbled as Anderson came over to stand beside her.

"Then we have to go in after them," Anderson

replied, slapping a fresh power pack into his kinetic shield generator. "We can't wait out here forever, and there's still a chance we'll find some of our own people alive down here."

"Or more mercs," O'Reilly muttered, replacing his own power pack.

The corporal was only saying what they were all thinking. For all they knew there was another full enemy squad deeper inside the base, and the two men who'd fled the battle had already managed to warn the reinforcements. But even though they might be walking into a trap, they couldn't turn back now.

The lieutenant gave the rest of the team a moment to gear up before shouting, "Dah, Shay—take the point. Let's move out!"

They advanced into the rough-hewn passage, maintaining a standard Alliance patrol formation—the two marines on point up front, Anderson and O'Reilly three meters behind them in the middle, and Lee three meters behind them watching their backs. They all had weapons raised and ready as they made slow but steady progress through the uneven, irregular tunnel that had been bored through the rock. They were officially in a hot zone now, and caution was more important than speed. One moment of careless inattention could cost all of them their lives.

Ten meters in, the corridor turned sharply to the left. The team stopped short at a hand signal from Dah, who crept forward and poked her head around the corner, momentarily exposing herself to possible enemy fire before ducking back. When she gave them the "all clear" they continued on.

Beyond the corner the passage continued for an-

other twenty meters before reaching a sealed security
door. The heavy metal barrier was closed and locked.
Anderson signaled to O'Reilly, and the corporal
moved forward to work his tech magic and override
the lockdown codes. The rest of the team assumed
standard positions for another flash-and-clear procedure.

"If those mercs are locking the security doors,"
Dah whispered to her commanding officer as they
waited for the door to open, "then that means they
have codes for the base. Someone on the inside must
have been working with them."

Anderson didn't reply, but he gave a grim nod. He
didn't like the idea that someone inside Sidon had betrayed the Alliance, but it was the only explanation
that made sense. The mercs had known the facility
was expecting an off-world shipment, and they must
have had the proper landing codes to get their ships
on the surface without raising any alarms. They'd
been familiar enough with the layout to clear out the
upper area and make their way to the elevators at the
back without letting anyone escape. And they had to
have access to restricted lockdown codes to seal the
security door. All the evidence pointed to the inescapable conclusion that there had been a traitor at
Sidon.

The door slid open and the team sprang into action,
using a flash grenade to blind anyone on the other
side, then charging in only to find the area beyond
empty. They were now standing in a large square room,
about twenty meters on each side. The shiny metal
walls, ceiling, and reinforced floor made it clear they
were now entering the heart of the research facility.

Everything had a sleek, modern feel; a sharp contrast to the rough-hewn natural tunnels they had just passed through. There was a hall leading off to the left, and another to the right.

"I've got a blood trail over here," O'Reilly called out on the left. "Looks fresh."

"We follow it," Anderson decided. "Lee and Shay, set up position here." He didn't like splitting up the team, but they didn't know the layout of the base. He didn't want any of the mercs doubling around behind them and making it back to the elevator. "Dah, O'Reilly—fall in!"

Leaving the two privates to guard the only way out, Anderson and the others set off down the hall on the left, moving ever deeper into the research complex. They passed several more intersections, but Anderson wasn't willing to split his squad up yet again. Instead, the three of them simply followed the blood trail. Along the way they passed a number of rooms, most of them small offices, judging by the desks and personal workstations. Like the dorms on the upper levels, each had been thoroughly ravaged by gunfire. The killing spree that began on the surface had continued unabated underground. And once again the mercs hadn't been content to leave their victims where they had fallen, but for some inexplicable reason had dragged them off.

It was five minutes later when they finally came across the source of the blood trail they'd been following. A turian lay facedown on the floor in the middle of a medium-sized room, bleeding profusely from a wound to his leg. Anderson recognized him as one of the mercs who had fled the recent battle. Approaching carefully, he knelt down beside the motionless figure to check for a pulse but found nothing.

There was only one other exit from the room, another sealed security door off to one side.

"You think his buddy's inside there?" Dah asked, using her assault rifle to point to the closed portal.

"I doubt it," Anderson replied. "He probably knew we'd be following the blood trail. I bet he ditched this guy at one of those other branches farther back. Probably waited for us to go by then made a mad dash back to the exit."

"I hope Shay and Lee are on their toes," Dah muttered.

"They can handle him," Anderson assured her. "I'm more interested in what's behind this door."

"Probably leads to the primary research lab," O'Reilly guessed. "Maybe we'll finally get some answers in there."

They rolled the dead merc out of the way; there was no sense taking the chance of someone tripping over his body if there was another firefight waiting for them beyond the door. Then, on Anderson's command, the corporal set to work overriding the security lockdown while the lieutenant and Chief Dah took position for another flash-and-clear operation.

Dah was the first one through this time, and once again there was nobody on the other side. Nobody alive, anyway.

"Sweet mother of mercy," she gasped.

Anderson stepped into the room and felt his stomach lurch at the gruesome spectacle before him. O'Reilly had been correct; they were standing in an enormous lab dominated by a massive central server.

The only way in or out was the door they had just come through, and like the rest of the base every piece of equipment in the room had been blasted beyond all hope of repair.

But none of that was what had evoked their reactions. At least thirty corpses were strewn about the room, most piled along the walls on either side of the entrance. Their uniforms marked them as Alliance personnel; the guards and researchers killed throughout the other sections of the facility. The mystery of where all the bodies had gone was solved, though Anderson still couldn't figure out why they'd all been dragged to this single location.

"Check for survivors, sir?" Dah asked, her voice not holding out much hope.

"Wait," Anderson said, holding up his hand to freeze his team in place. "Nobody move a muscle."

"Oh my God," O'Reilly whispered, just now recognizing what Anderson had already seen.

The entire room was wired with explosives. Not simple proximity mines, but countless ten-kilo detonation charges placed strategically around the lab. For Lieutenant Anderson, all the pieces suddenly fell into place.

There were enough explosives here to vaporize everything inside the room, including the bodies. That was why they'd been so carefully collected here. There'd be no way to positively ID the remains, meaning whoever betrayed Sidon would be presumed dead with all the others. They could assume a new identity and live off the profits of their crime with no chance of repercussions.

A soft electronic beep made Anderson realize that finding the traitor was the least of their problems.

"Timer!" O'Reilly hissed, his voice raw with fear and nervous energy.

A second later it beeped again, and the lieutenant knew the dying merc had lured them into a trap. The detonation sequence was counting down and their fate—survival or death—would very likely be determined by the next order he gave.

In the split second between beeps his mind analyzed and evaluated the situation. The size of the blast from the explosives would be enormous, more than enough to destabilize the entire underground complex. It would probably cause a cave-in, collapsing the huge natural chamber back by the elevator. Even if they were far enough away to survive the blast, they'd run out of air long before rescue workers would ever find them.

O'Reilly was a tech expert; there was a chance he could disarm the trigger before it went off. If they had enough time to find it. And if there wasn't a backup. And if it was a manufacturer he was familiar with. And if there weren't any built-in fail-safes to prevent manual overrides.

Too many ifs. Disarming it wasn't an option, which meant the only thing left for them to do was . . .

"RUN!"

Responding to his order, all three of them wheeled around and sprinted back down the halls the way they had come.

"Shay, Lee," Anderson shouted into his radio. "Get to the elevator. Now!"

"Aye-aye, sir!" one of them shouted back.

"Wait for us as long as possible, but if I give you the order, you go without us. Is that understood?"

There was silence on the other end of the radio—the only sounds were the clomping boots and heavy breathing of the three Alliance soldiers sprinting down the hall.

"Private! Do you hear me? If I say go, you damn well go whether we're there or not!"

He was rewarded with a reluctant, "Understood, sir."

They were racing through the halls as fast as they could run, slipping and skidding around corners in a desperate attempt to beat out the timer that could go off at any moment. There wasn't time to check for enemy ambushes; they just had to hope they didn't run into one.

Rounding the corner into the room where Anderson had earlier ordered Shay and Lee to wait for them, their luck finally ran out. Gunnery Chief Dah was in the lead, her long legs allowing her to eat up extra ground with every stride, and she had pulled a few meters ahead of her two male companions. She ran full speed into the room . . . and right into a spray of gunfire.

The lone surviving merc, a batarian, was waiting for them. He must have stumbled into the room after Shay and Lee had pulled back to the elevator on Anderson's command. Since then he'd been waiting patiently, just hoping for a chance to extract some form of petty revenge.

The force of the bullets picked Dah off her feet and sent her crashing to the ground in a heap. Her forward momentum caused her body to somersault across the floor until she stopped, crumpled and motionless in the corner.

Anderson was the second one into the room; he charged in with his weapon already firing. Normally, running straight at a stationary enemy with a loaded assault rifle was pure suicide, but the merc had foolishly kept his attention on Dah as she'd tumbled and fell—he wasn't even looking in Anderson's direction. By the time he tried to spin around and fire back at his charging foe the lieutenant was virtually on top of him; so close that even while running he was able to aim accurately enough to blow a hole in the batarian's chest.

O'Reilly arrived a split second later, coming to a stop when he saw Dah lying in a rapidly spreading pool of blood.

"Go!" Anderson shouted at him. "Get to the elevator."

O'Reilly gave a curt nod and took off, leaving Anderson to check on their fallen comrade.

The lieutenant dropped to one knee and rolled her over, then nearly jumped back in surprise when her eyes flickered open.

"Stupid bastard aimed too low," she said through gritted teeth. "Took me in the leg."

Anderson glanced down and saw that it was true. A few stray bullets had penetrated the kinetic barriers protecting her torso only to ricochet off the heavy plates of her body armor, inflicting no damage beyond small dents and discolorations. But her right leg, where the armor was thinner and the highest concentration of fire had drained the shields, had been reduced to pulp and hamburger.

"You ever have a piggyback, Chief?" Anderson asked her, tossing his weapons to the ground and rapidly stripping off his own body armor.

"I was never a piggyback kind of girl, sir," she replied, snapping off her belt and discarding every piece of equipment that wasn't strapped on.

"Nothing to it," he explained, reaching down to help her into a sitting position. She still had her body armor on, but they'd already wasted too much time. "All you gotta do is hold on."

He did his best to help her wrap her arms around his neck and shoulders, then stood up, momentarily staggering under the large woman's weight. He reached back to help support her weight, clutching her thighs and buttocks while her arms locked around his collar in fiercely strong grip.

"Giddy-up," she grunted, doing her best to hide the agony the movement was inflicting on her mangled limb.

Anderson took a few unsteady steps, struggling to find a way to move as quickly as possible while balancing the awkward load. By the time they emerged from the passage into the large stalactite-filled cavern he had found an awkward but effective cadence somewhere between a gallop and a trot. And then the timer detonated.

From the main laboratory in the heart of the research base an enormous ball of heat, fire, and force burst loose, laying waste as it swept through the complex. Doors were warped and ripped off hinges, floors buckled, walls melted.

Far away in the natural cavern the effects of the explosion were felt in three distinct stages. First, the

ground seemed to heave under Anderson's feet, sending him tumbling to the ground. Dah screamed as her
leg slammed against the floor, but her voice was
drowned out by the second phase of the explosion—
a deafening boom that echoed throughout the cavern
and drowned out every other sound. The final phase
was a wall of hot air propelled by the blast spilling out
from the passage to roll over them, pinning them to
the ground, burning their lungs and leaving them gasping for air.

Anderson struggled to breathe, and for a second he
nearly blacked out. He fought to maintain consciousness as the invisible hand squeezing his chest and pinning him to the ground slowly released its pressure
while the super-heated air expelled by the blast dis-
persed itself throughout the cavern.

They weren't out of danger yet. The force of the
blast had rocked the cavern. The strings of artificial
lights ripped loose, swaying wildly and casting bizarre, crazy shadows throughout the room. And
though his ears were still ringing, he could plainly
hear the loud, sharp cracks of stress fractures appear-
ing in the walls and ceiling as the cavern began to col-
lapse.

"O'Reilly!" he shouted into his radio, hoping the
three men in the elevator could still hear him. "This
place is caving in! Get to the surface! Now!"

"What about you and Dah?" The reply was barely
audible inside Anderson's helmet, though from the
tone it was clear the corporal was shouting.

"Send the elevator back down after you get to the
top," he snapped. "Now move! That's an order!"

Not waiting for a reply, Anderson scrambled over

to check on Gunnery Chief Dah. She had passed out;
the pain in her leg too much to bear on top of the
physical trauma of the explosion's aftershocks. Sum-
moning what was left of his strength, the lieutenant
managed to stand up, slinging her over his shoulders
in a fireman's carry.

He began a desperate, staggering race to freedom
as the chamber disintegrated around them. Stalactites
plunged down like enormous jagged limestone spears,
the fragile hold they had maintained on the ceiling for
thousands of years finally failing. Huge cracks were
spreading through the floor, walls, and roof, causing
great chunks of rock to shear off and tumble to the
floor where they exploded into dust and rubble on
impact.

Anderson did his best to block it all out. There was
nothing he could do but keep moving and pray they
weren't crushed from above, so he forced his mind to
focus solely on placing one foot in front of the other.
He wasn't sure he was going to make it. The swinging
strings of lights caused a strobelike effect that made it
difficult to keep his balance on the uneven ground.
He was bruised and beaten from the concussion of
the blast. Exhaustion and fatigue were setting in. The
muscles in his thighs and calves were burning.

The adrenaline rush he'd felt at the beginning of
the mission was gone: his body simply had nothing
left to give. He moved slower and slower, the unconscious woman draped over his shoulders feeling as
heavy as the massive slabs of rock raining down
around them.

When the elevator finally came into view he wasn't
surprised to see O'Reilly, Shay, and Lee still waiting

for him. Seeing their commander staggering along like the living dead, all three of them rushed out to help. Anderson was too exhausted to object. He simply let Dah slide from his shoulders into the grasp of the two privates, one taking her under the shoulders and the other under her hips.

With the burden removed he lost his balance and nearly fell over, but O'Reilly was there to catch him. Leaning on the corporal for support, he managed to take the last twenty steps into the elevator before collapsing in the corner.

The doors slammed shut and the car began the long journey up to the top. The ride was far from smooth: the elevator moved in fits and starts as the gears screeched and squealed. Nobody said anything, as if they were afraid mentioning their precarious position might make it worse. Anderson simply lay where he had fallen, panting and wheezing as he tried to catch his breath.

By the time they reached the top and spilled out into the safety of the surface he had recovered enough to speak.

"I told you not to wait for us," he chastised his team as they made their way back to the *Hastings*, the privates still carrying Dah's unconscious body between them. "I should bust each of you down a full rank for disobeying orders!" He paused to let the statement sink in. "That, or recommend you all for medals."

FOUR

First Lieutenant Kahlee Sanders was smart: she was one of the Alliance's top computer and systems technicians. She was attractive: other soldiers at the base were always trying to pick her up when she wasn't on duty. She was young: at twenty-six, she could expect at least another half century of healthy, productive years ahead of her. And she knew she was on the verge of making the biggest mistake of her life.

She glanced warily around the bar, sipping nervously at her drink as she pressed herself deeper into her small corner, trying not to draw attention. Average in both height and build, Kahlee's only really distinguishing feature was her shoulder-length blond hair—a genetically recessive trait, natural blonds were nearly extinct. But her hair was a dirty blond, with streaks edging toward shades of brown . . . and there were still plenty of humans who dyed their hair blond anyway. She didn't normally stand out in a crowd. That made it easy for her to escape notice here—the Black Hole was packed.

Most of the crowd was human. Not surprising, considering the bar was an upscale establishment within walking distance of the spaceports on Elysium, the Alliance's oldest and largest colony in the Skyllian Verge. But at least a third of the patrons were made up of other species. Batarians were the most predominant; she could see their narrow heads bobbing on their sinewy necks among the crowd. They had oversized nostrils and large, triangular noses that were almost flat against the face, the tip pointing straight down to their thin lips and pointy chin. Their faces were covered with hair so short and fine it looked like the soft velvet of a horse's nose, though the hair grew longer and thicker around the mouth. A flat stripe of ridged cartilage ran along the tops of their skulls and down the backs of their necks.

But the most unique characteristic of the species was undoubtedly the fact that they possessed two distinct sets of eyes. One pair was set wide in prominent bony sockets protruding from the corners of their face, giving their skulls a noticeable diamond shape. The second set of eyes was smaller and closer together, set higher on the face, just beneath the middle of the forehead. Batarians had a habit of looking at you with all four orbs simultaneously, making it difficult for a binocular species to know which pair to focus on during conversation. The inability to maintain eye contact was disconcerting for most other species, and the batarians always tried to exploit this advantage in situations involving bargaining and negotiations.

Like the Alliance, the batarian government was actively settling the Verge, trying to establish a foothold in a region ripe for expansion. But the Black Hole currently played host to a number of other aliens as well. She saw several turians among the crowd, their

features largely obscured by the hard, tattooed cara-
paces of flesh and bone that covered their heads and
faces like fierce pagan masks. She noticed the quick,
darting eyes of a small cluster of salarians across the
room. A pair of massive krogan loomed in the shadows near the door, like prehistoric dinosaurs standing
on their hind legs, guarding the entrance. A few ro-
tund volus waddled about the room. And a single
asari server, ethereal and beautiful, glided effortlessly
through the crowd, moving from table to table while
balancing a full tray of drinks.

Kahlee had come here alone, but it seemed as if
everyone else in the bar had arrived in a group. They
were leaning on the bar, or huddled around the high
tables, or milling about on the dance floor, or pressed
up against the walls. Everyone seemed to be having a
good time, laughing and chatting with friends, coworkers, or business associates. Kahlee was amazed they
could even hear one another. The constant din from
fifty simultaneous conversations rose up to the ceiling
and crashed down over her like a wave. She tried to
escape it by squeezing herself even farther back into
her own little corner.

When she'd first arrived she had thought the presence of the crowd would be comforting. Maybe she
could lose herself in the faceless mass of people. But
the drinks at the Black Hole were as potent as their
reputation, and even though she was only halfway
through her second glass, her senses were already
slightly dulled. Now there was too much noise, too
much motion. She couldn't keep a fix on what was
happening around her. Nobody here had any reason
to be suspicious of the young woman standing alone

in the corner, but she found herself constantly scanning the room to see if anyone was watching her.

At the moment nobody was even glancing in her direction. Not that this observation brought any comfort. She was in a tough spot, and a case of alcohol-fueled paranoia wasn't going to make things any easier. Kahlee set her drink down on a small counter built into the bar's wall and tried to collect her thoughts, taking stock of her situation.

Sixteen hours ago she had walked off the premises of the Sidon Research Facility without permission. Leaving the base was a minor infraction; things escalated when she didn't show up for her assigned shift eight hours later. Dereliction of duty was serious enough to go on her permanent record. And in another four hours her status would officially become UA—Unauthorized Absence—a crime punishable by court-martial, dishonorable discharge, and even imprisonment.

She picked up her half-finished drink and took another long sip, hoping the alcohol might help slow her racing thoughts. Everything had seemed so simple yesterday when she'd left. Kahlee had proof that her superiors at Sidon were conducting illegal research, and she was determined to report them.

She'd caught a shuttle leaving the base, flashing a pass she'd forged by hacking into the restricted security files, and arrived here on Elysium a few hours later. It was somewhere on that trip that she'd started having second thoughts.

With plenty of time to consider the full consequences of her actions, she began to see that things weren't as black and white as she'd first assumed. She had no idea how many people at the base might be implicated in a formal inquiry. What if people she worked with, people she considered her friends, were somehow involved? Did she really want to bring them down? Part of her felt like this was an act of betrayal.

But her hesitations went beyond loyalty to her fellow soldiers: she was taking a huge risk with her own career. She had evidence Sidon was conducting research way outside the scope of its official parameters; evidence obtained by illegally compromising top-security-clearance files, acting on nothing more than her initial suspicions and a wild hunch. Her hunch had turned out to be true, but technically her entire investigation had been an act of treason against the Alliance.

The more she'd thought about it, the more Kahlee realized she had no idea what she'd gotten herself into. She couldn't say if her superiors were acting alone, or if they were just following orders from someone higher up the chain of command. What if she reported them to the very person who'd ordered the illegal research conducted in the first place? Would anything change, or would it just be covered up? Was she possibly throwing away her career, and risking some serious jail time, for nothing?

In truth, if they really wanted to find her, it wouldn't have been that hard. She was on record boarding a shuttle heading to Elysium with her fake pass. But she doubted the Alliance would send anyone after her. Not until she was missing for more than twenty hours and it became a criminal offense. So she still had a little time to decide what to do.

Not that a few more hours would make much difference. She'd been struggling with this problem ever since she'd touched down. Kahlee was too wired to sleep, too afraid to go back to Sidon and face charges, too scared to press on. She kept moving from bar to bar, having a few drinks then walking it off to sober up. She never stayed in one place for long, fearful of drawing unwanted attention. Her path took her from bar to lounge to club as she hoped to find some sudden inspiration that would miraculously solve her problem.

She glanced up at the news vids showing on the screen set into the wall on the far side of the bar, her eye drawn by a familiar image. Although she couldn't hear what the broadcast was saying, she recognized a file photo of the Sidon Research Facility. Puzzled, Kahlee furrowed her brow and squinted, trying to read the rapidly moving type skimming across the bottom of the screen.

. . . ALLIANCE RESEARCH BASE ATTACKED . . .

Her eyes snapped wide in alarm and she slammed her glass down on the counter, spilling what remained of her drink. Ignoring it, she stepped out from her little corner and shoved her way through the crowd, heedlessly pushing and elbowing the other patrons out of her way until she was close enough to hear the newscaster's words.

"Details are still sketchy, but we have received official confirmation from Alliance sources that the Sidon Research Facility appears to have been the victim of a terrorist attack."

Anxious to hear more, Kahlee pressed forward,

jostling one of the other human patrons and causing him to spill his drink.

The man turned toward here, angrily exclaiming, "Hey, watch where you're . . ." He trailed off when he realized the bump had been delivered by a comely young woman.

Kahlee didn't even acknowledge him with a glance, keeping her eyes riveted on the screen overhead.

"The scene is still restricted pending the Alliance investigation, so we aren't able to bring you any live images . . ."

The man looked up at the screen, feigning interest in the hopes of forming a connection with her. "Gotta be the batarians," he said matter-of-factly.

The friend he'd been talking with chimed in as well, eager to impress the attractive newcomer to their conversation. "The Alliance has been predicting something like this for months," he said, assuming the tone of an unquestioned authority on the matter. "My cousin's in the military and he told me—"

A withering gaze from Kahlee shut him up. His silence secured, she turned back to the vid just in time to catch the tail end of the report.

". . . there are no reported survivors. In other news, the human ambassador to Camala recently held a press conference to announce the signing of a new trade accord . . ."

No survivors. The words left Kahlee numb, stunning her like a heavy blow to the back of the head. She had been at the base yesterday. Yesterday! If she hadn't run off on this foolish mission, she'd be dead right now. The room began to list to one side and Kahlee realized she was about to faint.

The man she had bumped into caught her as she teetered, holding her up while she struggled against the vertigo. "Hey, what's the matter?" His voice showed real concern. "You okay?"

"Huh?" Kahlee muttered, not even aware that most of her weight was being supported by a complete stranger. The man helped her stand straight, then let go—though he was poised to leap in again if she fell. He placed a hand on her arm to comfort her, or maybe to help her keep her balance.

"Did you know someone at the base? Did you have friends there?"

"Yes . . . I mean no." Too much booze, too little sleep, and the shock of what happened at Sidon had momentarily disabled her, but she was beginning to feel secure on her feet again. Her agile mind was clicking; the full implications of what had just happened were finally registering. She'd fled a top-security research base mere hours before it was attacked. She wasn't just a survivor . . . she was now a suspect!

The two men were looking at her with a mixture of puzzlement and concern. She smoothly disengaged herself from the hand on her arm and gave them an apologetic smile.

"I'm sorry. That story caught me off guard. I . . . I know people in the Alliance."

"Anything we can do?" the second man asked. She got the sense his offer was sincere, just a nice guy looking out for a fellow human. But right now all she wanted was to get away without doing anything else that could make anyone remember her.

"No, no. I'm all right. Thank you, though." She took a step back as she spoke. "I have to go. I'll be late for work. Sorry about your drink." She turned and disappeared back into the crowd, heading for the door. Glancing back over her shoulder, she was relieved to see neither of the men made any attempt to follow her. They simply shrugged, dismissing the bizarre encounter, then resumed their previous conversation.

It was dark and chilly outside as she stepped out from the bar. The news of Sidon's destruction had sobered her up, but she could still use a walk in the crisp night air to really clear her head.

The Black Hole was located on one of Elysium's main thoroughfares. It was still early in the evening, and the sidewalks were full of people. She moved quickly down the busy street, not heading in any particular direction, just feeling the need to be on the move. Her head was still spinning as she fought her way through the heavy pedestrian traffic. Slowly the paranoia began to creep back into her thoughts until she shied away from every passerby and jumped at every unexpected sound. She felt vulnerable out here with all these strangers, needlessly exposed.

A deserted side street offered temporary refuge. She darted down the narrow alley, stopping only when she had gone to the end of the block. The noise of people and monorails coming from the main drag was now only a faint murmur.

The news about Sidon changed everything. She had to reevaluate her situation. Had her disappearance somehow triggered the attack? It was hard to imagine it was mere coincidence, but she didn't see how the two events could be related.

One thing was certain: they'd be looking for her now. She had to cover her tracks. Find some way to book a flight off Elysium that couldn't be traced back to her. She'd need to find a fake ID, or bribe someone to let her board a ship illegally. If she stayed here much longer someone was bound to—

Kahlee screamed as she felt a heavy hand slam down on her shoulder. She was spun around and found herself staring into the chest of a terrifyingly large man with a vicelike grip. Looking up, she met his eyes, cold and hard.

"Kahlee Sanders?" It was more an accusation than a question.

Alarmed, she tried to take a step back, squirming and twisting away in an effort to break free. Her captor shook her once, roughly, and she winced in pain as his nails dug into the flesh of her collarbone.

"Lieutenant Kahlee Sanders, you're under arrest on suspicion of conspiring to commit treason against the Alliance."

In her surprise it had taken Kahlee a second to realize what the man was wearing. Now she clearly recognized his uniform: Alliance MP. They'd found her already. He must have spotted her on the main road and followed her into the deserted alley.

All the fight went out of her. Her head slumped forward as she surrendered to her fate. "I didn't do it," she whispered. "It's not what you think."

He grunted as if he didn't believe her, but he did drop his hand from her shoulder. She could feel the skin beneath her shirt bruising already.

Pulling out a pair of cuffs from his belt, he held them up for her to see. In a curt voice he ordered, "Turn around, Lieutenant. Hands behind your back."

She hesitated, then nodded. Resisting would only

make things worse. She was innocent, now she'd have to prove it in front of a military tribunal.

"Don't try to run," he warned. "I'm authorized to use lethal force if necessary." His words drew her attention down to the weapon on his hip even as she slowly turned her back to him, complying with his commands. From the corner of her eye she was just able to make out the Ahial Syndicate–manufactured Striker pistol holstered on his hip.

Her mind screamed out a warning even as she felt the cuff slap onto her right wrist. The Hahne-Kedar P7 was the standard-issue pistol for all Alliance personnel, not the Striker!

The realization came a millisecond after she felt the second cuff slap around her left wrist. Acting on instinct and adrenaline, Kahlee threw her head back violently. She was rewarded with a wet crunch as it smashed into the face of the fake Alliance MP.

She spun around as the man dropped to his knees, momentarily stunned by her unexpected attack. His arms dangled limply at his sides and a river of blood was pouring from his mouth and nose, creating a moist, dark stain on his face: the perfect target as she brought her knee up, inflicting even more damage to the injured area.

The blow knocked him backwards, and he slumped down onto his side, gurgling and choking as the blood clogged his throat. His body twitched and he flailed his legs, trying to ward off his attacker. But Kahlee was remorseless. She didn't know who this imposter was—mercenary or assassin—but she knew if she didn't get away from him, she was dead.

Calling on memories of the hand-to-hand combat

classes all Alliance personnel received during basic training, she easily avoided his feeble kicks. With her hands still cuffed behind her back her feet were her only weapon. She danced around the prone figure, moving in so she could deliver the steel toes and heavy heels of her combat boots to the vulnerable areas of his head and chest.

Her opponent rolled onto his stomach, trying to protect himself. Kahlee hesitated for a second, then spotted his hand fumbling at the holster of his gun. She leaped forward and stomped on his fingers, again and again, turning his digits into a mess of broken bones and mangled flesh.

She ignored the whimpers and burbling cries as the man tried to beg for mercy through blood and shattered teeth. He was still conscious, so he was still a threat. She kicked him hard in the temple, possibly fracturing his skull. His body spasmed once, then went limp. Another hard kick to the ribs evoked no reaction, assuring her he was really out.

She dropped down onto the ground beside the body, moving quickly in case somebody came into the alley to investigate the commotion. The fake MP had cuffed her hands behind her back, but he hadn't done a very good job of it. The metal rings were loose enough on her wrists to allow Kahlee to slide them several inches up and down her forearms—there was just enough play that she might be able to get free. Squirming and struggling, she managed to contort her body enough to slide her chained wrists down past her hip bones and along the backs of her thighs to her knees. She rolled onto her back and side, twisting so she could pull her feet through. Her wrists were still cuffed, but at least they were now in front of her.

Suppressing a gag reflex, she crawled on her hands and knees through the blood of her assailant until she was directly over his motionless body. He was still breathing in shallow, half-choked gasps. Kahlee let loose the breath she didn't even know she'd been holding. She felt no remorse over the savage beating she'd inflicted while fighting to save her own life, but she was glad she wouldn't have this man's death on her conscience.

Training and adrenaline had saved her. That, and the carelessness of her opponent. But as her adrenaline wound down and she took in the gruesome scene, she felt the first hints of panic. She was a soldier, but she'd never seen combat duty. She'd never encountered anything like this.

Come on, Sanders! The voice inside her head was that of her former drill instructor, though the words were her own. *You're not out of this mess yet.*

She gritted her teeth, determined to finish the job. Even so, Kahlee shuddered as she fumbled around the man's blood-soaked belt until she found the key to unlock her shackles. Releasing the cuffs proved even more difficult than sliding them around to her front, as she had to clasp the key in her teeth and try to fit it into the lock. But after several frustrating minutes she heard the click, and the bonds fell away from her left wrist. With one hand free it only took another second to unlock the other cuff and Kahlee was free.

Kahlee took a quick look around, relieved to see nobody had stumbled into the alley yet. She grabbed the gun from the man's holster, checked that the safety was on, and stuffed it beneath her jacket and into her belt. She stood up, then froze.

She didn't know who the unconscious man at her feet was working for, but it was obvious he had been specifically looking for her. That meant others probably were, too. They'd have the ports staked out, just waiting for her to try and get off-world. She was trapped. She couldn't even go back to the main street. Not with her clothes covered in blood.

There was only one option left. Taking another breath to calm her jangling nerves, Kahlee left her assailant's body where it lay, moving quickly in the direction away from the busy thoroughfare. She spent the rest of the night skulking through the back alleys of Elysium, careful to avoid detection, slowly making her way toward the house of the only person she could turn to for help. A man she promised her mother she'd never speak to again.

FIVE

Within a decade of its discovery by batarian surveyors, Camala had become one of the most important planets in the Skyllian Verge. Unlike most colony worlds, where initial populations were small and settlers tended to congregate around a single major city, Camala boasted two distinct metropolitan regions of over a million people each: Ujon, the capital, and the slightly larger Hatre, location of the world's primary spaceports.

The two cities were nearly five hundred kilometers apart, built on opposite sides of a wide, inhospitable desert—the source of Camala's rapid growth. For below the thin layer of orange sand and the hard, red rock underneath were some of the largest deposits of element zero in the Verge. The rich deposits of eezo—the galaxy's most valuable fuel source—drove Camala's economy, drawing in colonists eager to seek their fortunes working at the hundreds of mining and refinery operations scattered across the empty desert. The majority of the world's population were batarians, and only they enjoyed the full privileges of true citizenship under local law. But like any colony world with a prosperous economy, there was always a steady influx of visitors and immigrants from every recognized species across Citadel space.

Camala was easily the wealthiest of the batarian colony worlds, and Edan Had'dah was one of the wealthiest batarians on Camala. He was quite likely among the ten richest individuals in the entire Skyllian Verge, and he wasn't afraid to show it. Normally he wore the latest in cutting-edge fashions: asari-designed ensembles made with the finest materials imported from Thessia itself. His preference ran to the opulent and extravagant—flowing black robes highlighted with splashes of red to bring out the hues of his skin. But for the meeting tonight he had donned a simple brown suit covered by a drab gray overcoat. For someone as infamously ostentatious as Edan Had'dah, his plain garb was an almost impenetrable disguise.

Typically, Edan would be enjoying a soothing nightcap at this hour, sipping the finest of hanar liquors in the den of his mansion in Ujon. But this night was positively atypical. Instead of relaxing in comfort and luxury, he was stuck sitting on a hard chair in a dingy warehouse in the desert outside Hatre, waiting for the Verge's most infamous bounty hunter to arrive. Edan didn't like waiting.

He wasn't waiting alone. At least a dozen other men, all members of the Blue Sun mercenary gang, were milling about the warehouse. Six of them were batarian, two were turian, and the rest were human.

Edan didn't like humans, either. Like his own species, they were bipedal. Similar in height, the humans were thicker in the torso, arms, and legs. They had short, stubby necks and square, blockish heads.

And like all binocular species, their faces seemed lacking in character and intelligence. Instead of nostril slits they had an odd jutting protuberance for a nose. Even their mouths were strange, their lips so full and puffy it was a wonder they didn't slur their speech. He actually thought they closely resembled the asari—another race Edan didn't like.

But he wasn't one to let personal prejudice get in the way of business. There were several other so-called private security organizations for hire in the Skyllian Verge, and most of them charged a lot less than the Blue Suns. But the Suns had developed a reputation for being both discreet and ruthlessly efficient. Edan had used them several times in the past when "unconventional" business opportunities had presented themselves, so he knew from personal experience that their reputation was well earned. He wasn't about to trust a mission as important as this one to someone else simply because the Suns had recently started taking on humans. Even though it had been a human member of the group who had screwed up on Elysium.

Normally Edan would never meet directly with the mercenaries he employed. He preferred to work through agents and go-betweens to keep his identity hidden—and also to avoid dealing with those who were socially beneath him. But the man he was hiring tonight had insisted on meeting him in person. Edan had no intention of bringing a bounty hunter into his home . . . or of meeting with him alone. So he'd donned the nondescript clothes, left his mansion, and traveled hundreds of kilometers by private plane to the outskirts of Ujon's twin city on the other side of the desert. Now he was spending the night in a cold, dusty warehouse filled with soldiers for hire, sitting in a chair that was causing his back to ache and his legs to go numb. And the bounty hunter was over an hour late!

But it wasn't as if he could change his mind. He was in too deep. The Blue Suns in the warehouse knew his identity; now he'd have to keep them around as his personal bodyguards until this job was finished. It was the only way to make sure they didn't reveal his identity to the rest of the Blue Sun crew. What happened at Sidon was going to draw attention, and Edan couldn't take the risk of someone exposing his involvement. He also needed to make sure there were no loose ends that could link him to the attack, which was why he had agreed to this meeting.

"He's here." Edan jumped slightly at the voice. One of the Blue Suns—a fellow batarian—had crept up silently behind him and was now standing close enough to whisper in his ear.

"Bring him in," he replied, quickly regaining his composure. The merc nodded and left the room as his employer stood up, grateful to be out of the uncomfortable chair. A moment later the guest of honor finally appeared.

He was easily the most impressive krogan Edan had ever seen. At two and a half meters tall and nearly two hundred kilograms, he was large even by the standards of his reptilian species, but not enormous. Like all krogan, the top of his spine was slightly curved, giving him a hunchbacked appearance. The effect was further enhanced by the heavy frill of bone and scaled flesh growing from his upper back, collar, and shoulders like a thick shell, from which his blunt head protruded. Rough, leathery plates covered the crown of his skull and nape of his neck. His features were flat and brutish, almost prehistoric. He had no visible nose or ears and his eyes were small and set wide on either side of his head, though they gleamed with a cruel cunning.

A krogan could live for several centuries, his or her complexion growing duller and darker with age; this one's skin was all mottled browns and tans, with almost no remaining trace of the pale yellow and green markings common to younger members of the species. A labyrinth of discolored welts and scars crisscrossed his face and throat, ancient battle wounds forming a disfiguring pattern, as if all his veins were on the verge of bursting through the surface of his skin. He wore light body armor, but he carried no weapons—those would have been removed at the door, as per Edan's previous orders. Despite being unarmed he still radiated an aura of menace and destruction.

The krogan walked with an odd, lumbering grace; a force of nature rolling across the floor of the warehouse, merciless and unstoppable. Four Blue Suns escorted him in, two marching on either side. They were there to intimidate the bounty hunter and dissuade him from any aggressive responses if the negotiations went poorly. But it was clear that they were the ones who felt intimidated. Their tension was obvious in every step; they moved as if they were standing on the edge of a volcano about to erupt. One of them, a young human with a Blue Sun tattoo covering his left eye, kept reaching down to the pistol at his side as if trying to draw courage from the mere act of touching it.

Edan would have found their discomfort amusing if he hadn't been relying on them for protection. The batarian decided he would do everything in his power to make sure this meeting went smoothly.

As the krogan approached, his lips pulled back in a snarl, exposing his serrated teeth . . . or maybe it was a smile. He stopped a few steps away, still flanked on either side by the four mercenaries.

"My name is Skarr," he growled, his voice so deep it sent thrumming vibrations across the floor.

"I am Edan Had'dah," the batarian replied, giving a slight tilt of his head to the left, a gesture of admiration and respect among his species. Skarr tilted his own head in response, but he leaned to the right: a greeting usually directed at inferiors.

Edan bristled involuntarily. Either Skarr was insulting him, or the krogan didn't understand the significance of the gesture. He chose to proceed as if it was the latter explanation, though from what he knew of Skarr there was a good chance it was the former.

"I don't normally agree to meet with the people I hire," he explained, "but in your case I chose to make an exception. Based on your reputation, your skills are worth bending the rules for."

Skarr dismissed the compliment with a derisive snort. "Based on your reputation I thought you'd be better dressed. You sure you can afford me?"

There were some shocked murmurs from the other batarians in the room. Casting aspersions on the monetary worth of a social better was a grave insult among their culture. Again, Edan wondered if Skarr had done this on purpose. Fortunately, he was used to dealing with the less-cultured species of the galaxy, and he wasn't hiring Skarr because of his renowned etiquette.

"Rest assured, I have sufficient funds to pay you," he replied, his voice calm and even. "It is a simple job."

"This have anything to do with the Sidon base?"

Edan's inner eyes blinked once, registering his surprise. Negotiation was a subtle dance of deception and misinformation, each party holding secrets from the other in an effort to gain the upper hand. And Edan had just slipped up. His involuntary reaction had revealed a fact he'd meant to keep hidden . . . if the krogan was smart enough to pick up on it.

"Sidon? Why would you think that?" he asked, keeping his voice carefully neutral.

Skarr shrugged his massive shoulders. "Just a hunch. And my price just went up."

"Your involvement only requires you to find and eliminate your target," Edan countered. His voice gave nothing away, but inside he was silently cursing himself for losing the first round of bargaining.

"Target? Just one?"

"Just one. A female human."

The krogan turned his head from side to side, scanning the dozen or so Blue Sun mercs scattered about the warehouse. "You've got a lot of men here. Why don't you make them do your dirty work?"

Edan hesitated. He preferred to ask the questions; he didn't like answering them. He was wary of making another mistake in their negotiation. But even his reluctance gave away more than he intended.

Skarr barked out a laugh. "These *hrakhors* screwed it up, didn't they?"

Every merc in the warehouse tensed up at his words, confirming them as fact. Not that it mattered. Somehow Edan knew Skarr would see through any false denials, so he simply nodded, conceding another point to his opponent.

"What happened?" the krogan wanted to know.

"I hired the Blue Suns to find her and bring her in for interrogation," Edan admitted. "One of them spotted her on Elysium. They found him several hours later crawling around a side street, looking for his teeth."

"That's what happens when you're too cheap to hire a real professional."

One insult too many.

The man with the tattoo whipped his pistol out and slammed the butt against the side of the krogan's skull. The force of the blow rocked Skarr's head to the side, but it did not knock him off his feet. He wheeled around with a deafening roar, catching his attacker with a vicious backhand that broke the young man's neck.

The other three mercs fell on Skarr before their comrade's body hit the ground, their combined weight dragging the big alien to the floor. Before the meeting, Edan had given them strict orders not to kill Skarr unless absolutely necessary . . . he needed him to track down the missing woman. So instead of shooting the bounty hunter all three were piled on top of him, pinning him to the ground as they tried to pistol whip him into unconsciousness.

Unfortunately, nobody had told Skarr *he* couldn't kill *them*. A long, jagged blade appeared in his hand, materializing from some secret hiding place in a boot, belt, or glove. Edan jumped back from the fray as the blade gashed open the throat of one merc. The return arc sliced through the vulnerable joint between the knee and thigh in the body armor of a second, severing his femoral artery. As he instinctively clutched at the gushing wound with both hands Skarr drove the blade into his chest, piercing his protective vest and puncturing his heart.

The blade momentarily stuck in the rib cage as the krogan tried to pull it out, giving the last surviving merc, another human, the chance to roll away from the pile and scramble to his feet, safely out of the knife's range. The human whipped out his pistol and pointed it at the gore-covered bounty hunter, who was still on the floor.

"Don't move!" the man screamed, his voice cracking with fear.

Skarr's head snapped from side to side, ignoring the enemy in front of him as he took stock of the eight other mercs in the warehouse. Every single one of them had their assault rifles trained on him, ready to fire. The knife dropped to the floor and Skarr raised his empty hands above his head as he slowly stood up. He turned to face Edan as the merc with the pistol took a few steps farther back, just to be safe.

"So what happens now, batarian?"

Edan finally had the upper hand in their negotiations, and he was eager to press his advantage. "Maybe I should just order them to kill you where you stand." He kept his inner eyes focused on Skarr, but let the other pair glance around the room to draw attention to the fact that the bounty hunter was surrounded.

The krogan merely laughed at the empty threat. "If you wanted me dead, they'd have shot me before I had a chance to pull my knife. But they didn't. You must have given them orders not to take me out, so I figure I'm worth more to you than a handful of dead mercs. My price just went up again."

Even with a warehouse full of armed mercenaries pointing their weapons at him, the krogan was perceptive enough to turn the situation to his profit. Underestimating Skarr's intelligence was a mistake Edan vowed he wouldn't make again. He wondered how many other people had underestimated Skarr in the past . . . and what it had cost them.

"You could've made a lot of money in my line of work, Skarr." He made no attempt to hide his grudging respect.

"I make a lot of money in this line of work. And I get to kill people as one of my perks. So let's stop screwing around and make a deal."

Edan gave a slight nod and blinked all four of his eyes at once, signaling the mercs to lower their weapons. They weren't happy that Skarr had killed three of their comrades, but loyalty meant less to them than money. And with the three dead, their cut just got larger.

Only the young human closest to the krogan, the one with the pistol, didn't comply. He looked around in disbelief at the others, his weapon still aimed directly at Skarr.

"What are you doing?" he shouted to the others. "We can't just let him get away with this!"

"Don't be stupid, boy," Skarr spat out. "Killing me won't bring your dead friends back. It's just bad business."

"You shut up!" he snapped back, focusing all his attention on Skarr.

The krogan's voice dropped to a menacing whisper. "Think hard about your next move, human. Nobody else is going to step in. It's just you and me."

The merc was trembling now, but he managed to keep the pistol aimed at his target. Skarr didn't seem concerned.

"You've got to the count of three to drop that gun."

"Or what?" the merc screamed. "You make one move and you're dead!"

"One."

Edan noticed the krogan was suddenly surrounded by a faint aura, barely visible even with the benefit of two pairs of eyes. There was a subtle waver around the bounty hunter, as if the light in the room were being ever so slightly distorted as it passed through the surrounding air.

Skarr was a biotic! The krogan was one of those rare individuals capable of manipulating dark energy, the imperceptible quantum force that pervaded all the so-called empty space in the universe. Normally too weak to have any noticeable effects on the physical world, dark energy could be concentrated into extremely dense fields by biotics through mental conditioning. With their natural talents augmented by thousands of microscopic amplifiers surgically implanted throughout their nervous system, biotic individuals could use biofeedback to release the accumulated power in a single directed burst. Which was exactly what Skarr was doing; stalling for time as he gathered enough power to unleash it against the young man still foolishly holding a gun on him.

But the merc didn't realize what was happening. Humanity didn't have any individuals with latent biotic abilities; Edan suspected he wasn't even aware such a power existed. But he was about to find out.

"Two."

The merc opened his mouth to say something else, but he never got the chance. Skarr thrust a clenched fist in his direction, and the air rippled as a wave of invisible dark energy surged out and over his adversary. The unsuspecting human was picked up off his feet and thrown backwards several meters. He landed heavily on the floor, knocking the wind out of his lungs and sending the pistol flying from his hand.

He was stunned only for a second—plenty of time for Skarr to cross the distance between them and wrap his three-fingered hand around the merc's throat. He raised the human to the ceiling, easily holding him with one arm as he slowly crushed his windpipe. The merc kicked his dangling heels and clawed at the scaly forearm choking the life from him to no avail.

"Your death comes at the hands of a true krogan Battle Master," Skarr casually informed him as his victim's face turned bright red, then blue. "I hope you appreciate the honor."

The rest of the Blue Suns stood by and did nothing,

watching the whole affair with cold disdain. From their expressions Edan could tell they weren't enjoying the spectacle, but none of them was willing to step in and put a stop to it. Not if it meant offending their employer . . . or incurring the krogan's wrath.

The merc's struggles grew weaker, then his eyes rolled back up into his skull and he went still. Skarr shook him once then gave a final squeeze, completely collapsing his trachea before dropping him disdainfully to the floor.

"I thought you said he had to the count of three," Edan remarked.

"I lied."

"An impressive display," Edan admitted, nodding his head in the direction of the bodies. "I only hope you have similar results with Kahlee Sanders. Of course, you'll have to find her, first."

"I'll find her," the krogan replied with absolute conviction. "That's what I do."

Jon Grissom woke to the sound of someone pounding on his door in the middle of the night. Grumbling, he rolled out of bed and threw on a tattered housecoat, though he didn't bother tying it closed. Any visitor rude enough to get him out of bed at this hour could damn well suffer through seeing him in his boxers.

He'd actually been expecting something like this ever since he'd heard Sidon had been attacked. Either someone from Alliance brass showing up to try and convince him to make some kind of public appearance or official statement, or some reporter looking to get the reaction of one of humanity's most recognizable icons. Whichever it was, they were out of luck. He was retired now. He was done being a hero; he was sick of being some kind of symbol for all of humanity. Now he was just a cranky old man living off his officer's pension.

He flicked on a light in the hall and winced at the brightness, still trying to shake off the last vestiges of groggy sleep. He plodded his way slowly from the bedroom—tucked away in the back of his small, single-story dwelling—toward the front door. The pounding continued, growing more insistent and frantic.

"Goddammit, I'm coming!" he shouted, but he didn't bother to pick up his pace. At least the noise wouldn't wake the neighbors—there weren't any. Not close enough to hear, anyway. As far as he was concerned, that was the main selling feature of the house.

Elysium had seemed like a good place to retire. The colony was far enough away from Earth and other major settlements to dissuade people from making the trip out of simple curiosity. And with a population of several million, Elysium was large enough for him to just disappear among the masses. Not to mention it was safe, stable, and secure. He could have found somewhere even more remote, but on a less established colony he'd run the risk of being looked at as some type of savior or de facto leader whenever something went wrong.

It wasn't perfect, though. When he'd first arrived on Elysium five years ago, local politicians had pestered him constantly, either wanting him to run on their party's behalf or looking for an endorsement of their own candidacy. Grissom chose to remain completely fair and unbiased: he told every single one of them to go to hell.

After the first year people stopped bothering him. Every six months or so he'd still get a short video message from the Alliance encouraging him to come back and help serve humanity. He was only in his fifties: too young to sit around and do nothing, they'd say. He never bothered to reply. Grissom figured he'd already done plenty to serve humanity. His military career had always come first; it had cost him his family. But that was just the beginning. There was the five-year media circus that had followed his pioneering journey through the Charon relay, thousands upon thousands of interviews. Things only got worse after his efforts during the First Contact War: more interviews; public appearances; private conferences with admirals, generals, and politicians; official diplomatic ceremonies to meet with representatives of every freaky mutant species of alien the Alliance ran into. Now he was done. Let someone else take the banner and run with it—he just wanted to be left the hell alone.

And then some jackasses had to go and attack an Alliance base right on Elysium's doorstep, galactically speaking. It was inevitable somebody would figure this was a good enough excuse to resume bothering him again. But did they have to do it in the middle of the goddamned night?

He was at the door, and the pounding hadn't let up at all. If anything, it had gotten more urgent and intense the longer he took. As he unlocked the door, Grissom decided he would tell the visitor to piss off if they were from the Alliance. If it was a reporter, he'd punch him—or her—right in the mouth.

A terrified young woman stood at the door, shaking in the cold darkness. She was covered in so much blood, it took him a second to recognize her.

"Kahlee?"

"I'm in trouble," she said in a quavering voice. "I need your help, Dad."

SIX

"Citadel control says we are cleared for landing" came the helmsman's voice over the shipboard intercom. "ETA to docking, seventeen minutes."

Through the *Hastings*'s primary viewport, Anderson could see the Citadel in the distance, the magnificent space station that served as the cultural, economic, and political center of the galaxy. From here, several thousand kilometers away, it resembled a five-pointed star: a quintet of long, thick arms extending out from a hollow central ring.

Though he'd seen it many times before, Anderson still marveled at its sheer size. The middle ring was ten kilometers in diameter; each arm was twenty-five kilometers long and five kilometers in breadth. In the twenty-seven hundred years since the Council was established on the Citadel, great cosmopolitan metropolises known as the wards had been constructed along each arm, entire cities built into the station's multi-level interior. Forty million people from every species and sector across the known galaxy now made their homes there.

There was quite simply no other station to compare it to; even Arcturus would be dwarfed in its presence. But it wasn't just its size that made it so amazing: like the mass relays, the Citadel had originally been created by the Protheans. Its hull was formed of the same virtually indestructible material used to construct the mass relays—a technological feat no other species had equaled since the Protheans' mysterious extinction fifty thousand years ago. Even with the most advanced weaponry it would take days of steady, concentrated bombardment to do any significant damage to the hull.

Not that anyone would ever consider attacking the Citadel. The station was located at the heart of a major mass relay junction deep inside a dense nebula cloud. This gave it several natural defenses: the nebula was difficult to navigate—it would slow any enemy fleets and make it difficult for them to launch any sort of organized attack. And with several dozen mass relays in the vicinity, reinforcements from virtually every region of the galaxy were only minutes away.

If anyone did penetrate these exterior defenses, the station's long arms could fold up around the central ring, drawing together to transform the Citadel from a five-armed star into a long cylindrical tube. Once the arms were closed, the station was all but impregnable.

The final layer of protection was provided by the Council Fleet, a joint force of turian, salarian, and asari vessels that was always on patrol in the vicinity. It only took Anderson a few seconds to pick out the flagship, the *Destiny Ascension*. An asari dreadnought, the *Ascension* was more than just a majestic symbol of the Council's power. Four times the size of anything in the human fleet, and with a crew approaching five thousand, the *Destiny Ascension* was the most formidable warship ever constructed. Like the Citadel itself, it was without peer.

Of course, the ships of the Council Fleet were not the only vessels in the area. The Serpent Nebula was the nexus of the galaxy's mass relay network—all roads eventually led to the Citadel. Traffic here was constant and crowded: this was one of the few places in all the galaxy where there was a real threat of crashing into another vessel.

Congestion was particularly heavy at the free-floating discharge stations. Generating the mass effect fields necessary to run at FTL speeds caused a powerful charge to build up inside a ship's drive core. Left unchecked the core would oversaturate, resulting in a massive energy burst being released through the hull— a burst powerful enough to cook anyone on board who wasn't properly grounded, burn out all electronic systems, and even fuse the metal bulkheads.

To prevent such a calamity most ships were required to discharge their drive cores every twenty to thirty hours. Typically this was done by grounding on a planet or dispersing the buildup through close proximity to the magnetic field of a large stellar body, such as a sun or gas giant. However, there were no astrological bodies of sufficient size in the nearby vicinity of the Citadel. Instead, a ring of specially designed docking stations allowed ships to link in and release the energy in their drive cores before continuing on using conventional sub-FTL drives.

Fortunately, the *Hastings* had discharged her core when she'd first arrived in the region over an hour ago. Since then she'd been in a holding pattern, patiently waiting for the clearance they had only just now received.

Anderson didn't need to worry about the crew's performance on a routine approach like this; they'd done it hundreds of times before. Instead, he just shut his mind off and enjoyed the view as the Citadel drew slowly closer, looming ever larger in the viewport. The lights from the wards twinkled and shone; their piercing illumination a counterpoint to the hazy, swirling brightness of the nebula cloud that served as the backdrop to the scene.

"It's beautiful."

Anderson jumped, startled by the voice coming from right behind him.

Gunnery Chief Dah laughed. "Sorry, Lieutenant. Didn't mean to scare you."

Anderson glanced down at the bandages and walking brace that encased her leg from the upper thigh all the way down to her ankle.

"You're getting pretty good on that thing, Chief. I didn't even hear you sneaking up on me."

She shrugged. "Medic said I'm going to make a complete recovery. I owe you one."

"That's not how it works," Anderson replied with a smile. "I know you'd have done the same for me."

"I like to think so, sir. But thinking it and doing it aren't the same. So . . . thanks."

"Don't tell me you came all the way up here from the infirmary just to thank me."

She grinned. "Actually, I came to see if you'd give me another piggyback ride."

"Forget it," Anderson replied with a laugh. "I

nearly threw my back out hauling your ass out of there. You really need to shed a few pounds."

"Careful, sir," she warned, lifting her braced leg an inch off the floor. "I can deliver a pretty good kick with this thing."

Anderson turned back to the viewport, grinning. "Just shut up and enjoy the view, Dah. That's an order."

"Yes, sir."

It only took a few minutes for Anderson to clear customs after they landed. They had touched down at an Alliance port, and military personnel were given top priority whenever they came in from a mission. The Citadel security officers checked his Alliance ID and verified it by scanning his thumbprint, then gave a cursory check of the pack carrying his personal belongings before waving him through. Anderson was pleased to see they were both human; last month there had still been a few salarian officers assigned to the Alliance ports due to species staff shortages. C-Sec had promised to recruit more humans into their ranks; it looked like they'd been true to their word.

Leaving the ports behind, he stepped onto the elevator that would bring him up to the main level. He yawned once; now that he was off duty the fatigue he'd been holding at bay during the entire mission began to wash over him. He couldn't wait to get back to his private residence in the wards. Considering how much time he spent on patrol, it could be argued that paying rent for an apartment on the Citadel was an extravagant expense. But he felt it was important to have a place he could call his own, even if he was only home one week out of four.

The elevator stopped, the doors opened, and Anderson stepped out into the pandemonium of light and sound that was the wards. Throngs of people filled the pedways, individuals of every species coming and going in all directions. Rapid-transit cars zoomed by overhead on the monorail, each one filled with commuters, students, and general gawkers taking the high-speed tour. The lower streets were packed with smaller ground-transport vehicles weaving in and out of the designated thoroughfares, each driver in more of a hurry than the last. It was always rush hour on the Citadel.

Fortunately he didn't need to flag a driver down or head to a transit stop. His apartment was only twenty minutes away by foot, so he simply hiked his gear up over his shoulder and fell in with the mob, jostling and shoving with the rest of the maddening crowds.

As he walked, his senses were under constant assault from an endless stream of electronic advertisements. Everywhere he looked there were flashing holographic images, futuristic billboards promoting a thousand different companies on a hundred different worlds. Food, beverages, vehicles, clothes, entertainment: on the Citadel, everything was available for purchase. However, only a handful of the ads were geared specifically to humans; they were still a minority on the station, and corporations preferred to spend their advertising dollars on species with a larger market share. But with each passing month Anderson noticed more and more of his own kind among the hustling, bustling masses.

Anderson knew that it was important for humans to integrate themselves with the rest of the interstellar community. What better place to do it than the Citadel, where all the disparate cultures in Council space were on display? That was the real reason Anderson kept his apartment in the wards. He wanted to understand the other species, and the quickest way to do that was to live among them.

He reached his building, pausing at the main door to speak his name so the voice recognition system would let him in. His apartment was on the second level, so he eschewed the elevator and lugged his pack up the staircase. At the door to his personal quarters he again gave his name, then staggered into the room and dropped his gear in the center of the floor. He was too tired to turn on the lights as he made his way through the small kitchen to the single bedroom at the back; barely registering the faint whoosh as the apartment door automatically closed behind him. When he reached the bedroom he didn't even bother to undress—he simply collapsed on the bed, exhausted but glad to be home.

Anderson woke several hours later. Night and day meant little in the perpetual activity of the Citadel, but when he rolled over to check the clock by his bed the digital readout said 17:00. On human colonies and out on patrol the Alliance still used the familiar twenty-four-hour clock based on Terran Coordinated Universal Time, the protocol established in the late twentieth century to replace the archaic Greenwich Mean Time system. On the Citadel, however, everything operated on the galactic standard of a twenty-hour day. To further complicate things, each hour was divided into one hundred minutes of one hundred seconds . . . but each second was roughly half as long as the ones humans were used to.

The net result was that the twenty-hour galactic standard day was about fifteen percent longer than the twenty-four-hour day as calculated by Terran Coordinated Universal Time. Just thinking about it made Anderson's head hurt, and it played havoc with his sleep patterns. This was to be expected, given that he'd been preconditioned by several million years of Terran evolution.

Three more hours and the day would roll into tomorrow, when he was supposed to present himself to the ambassador for a debriefing on Sidon. He didn't have to be there until 10:00, however, which meant that he had plenty of time to kill. He'd probably need to catch a few more hours of sleep before the meeting, but he wasn't tired now. So Anderson rolled out of bed, shed his clothes, and tossed them into the small laundry machine. He had a quick shower, changed into fresh clothes—civvies—then logged on to his data terminal to check for news updates and messages.

Communication across an entire galaxy was no simple matter. Ships could use mass effect drives to exceed the speed of light, but signals transmitted through the cold vacuum of space by conventional means would still take years to travel from one solar system to another.

Transferring information, personal messages, or even raw data across thousands of light-years expediently could only be accomplished in one of two ways. Files could be transported by courier drones, unmanned ships programmed to travel through the mass relays network by the most direct routes possible. But courier drones weren't cheap to produce or operate: fuel was expensive. And if they had to pass through several relays it could take hours for them to arrive at their destination. The solution wasn't practical for back-and-forth communications.

The other option was to transmit data via the extranet, a series of buoys placed across the galaxy that were specifically designed to enable real-time communication between systems. Information could be sent by a conventional radio signal to the nearest array of communication buoys. The buoys were telemetrically aligned with a similar array hundreds or even thousands of light-years away, connected by the tight beam projection of a mass effect field; the space-age equivalent of the fiber-optic cables used on Earth in the late twentieth century. Within this narrow corridor, signals could be projected several thousands times faster than the speed of light. Data in the form of radio signals could be relayed from one array to the next virtually instantaneously. Once the arrays were properly aligned, it was even possible to speak to someone on the opposite end of the galaxy with a lag of only a few tenths of a second.

However, while the extranet's buoy arrays made communication possible, it still wasn't exactly feasible for the vast majority. Trillions of people on thousands of worlds were accessing the extranet every second of every day, overloading the finite bandwidth capabilities of the com arrays. To accommodate this, information was sent in carefully measured bursts of data, and space in each burst was parceled out in a highly regulated priority system. Top priority in each burst was given to organizations directly responsible for preserving galactic security. Next came the various official governments and militaries for each and every species in Council space; then the assorted media conglomerates. Anything left over was parceled off and sold to the highest bidder.

Virtually all of the unused space on every burst was purchased by extranet provider corporations, who then divided their allocated space into thousands of tiny packages that were resold to individual subscribers. Depending on the provider and how much an individual was willing to pay, it was possible to get personal updates from hourly, daily, or even weekly bursts.

Not that Anderson had to be concerned about any of that. As an Alliance officer his private extranet account received official bursts every fifteen minutes. Piggybacking personal messages onto the official bursts was one of the perks of his rank.

There was only one message waiting for him in his in-box. He frowned, recognizing the sender's address. It wasn't exactly a surprise, but he wasn't happy to see the file. For a second he considered ignoring it, but he knew he was being childish. Better to just get it over with.

He opened the file, downloading a series of e-docs and a short prerecorded video message from the divorce attorney.

An image of Ib Haman, his lawyer, appeared on the terminal's screen as the video began to play. Ib was a portly, balding man in his sixties. He was wearing an expensive-looking suit and was seated behind his desk in an office Anderson had become all too familiar with over the last year.

"Lieutenant. I won't bother with the formality of asking how you're doing . . . I know this hasn't been easy for you or Cynthia."

"Damn right," Anderson muttered under his breath as the message continued.

"I've sent you copies of all the documents I had you sign the last time we met. Cynthia's signed them now, too."

The man on the screen glanced down and shifted some papers on the desk in front of him, then looked back up at the camera.

"You'll also see a copy of my fee. I know this isn't much consolation right now, but just be glad you two didn't have any children. It could have been a lot worse—and a lot more expensive. When custody becomes an issue the proceedings rarely go this smoothly."

Anderson snorted. Nothing about this mess had felt "smooth" to him.

"The marriage will be officially absolved on the date indicated in the documents. I suspect that by the time you get this message your divorce will be final.

"If you have any questions please feel free to contact me, Lieutenant. And if you ever need me for—"

The message terminated abruptly as Anderson deleted it and dragged it into the trash. He didn't plan on ever talking to Ib Haman again. The man was a good attorney; his prices were reasonable and he'd been fair and unbiased throughout the divorce. In fact, he'd been nothing but the model of efficiency and professionalism. And if he was standing in the apartment right now, Anderson would have punched him in the face.

It was a funny thing, Anderson thought as he shut the terminal down. He'd just participated in two of humanity's oldest and most enduring customs: marriage and divorce. Now it was time for an even older tradition: he was going to the bar to get drunk.

SEVEN

Chora's Den was the only bar within walking distance of Anderson's apartment. It wasn't exactly a dive, though it did have a certain seedy feel to it. That was part of its charm, along with supple dancers and stiff drinks. But what Anderson liked most about it was the clientele.

At any given time the Den could be busy, but it was never packed. There were plenty of more popular clubs in the wards where people could go to be seen . . . or to be part of the scene. People came here to eat, drink, and relax; average, everyday people who lived and worked in the wards. The common folk, if you could call such an interesting menagerie of aliens common.

Of course, even humans were alien here. Anderson was instantly aware of this as he came through the door. Dozens of eyes turned to look at him, many staring with open curiosity as he paused at the entrance.

It wasn't that humans were particularly strange-looking. Species like the hanar, translucent beings that resembled three-meter-tall jellyfish, were the exception rather than the rule. Most of the space-faring species in the galaxy were bipeds between one and three meters in height. There were a number of theories to explain this resemblance: some were mundane; others highly bizarre and speculative.

Given that most species at the Citadel had ascended to interstellar flight through the discovery and adaptation of caches of Prothean technology on planets within the same solar system as their respective home worlds, many anthropologists believed the Protheans had played some role in evolution throughout the galaxy.

Anderson, however, subscribed to the most generally accepted theory that there was some evolutionary advantage to the biped form that resulted in its proliferation across the galaxy. The caches of technology were easily explained: it was only natural for the Protheans to study intelligent but primitive races that bore some similarity to themselves. The various species, such as humans, had evolved first, and then the Protheans had arrived to study them, not the other way around. The theory of parallel evolution was further supported by the fact that most life-forms on the Citadel were carbon-based, highly dependant on water, and breathed a mixture of gases similar to those found on Earth.

In fact, virtually all inhabitable planets in the galaxy were fundamentally similar to Earth in several key characteristics. They tended to exist in systems with suns that fit the type-G classification according to the traditional Morgan-Keenan system still used by the Alliance. Their orbits all fell in the narrow range known as the life-zone: too close to the sun and water would exist only as a gas, too far away and it would be permanently trapped in frozen form. Because of this, the time it took the home world of almost every major species to complete one orbit around its sun varied by only a few weeks. The galactic standard year—an average of the asari, salarian, and turian years—was only 1.09 times longer than Earth's.

No, Anderson thought as he crossed the floor to an open seat on the bar, *it wasn't their appearance or unusual physical characteristics that made humans stand out. They were simply the newcomers, and they'd made one hell of a first impression.*

A pair of turians fixed their avian eyes on him, following his every move like hawks ready to swoop down on an unsuspecting mouse. Turians were roughly the same height as humans, but much thinner. Their bones were slender and their frames were sharp and angular. Their three-fingered hands looked almost like talons, and their heads and faces were covered by a rigid mask of brown-gray cartilage and bone, which they tended to mark with striping and tribal tattoos. It flared out from the top and back of the skull in short, blunted spikes and extended down to cover the forehead, nose, upper lip, and cheeks, making it difficult to distinguish between individual members of the species. Looking at turians always reminded Anderson of the evolutionary link between dinosaurs and birds.

He met their gaze for a second then quickly looked away, doing his best to ignore them. He was in a foul mood tonight, but he wasn't about to try and revive the First Contact War. Instead, he turned his attention to the asari dancer on the stage in the center of the bar.

Of all the species in Council space, the asari were the

most widespread . . . and the ones who most closely resembled humans. Human women, anyway: tall and slender, with well-proportioned figures. The asari were an asexual species—the concept of gender didn't really apply. But to Anderson's eye they were clearly female. Even their facial features were human . . . although they had an angelic, almost ethereal quality to them. Their complexion was tinged with a blue or greenish hue, but pigment modification was a simple enough procedure that it was possible to see humans of similar skin color, too. Only the backs of their heads betrayed their alien origins. Instead of hair, they had wavy folds of sculpted skin . . . not entirely unattractive, but a disconcertingly alien feature on a species that was otherwise so human in appearance.

The asari were something of a paradox for Anderson. On the one hand they were an aesthetically captivating species. They seemed to embrace this aspect of themselves, and often took to the openly alluring or sensually provocative professions. Asari frequently performed as dancers or served as consorts for hire. On the other hand, they were the most respected, admired, and powerful species in the galaxy.

Renowned for their wisdom and foresight, the asari, by all accepted accounts, were the first species after the Prothean extinction to achieve interstellar flight. They were also the first to discover the Citadel, and they were a founding member species of the Council. The asari controlled more territory and wielded more influence than any other race.

Anderson knew all these facts, yet he often found it difficult to reconcile their dominant role in galactic politics with the enthralling performance of an asari on the stage. He knew the failure was his: a product of his human biases and ill-conceived expectations. It was stupid to judge an entire species on the basis of an individual. But it went deeper than an impression formed by watching a few dancers: the asari looked female, so they were victims of stereotypical human anti-matriarchal tendencies.

At least he was aware of his prejudice, and he did his best to fight against it. Unfortunately he knew there were plenty of other humans who felt the same way and were more than willing to give in to their biases. Just further proof that they still had a lot to learn about the rest of the galaxy.

As he continued to watch the dancer performing on stage, Anderson found the subtle differences in their physiology easy to ignore. He'd heard plenty of graphic tales of interspecies sexual relations, he'd even seen a few vids. He prided himself on keeping an open mind, but that kind of thing normally repulsed him. With the asari, however, he could understand the attraction. And from everything he'd heard, they were highly skilled lovers as well.

But that wasn't why he was here, either.

He turned away from the stage just as the volus bartender waddled up to serve him. The volus home world had a gravity nearly one and a half times that of Earth, and because of this the volus were shorter than humans, their bodies so thick and heavy they almost appeared to be spherical. While the turians evoked hawks or falcons, the volus reminded Anderson of the manatees he had seen at the marine preserve during his last visit to Earth: slow, lumbering, and almost comical.

The atmosphere on the Citadel was thinner than they were used to, so they tended to wear rebreather masks, obscuring their faces. But Anderson had been in Chora's Den enough times to recognize this particular volus.

"I need a drink, Maawda."

"Of course, Lieutenant," the bartender replied, his voice wheezing through the rebreather and the folds of skin at his throat. "What type of beverage do you desire?"

"Surprise me. Something new. Make it strong."

Maawda pulled a blue bottle from the shelves behind the bar and a glass from beneath the counter.

"This is elasa," he explained as he filled the glass with a pale green liquid. "From Thessia."

The asari home world. Anderson nodded, then took a tentative sip. The drink was sharp and cold, but it wasn't exactly unpleasant. The lingering aftertaste was particularly strong, and markedly different from the first sip. It was a bitter flavor, with an undertone of tangy sweetness. If he had to use one word to describe it, he would have said "poignant."

"Not bad," he said approvingly, taking another sip.

"Some call it Sorrow's Companion," Maawda noted, settling himself and leaning in on the counter across from his customer. "A melancholy drink for a melancholy man."

The lieutenant couldn't help but smile at the situation: a volus bartender spotting depression in his human customer, and feeling enough compassion to ask what was wrong. Further proof of what Anderson truly believed: despite all the obvious physical and cultural differences, at their core nearly every species shared the same basic needs, wants, and values.

"I got some bad news today," he answered, running a finger around the rim of his drink. He didn't know a lot about volus culture, so he wasn't quite sure how to explain his situation. "Do you know what marriage is?"

The bartender nodded. "It is a formalized union between partners, yes? An institutionalized recognition of the mating process. My people have a similar tradition."

"Well, I just got divorced. My wife and I are no longer together. My marriage is officially over as of today."

"I am sorry for your loss," Maawda wheezed. "But I am also surprised. In all the times you have come in before you have never mentioned any kind of partner."

Therein lay the problem. Cynthia was back on Earth, and Anderson wasn't. He was either here on the Citadel or out patrolling the Verge. He was a soldier first, and a husband second . . . and Cynthia deserved better.

He downed the rest of his drink in a single gulp, then slammed the glass back down on the bar. "Hit me again, Maawda."

The bartender did as instructed. "Perhaps this situation is only temporary, yes?" he asked as he refilled Anderson's cup. "Maybe in time you will resume this partnership?"

Anderson shook his head. "No chance of that. It's over. Time to move on."

"Easy to say, not so easy to do," the volus replied knowingly.

Anderson took another drink, but he was back to sipping. It wasn't wise to overdo it on a new drink; every concoction had its own unique effects. He could already feel an unusual sensation spreading through him. A numbing warmth crawled its way up from his stomach and out along his arms and legs, making his toes tingle and his fingers itch. It wasn't uncomfortable, just unfamiliar.

"Just how strong is this stuff?" he asked the bartender.

Maawda shrugged. "Depends on how much you drink. I can leave the bottle if you wish to crawl out of here."

The volus's offer sounded like a hell of an idea. Anderson wanted nothing more than to drink until everything went away: the dull, aching pain of the divorce; the gruesome images of the dead bodies at Sidon; the lingering, indefinable stress that always dogged him in those first few days after he came off patrol. But he had a meeting in the morning with the human ambassador to the Citadel, and it wouldn't be professional to show up with a hangover.

"Sorry, Maawda. I better go. Early meeting tomorrow." He polished off his drink and stood up, relieved to see the room wasn't spinning around him. "Put it on my account."

With one last, lingering look at the asari dancer he turned and headed toward the door. The two turians glared at him as he passed their table, and one of them muttered something under his breath. Anderson didn't need to understand the words to know he was being insulted.

He hesitated, his fists involuntarily clenching as he felt his temper rise. But only for a second. Showing up at tomorrow's meeting hung over was bad; having to explain why C-Sec had picked him up for beating the crap out of two turians who didn't know enough to keep their mouths shut was worse.

That was one of the burdens of being an Alliance officer. He was a representative of his species; his actions reflected on humanity as a whole. Even with a mind full of dark thoughts and a belly full of stiff booze, he didn't have the luxury of kicking their asses. Taking a deep breath, he simply walked away, swallowing his pride and ignoring the harsh, mocking laughter coming from behind him because it was his duty.

Always a soldier first.

EIGHT

Anderson was up at 07:00. He had a slight headache, the mild aftereffects of his late-night visit to Chora's Den. But a three-mile run on the treadmill he kept stashed in the corner of the apartment and a steaming hot shower purged the last remnants of the elasa from his system.

By the time he changed into his uniform—cleaned and pressed from the night before—he felt like his old self. He'd pushed all thoughts of Cynthia and the divorce into a small compartment in the back of his mind; it was time to move on. There was only one thing that mattered this morning: getting some answers about Sidon.

He walked through the streets to the public-transport depot. He showed his military ID, then boarded the high-speed elevator used to shuttle people from the lower levels of the wards to the Presidium high above.

Anderson always enjoyed visiting the Presidium. Unlike the wards, which were built along the arms extending out from the Citadel, the Presidium occupied the station's central ring. And although it housed all the government offices and the embassies of the

various species, it was a sharp contrast to the sprawling metropolis he was leaving behind.

The Presidium had been designed to evoke a vast
parkland ecosystem. A large freshwater lake dominated the center of the level, rolling fields of verdant
grass ran the length of its banks. Fabricated breezes,
gentle as spring zephyrs, caused ripples on the lake
and spread the scent of the thousands of planted trees
and flowers to every corner of the Presidium. Artificial sunlight streamed down from a simulated blue
sky filled with white, puffy clouds. The illusion was so
perfect that most people, including Anderson, couldn't
distinguish it from the real thing.

The buildings where the business of government
was conducted had been similarly constructed with
an eye to natural aesthetics. Set along the gently curv-
ing arch that marked the edge of the station's central
ring, they blended unobtrusively into the background.
Broad, open walkways meandered back and from building to building, echoing the landscape of the carefully
manufactured pastoral scene at the Presidium's heart—
the perfect combination of form and function.

However, as Anderson stepped off the elevator and
onto the level, he was reminded that it wasn't the
organic beauty that he most appreciated about the
Presidium. Access to the Citadel's inner ring was
generally restricted to government and military officials, or those with legitimate embassy business. As a
result, the Presidium was the one place on the Citadel
where Anderson didn't feel like he was under constant siege from the rushing, crushing crowds.

Not that it was empty, of course. The galactic bureaucracy employed thousands of citizens from every race that maintained an embassy on the Presidium, including humanity. But the numbers here were a far cry from the millions who populated the wards.

He reveled in the peaceful tranquillity as he strolled along the lakeside, slowly working his way toward his meeting at the human embassy. Far in the distance he could see the Citadel Tower, where the Council met with ambassadors petitioning them on matters of interstellar policy and law. The Tower's spire rose in majestic solitude above the rest of the buildings, barely visible at the point where the curve of the central ring created a false horizon.

Anderson had never been there himself. If he ever wanted to petition the Council, he'd have to go through the proper channels; most likely the ambassador would end up doing it on his behalf. And that was just fine by him. He was a soldier, not a diplomat.

He passed by one of the keepers, the silent, enigmatic race that maintained and controlled the inner workings of the Citadel. They reminded him of oversized aphids: fat green bodies with too many sticklike arms and legs, always scuttling from one place to another on some task or errand.

Little was known about the keepers. They existed nowhere in the galaxy but on the Citadel; they had simply been there waiting when the asari had discovered the station almost three thousand years ago. They had reacted to the arrival of the new species as servants might react to a master returning home: scurrying and scrambling to do everything possible to make it easier for the asari to familiarize themselves with the Citadel and its operations.

All efforts to directly communicate with the keep-ers were met with mute, passive resistance. They seemed to have no purpose to their existence beyond servicing and repairing the Citadel, and there was an ongoing debate as to whether they were truly intelli-gent. Some theories held that they were in fact organic machines, genetically programmed by the Protheans to care for the Citadel with a single-minded fanaticism. They functioned purely on instinct, the theory claimed, so unaware they didn't even realize their original creators had vanished fifty thousand years ago.

Anderson ignored the keeper as he went by—a typi-cal reaction. They were so ubiquitous on the station, and so unobtrusive and unassuming, that most peo-ple tended to just take them for granted.

Five minutes later he had reached the building that served as the human embassy. He went inside, the corners of his mouth rising up in a slight grin when he saw the attractive young woman sitting behind the reception desk. She looked up as he approached, re-turning his coy smile with a radiant one of her own.

"Good morning, Aurora."

"It's been a while since I've seen you around here, Lieutenant." Her voice was as pleasing to the ear as her appearance was to the eye: warm, inviting, confident—the perfect welcome to any and all embassy visitors.

"I was beginning to think you were avoiding me," she teased.

"No, I'm just trying to stay out of trouble."

With a free hand she tapped a few keys on her ter-minal and glanced over at the screen. "Uh-oh," she said, feigning a deep and troubling concern, "you've got a meeting with Ambassador Goyle herself."

She arched an eyebrow, playfully taking him to task. "I thought you said you were staying out of trouble."

"I said I was *trying* to stay out of trouble," he countered. "I never said I was succeeding."

He was rewarded with a light laugh that was probably polished and practiced, but nonetheless sounded warm and sincere.

"The captain's already here. I'll let them know you're coming."

Anderson nodded and headed up the stairs toward the ambassador's office, his step somewhat lighter than it had been a few moments before. He wasn't foolish enough to read anything into their exchange. Aurora was just doing her job: the receptionist had been hired for her ability to make people feel comfortable and at ease. But he wouldn't deny that he enjoyed their flirtations.

The door to the ambassador's office was closed. Aurora had said they were expecting him, but he still paused to knock.

"Come in" came a woman's voice from the other side.

As soon as he entered he knew the meeting was serious. There were several comfortable chairs and a small coffee table in the office, not to mention the ambassador's desk. But both the captain and the ambassador were standing as they waited for him.

"Please close the door behind you, Lieutenant." Anderson did as the ambassador instructed, then stepped into the room and stood stiffly at attention.

Anita Goyle was the most influential and important individual in human politics, and she definitely projected an image of power. Bold and confident, she was a striking woman in her early sixties. She was of medium build, with long silver hair—tied up in a stylish bun—and high, elegant cheekbones. Her features were Middle Eastern, though she had deep emerald eyes that stood out in sharp contrast to her mocha skin. Right now those eyes were fixed directly on Anderson, and he had to fight the urge to fidget under their piercing gaze.

"At ease," his captain said. Anderson complied, widening his stance and clasping his hands behind his back.

"I'm not going to play games with you, Lieutenant," the ambassador began. She had a reputation for cutting through the usual political bs; that was one of the things Anderson admired about her. "We're here to try and figure out what went wrong at Sidon, and how we're going to fix it."

"Yes, ma'am," he replied.

"I want you to speak freely here. You understand, Lieutenant? Don't hold anything back."

"Understood, ma'am."

"As you know, Sidon was one of our top-security-clearance installations. What you hopefully didn't know was that it was the primary Alliance facility for AI research."

It was difficult for Anderson not to show his surprise. Attempting to develop artificial intelligence was one of the few things specifically banned in the Citadel Conventions. Developing purely synthetic life, whether cloned or manufactured, was considered a crime against the entire galaxy.

Experts from nearly every species predicted that

true artificial intelligence—such as a synthetic neural network with the ability to absorb and critically analyze knowledge—would grow exponentially the instant it learned to learn. It would teach itself; quickly surpassing the capabilities of its organic creators and growing beyond their control. Every single species in the galaxy relied on computers that were linked into the vast data network of the extranet for transport, trade, defense, and basic survival. If a rogue AI program was somehow able to access and influence those data networks, the results would be catastrophic.

Conventional theory held that the doomsday scenario wasn't merely possible, it was unavoidable. According to the Council, the emergence of an artificial intelligence was the single greatest threat to organic life in the galaxy. And there was evidence to support their position.

Three hundred years ago, long before humanity appeared on the galactic scene, the quarian species had created a race of synthetic servants to serve as an expandable and expendable labor force. The geth, as they were called, were not true AIs: their neural networks were developed in a way that was highly restrictive and self-limiting. Despite this precaution, the geth eventually turned on their quarian masters, validating all the dire warnings and predictions.

The quarians had neither the numbers nor the ability to stand against their former servants. In a short but savage war their entire society was wiped out. Only a few million survivors—less than one percent of their entire population—escaped the genocide, fleeing their home world in a massive fleet, refugees forced to live in exile.

In the aftermath of the war, the geth became a completely isolationist society. Cutting off all contact with the organic species of the galaxy, they expanded their territory into the unexplored regions behind a vast nebulae cloud known as the Perseus Veil. Every attempt to open diplomatic channels with them failed: emissary vessels sent to open negotiations were attacked and destroyed the moment they entered geth space.

Fleets from every species in Citadel space massed on the borders of the Veil as the Council prepared for a massive geth invasion. But the expected attack never came. Gradually the fleets were scaled back, until now, several centuries after the quarians were driven out, only a few patrols remained to monitor the region for signs of geth aggression.

However, the lesson of the quarians had not been forgotten. They had lost everything to the synthetic creatures they created . . . and on top of this, the geth were still less advanced than a true AI.

"You look like you have something to say, Lieutenant."

Anderson had done his best to keep his face from betraying his feelings, but the ambassador had seen right through his facade. There was a reason she was the most powerful politician in the Alliance.

"I'm sorry, ma'am. I'm just surprised we're conducting AI research. Seems pretty risky."

"We are well aware of the dangers," the ambassador reassured him. "We have no intention of unleashing a fully formed AI on the galaxy. The goals of the project were very specific: create limited AI simulations for observation and study.

"Humanity is the underdog now," she continued. "We're expanding, but we still don't have the numbers or the fleets to match the major species vying for power in Council space. We need some kind of advantage. Understanding AI technology would help give us the edge we need to compete and survive."

"You of all people should understand," the captain added. "Without rudimentary AI technology we'd all be living under turian rule right now."

It was true. Alliance military strategy relied heavily on highly advanced combat simulation programs. Collating millions of variables each second, the simulations would analyze a massive data bank of scenarios, helping to provide constant updates on optimized tactics and strategies to the commanders of each Alliance vessel. Without the combat simulators, humanity wouldn't have stood a chance against the larger, more experienced turian fleets in the First Contact War.

"I understand your concern," Ambassador Goyle explained, possibly sensing Anderson still wasn't wholly convinced. "But Sidon base was operating under the strictest security and safety protocols. The project head, Dr. Shu Qian, is the galaxy's foremost expert on artificial intelligence research.

"He personally oversaw every aspect of the project. Qian even insisted that the neural networks we used to create the AI simulations be completely self-contained. The data had to be registered and recorded by hand, then manually entered into a separate system to ensure there was no chance of cross-contamination with the neural network. Whatever happened, there was no way for the AI simulations to affect anything outside the restricted data systems within the base. Every possible precaution was taken to make sure nothing could possibly go wrong."

"And yet something did."

"You're out of line, Lieutenant!" the captain barked.

The ambassador held up her hand as she jumped to his defense. "I told him to speak freely, Captain."

"I meant no disrespect, ma'am," Anderson said by way of apology. "You don't need to justify Sidon's existence to me. I'm just a grunt who got sent in to clean up the mess."

An awkward silence followed, finally broken by the ambassador. "I've read your report," she said, tactfully changing the direction of the conversation. "You don't seem to think this was a random attack."

"No, ma'am. I'd say Sidon was specifically targeted. I just didn't know why until now."

"If that's true, there's a good chance whoever attacked Sidon was also after Dr. Qian specifically. His work in the field is unparalleled; nobody understands synthetic intelligence better than he."

"You think Dr. Qian's still alive?"

"My gut says he is," the ambassador answered. "I think whoever attacked Sidon destroyed the base to cover their tracks. They wanted us to think everybody inside was dead so we wouldn't bother looking for Qian."

The lieutenant had assumed the explosion was meant to hide the identity of the traitor, but it could also have been used to hide the fact that Qian wasn't among the dead. There wasn't any way to prove the theory, of course, but like the ambassador, Anderson had learned to trust his gut. And his gut said she was right.

"Do you think Dr. Qian could be convinced to use his research to help someone outside the Alliance develop an AI?" he asked.

"Dr. Qian isn't a soldier," she replied, a look of grim concern on her face. "He has a brilliant mind, but it's in the body of a frail old man. He might be brave enough to refuse to help a nonhuman species, even if they threatened to kill him. But a few weeks of torture would break his resistance."

"So we're working against the clock."

"Seems that way," the ambassador admitted. "I noticed something else in your report," she continued, smoothly changing her focus yet again. "You said you believe the attackers had help from someone working on the project?"

"Yes, ma'am."

"We may know who that person is," the captain chimed in.

"Sir?"

It was the ambassador who answered him. "One of our top technicians left the base UA just hours before the attack. Kahlee Sanders. We have reports she was last seen on Elysium, but she's dropped off the grid since then."

"You figure if we find her, we find Dr. Qian?"

"We won't know that until you find her, Lieutenant."

Anderson was surprised. "You're sending the *Hastings* to track her down?"

"No," the ambassador replied. "Just you."

Instinctively he turned toward his captain. "Sir, I don't understand."

"You're the best damn XO I've ever served with,

Anderson," the captain said. "But the ambassador's asking that you be reassigned."

"Understood, sir." He tried to keep his voice professional, but Goyle must have picked up on his disappointment.

"This isn't a punishment, Lieutenant. I've looked over your service records. Head of your class at Arcturus. Three different medals of merit during the First Contact War. Numerous commendations throughout your career. You're the best the Alliance has to offer. And this is the most important mission we've ever had."

Anderson gave an emphatic nod. "You can count on me, Ambassador." He was a soldier, sworn to defend humanity. This was his duty, and it was an honor to accept the burden being placed upon him.

"You're going to be working on this alone," the captain told him. "The more people we send after Sanders, the more chance somebody outside this room finds out what we were doing at Sidon."

"Officially this mission doesn't even exist," the ambassador added. "Humanity's still the new kid on the block. We're bold, we're brash, and every other race is just waiting for us to screw up.

"I don't have to tell you what it's like out there in the Verge, Lieutenant. You've seen how hard it is to establish a colony and make it stick. We're clawing and scraping and fighting for every little gain we make, just trying to survive. But if the Citadel gets wind of this, things will get a whole lot tougher.

"If we're lucky, we'll get off with an official rebuke and major trade sanctions, crippling our economy. If we're unlucky, they could revoke our embassy here on the Citadel. They could make it illegal for any other Council species to deal with us on any level.

"Humanity's not strong enough to make it out there completely on our own. Not yet."

"I know how to be discreet," Anderson assured her.

"It's not just you. Kahlee Sanders knows something about this. So does whoever was involved in the actual attack. How long until one of these people runs across a Spectre?"

Anderson frowned. The last thing they needed was for a Spectre to become involved. Elite agents of the Citadel's covert Special Tactics and Recon branch, Spectres answered directly to the Council itself. Highly trained individuals authorized to act above and outside the law, the Spectres had one simple mandate: protect galactic stability at any and all costs. The Skyllian Verge—a largely unsettled border region of Council space that was a known haven for rebels, insurrectionists, and terrorist groups—was exactly the kind of place where Spectres would be most active. And a rogue faction in possession of the galaxy's foremost expert on AI technology was exactly the kind of threat Spectres excelled in hunting down and eliminating.

"If a Spectre somehow finds out about this, they'll have to report it to the Council," Anderson said, choosing his words carefully. "How far am I supposed to go to keep this secret?"

"Are you asking if we're ordering you to kill an official agent of the Council?" the captain asked.

Anderson nodded.

"I can't make that decision for you, Lieutenant,"

the ambassador told him. "We trust your judgment. If the situation comes up, it'll be your call.

"Not that I think it'll matter," she added ominously. "By the time you find out a Spectre's gotten involved, you'll probably already be dead."

NINE

Night was approaching on the planet of Juxhi. The dim orange sun was setting on the horizon and Yando, the smaller of the world's two moons, was already approaching its zenith. For the next twenty minutes darkness would reign. Then Budmi, Yando's larger twin, would begin to rise, and the darkness would give way to an eerie twilight.

Saren Arterius, a turian Spectre, waited patiently for the sun to disappear. For several hours Saren had been perched atop a rock outcropping, staking out a small, isolated warehouse in the desert on the outskirts of Phend, Juxhi's capital city. Built in the sheltering stones of a small canyon, the run-down building was completely unremarkable, except for the fact that an illegal weapons deal was about to go down there.

The buyers were already inside: a group of gun-toting thugs with basic military training known as the Grim Skulls, one of the many private security organizations active in the Verge. The Skulls were small, a few dozen criminal mercenaries who had never been worth Saren's attention before tonight. Then they'd made the mistake of thinking they could purchase a stolen shipment of military-grade weapons that had disappeared from a turian transport freighter.

His ears caught the sound of an engine in the distance, and a few minutes later a six-wheeled ATV rolled up and came to a stop beside the shed. A half-dozen men got out; two were turian, the others human. Even in the dim light, Saren recognized one of the turians immediately: a dockworker from the Camala ports.

He'd been following the dockworker for days, ever since he checked the duty logs to see who was on shift when the shipment went missing. Only one worker hadn't shown up for work the next day; figuring out who the thief was had been embarrassingly easy.

Tracking him down wasn't much harder. This entire operation reeked of amateurs in over their heads, from the theft to the buyers. Normally Saren would've turned the matter over to local authorities and moved on to something bigger. But turians selling weapons to humans was something he took personally.

The door to the shed opened, and four of the figures, including both turians, unloaded a crate from the back of the ATV and carried it inside. The other two took up sentry positions beside the door.

Saren shook his head in disbelief as he snapped his night-vision goggles into place. What possible use was there in leaving two men to stand guard outside a warehouse in the middle of nowhere? They had no cover; they were completely exposed.

Raising his Izaali Combine–manufactured sniper rifle to his eye, he fired two shots and both sentries slumped to the ground. Moving with an almost casual efficiency, he collapsed the sniper rifle and slid it back into the designated slot on his backpack. A more professional operation would have someone on the inside periodically checking on the sentries . . . or wouldn't have left them out there in the first place.

It took him ten minutes to clamber down from his perch on the rock face. By then the twin moons were both visible, giving enough illumination for him to stash his goggles back into his pack.

Whipping out the Haliat Arms semiautomatic assault rifle from where it clicked into place on his thigh, he approached the building's entrance. He'd scouted the warehouse earlier; he knew there were no windows and no other doors. Everyone inside was trapped—further proof he was dealing with idiots.

He pressed himself against the door, listening carefully. Inside he could hear angry bickering. Apparently nobody had the foresight to spell out the terms of the exchange before the meeting; either that or somebody was trying to renegotiate the deal. Professionals didn't make that mistake: get to the meeting, make the exchange, and get out. The longer you're there, the more chance something's going to go wrong.

Saren pulled three incendiary grenades from his belt, primed them, and began to count silently to himself. When he reached five he yanked open the door, tossed all three grenades in, slammed the door shut, and ran for cover behind the ATV.

The explosion blew the door off its hinges, sending smoke, flame, and debris shooting out the opening. Inside he heard screams and the sound of gunfire as the terrified men inside panicked. Burned and blinded, they started shooting wildly, each side convinced they'd been betrayed by the other. For a full twenty seconds the echo of gunfire reverberating off the warehouse's metal walls drowned out every other sound.

Then everything went still. Saren aimed his weapon at the door, and was rewarded a few seconds later when two men came charging out, guns blazing. He took the first square in the chest with a short burst from his assault rifle, then ducked behind the tail end of the ATV for cover as the surviving merc returned fire. A quick roll brought Saren to the front of the vehicle, and when he popped up his enemy still had his weapon aimed at the back end, waiting for Saren to reemerge. At point-blank range the rounds from Saren's assault rifle sheared off half of the guy's head.

For good measure, Saren lobbed two more grenades into the open door. Instead of a fiery explosion, these released a noxious cloud when they detonated. He heard more shouts and screams, followed by choking coughs. Three more mercs stumbled out of the shed one by one, each blind and gagging from the poison gas. Not one of them even returned fire as Saren mowed them down.

He waited a few more minutes, letting the deadly fog clear, then sprinted from his position behind the truck to the edge of the door. He poked his head inside for an instant, then ducked back out of the way.

The warehouse was littered with a dozen bodies. Some had been shot, several were burned, and the rest were twisted into horrific contortions from the gas causing their muscles to seize and spasm as they died. Several weapons were scattered about, dropped by their owners in their death throes. The crate they had carried inside on their arrival sat in the middle of the floor, unopened. Aside from that, the warehouse was empty.

Assault rifle in hand, Saren made his way from body to body, slowly working his way from the door toward the back of the warehouse as he checked for signs of life. With the toe of his shoe, he rolled over a charred turian who had fallen near the crate. One half of his face was burned, the carapace crispy and brittle. The flesh beneath it had melted, fusing the eyelids on the left side together. A small moan escaped his lips, and his good eye fluttered open.

"Who . . . who are you?" he croaked.

"A Spectre," Saren replied, standing over him.

He coughed, spewing up dark phlegm that was mostly a mix of blood and poison.

"Please . . . help me."

"You are in violation of interstellar law," Saren recited in a cold, passionless voice. "You are a thief, a smuggler, and a traitor to our species."

The dying man tried to say something, but only coughed again. His breath was labored: the acrid smoke from the incendiary grenades had seared his lungs, damaging them so badly he hadn't been able to breathe in enough of the poison gas to kill him. If he received immediate medical attention there was still a small chance he might survive . . . but Saren had no intention of taking him to a hospital.

Snapping his assault rifle back into the slot on his thigh, Saren dropped down on one knee and leaned in close to the other turian's flame-ravaged features. "You steal weapons from your own people, and then you sell them to *humans*?" he demanded in a fierce whisper. "Do you know how many turians I saw die by human hands?"

It took a tremendous effort, but somehow the burned man managed to mutter four faint words in feeble protest through his scorched lips. "That . . . war . . . is . . . over."

Saren stood up and pulled his pistol in one smooth motion. "Tell that to our dead brothers." He fired two shots into the turian's head, ending the conversation.

Pistol still in hand, he resumed his inspection of the bodies. He noticed two human corpses near the back wall of the warehouse, noticeably less gruesome than the others. The grenades had detonated up near the front of the building and these mercs had taken less damage. Even the poison would have dissipated by the time it reached all the way back here, explaining why the bodies weren't twisted and contorted like the others. They must have been killed by friendly fire.

He approached the first one carefully, then relaxed when he saw clear evidence that the man was truly dead: six finger-sized holes in a tight pattern showed where the close-range blast of a scatter gun had torn through the front of his protective vest, creating a single fist-sized hole as the rounds exited his back.

The final corpse had fallen facedown in a pool of his own blood. The scatter-gun that must have inadvertently killed the man beside him lay on the ground . . . a hair's breadth away from the body's limp, lifeless hand.

Saren froze, suddenly wary. Something wasn't right. His eyes scanned the motionless figure, seeking out the lethal wound. There was a gaping hole in the side of his upper thigh, the likely source of all the blood, but because of how he'd landed, no other injuries were visible.

His eyes snapped back to the thigh: blood still should have been dripping from the wound, but the flow was staunched. As if someone had sealed it with a quick application of medigel.

"Move your hand away from your weapon and roll over," Saren called out, raising his pistol and holding it in both hands as he aimed it at the corpse, "or I'll shoot you right now."

After a second, the hand slowly drew back from the scatter-gun. The man rolled onto his back, gasping loudly for air: he'd been holding his breath as Saren approached, trying to play dead.

"Please don't kill me," he begged as Saren took a step toward him, the pistol trained on the spot right between his eyes. "I didn't even fight in the First Contact War!"

"Some Spectres arrest people," Saren said, his tone casual. "I don't."

"Wait!" the man screamed, scrambling back until he was pressed up against the wall. "Wait! I have information!"

Saren didn't say anything. Instead, he lowered the gun and gave a short nod.

"It's another group of mercs. The Blue Suns."

Every Spectre working in the Verge knew the Blue Suns were a force to be reckoned with. A small but well-known group, their members were both experienced and professional. The exact opposite of this crew.

"Go on."

"They're up to something. Something big."

"What?"

"I . . . I don't know," the man stammered, wincing as if he expected to be shot for the admission. After the second it took him to realize he was still alive, he plowed forward, speaking quickly.

"That's how we got in on this buy. The Blue Suns were supposed to take the shipment, but they pulled out. I heard they got a major job in the works. Something they didn't want to risk by drawing the attention of a Spectre with a weapons buy."

Saren was intrigued. Whatever they were up to had to be big: the Blue Suns almost never turned their backs on a deal they'd already negotiated. If they were trying that hard to keep Spectres out of the picture, it meant he damn well better find out what was going on.

"What else?"

"That's all I know," the man said. "I swear! If you want more you need to look at the Blue Suns.

"So . . . do we have a deal?"

Saren gave a derisive snort. "Deal?"

"You know . . . I give you information about the Blue Suns and you let me live."

The Spectre raised his pistol again. "You should've negotiated before you spilled your guts. You've got nothing left to bargain with."

"What? No, please! Don't—"

The pistol put an end to his protests, and Saren turned and walked calmly back outside, leaving the carnage of the warehouse behind. He'd alert the local authorities once he got back to Phend so they could retrieve the stolen weapons . . . and clean up the mess.

Saren's mind was already on his next job. Initially

he'd dismissed the news of Sidon's destruction. He figured it would eventually lead back to some radical splinter group of batarian rebels, a retaliation against humanity's efforts to push their main rivals out of the Verge. But if the attack wasn't the work of political terrorists, then the Blue Suns were one of the few private security organizations with the capability to pull it off.

Saren had every intention of finding out who had hired them and why. And he knew just where to start his investigation.

Anderson had spent the better part of two days reviewing Kahlee Sanders's personnel file, trying to make sense of it.

The physical data was straightforward: age, 26; height, 5 feet 5 inches; weight, 120 pounds. The ID picture in her file showed she had predominantly Caucasian features: complexion, fair; eyes, light brown; hair, dark blond. She was attractive, but Anderson doubted anyone would ever have called her cute. There was a hard edge to her expression, as if she were looking for a fight.

That wasn't surprising, given her personal background. According to the file she had grown up in the Texan megapolis formed by the union of Houston, Dallas, and San Antonio; one of the poorer regions on Earth. She was raised by a single mother, a factory worker making minimum wage. Enlisting with the Alliance had probably been her only chance to get a better life, though she hadn't signed up until the age of twenty-two, shortly after her mother's death.

Most recruits signed up before they were twenty.

Anderson had joined the day he turned eighteen. But despite her late start, or maybe because of it, Kahlee Sanders had excelled at basic training. She was competent in hand-to-hand combat and weapons training, but her true aptitude had been in the technology fields.

According to her file she'd taken entry-level computing courses in the years leading up to her enlistment, and once she joined she threw herself into the study of advanced programming, data communication networks, and prototype systems architectures. She finished at the top of her class, completing a three-year program in only two.

Personality tests and psych evaluations showed she was intelligent, with a strong sense of personal identity and self-worth. Evaluations from peers and superior officers showed she was cooperative, popular, and an asset to any team she worked with. It was no wonder she'd been assigned to the Sidon project.

And that's why none of this felt right. Anderson knew the difference between a good soldier and a bad one. Kahlee Sanders was definitely a good soldier. She may have initially joined the Alliance as an escape, seeking a better life than the one she had on Earth. But she had found exactly what she was looking for. She'd experienced nothing but success, accolades, and rewards since joining the military. Plus, with her mother gone, she had no other family and no real friends outside her fellow soldiers.

Anderson couldn't come up with a single reason she would turn against the Alliance. Even greed didn't make sense: everyone at Sidon was pulling down a top salary. Besides, Anderson knew enough about human nature to understand that it took more than simple greed to convince a person to aid in the slaughter of the people they lived and worked with every day.

One more thing bothered him about this. If Sanders was the traitor, why had she disappeared the day before the attack and drawn attention to herself? All she had to do was show up for her regular shift and it would have been assumed that she was one of the bodies vaporized in the explosion. It felt like someone was setting her up.

But he couldn't deny that her sudden disappearance was too suspicious to be dismissed as mere coincidence. He needed to figure out what was going on, and so far his only possible clue was what wasn't in her file. Kahlee Sanders's father was officially listed as "unknown." In this day and age of universal birth control to deal with rising populations, as well as massive DNA data banks, it was virtually impossible not to know the identity of a child's parents . . . unless it was being specifically hidden.

Digging deeper into official files had shown all references to Kahlee Sanders's father had been purged: hospital records, immunization reports . . . everything. It was as if someone had actively tried to cut him out of her life. Someone with enough importance to falsify government documents.

Kahlee and her mother both had to be part of the cover-up. If her mother had wanted the father's identity exposed, there would have been no way to stop her. And Kahlee could easily have gotten a DNA test anytime she wanted. They had to know, but for some reason they didn't want anyone else knowing.

However, neither one of them had the kind of financial resources or political clout it would take to pull something like that off. Which meant someone else—probably the father—had also been involved. If Anderson could figure out who the father was, and why he'd been expunged from all official records, it might help him figure out how Kahlee Sanders was tied up in the attack on Sidon.

Unfortunately, he'd exhausted all official channels. Fortunately, there were other ways to dig up buried secrets. Which was why he was now standing in a dark alley in the wards, waiting to meet with an information broker.

He had shown up a few minutes early, eager to see what the broker's search would turn up. Not surprisingly, his contact wasn't here yet. He spent the next few minutes waiting, occasionally pacing back and forth as the seconds dragged by.

A figure stepped into view just as his watch beeped on the hour, materializing from the shadows. As she approached, it quickly became clear that she was a salarian. Shorter and thinner than humans, salarians resembled a cross between some kind of lizard or chameleon and the "grays" described by alleged victims during the rash of fictitious alien abductions reported back on Earth in the late twentieth century. Anderson wondered if she'd been there the whole time, observing him as she waited patiently for the moment of their appointed meeting to arrive.

"Did you find anything?" he asked the woman he had hired to scour the extranet for any clues as to the identity of Kahlee Sanders's father.

Trillions of tetragigs of data were transmitted in

bursts across the extranet every day; there had to be something useful buried in there. But searching a functionally infinite amount of data for a specific piece of information could be an exercise in pointless frustration. It would take days to collect, process, and scan every burst . . . and even then the output might be millions and millions of pages of hard copy. That's where information brokers came in—specialists who used complex algorithms and custom-designed search engines to limit and sort the data. Mastering the extranet was as much an art as a science, and salarians excelled at the art of gathering confidential information.

The salarian blinked her large eyes. "I warned you there might not be much to find," she said, speaking quickly. Salarians always spoke quickly. "Records from before your species linked to the extranet are sporadic."

Anderson had expected as much. Archives from the days predating the First Contact War were slowly being added to the extranet by various government agencies, but the input of old records was a minor priority for every administration. Given Sanders's age, it was likely her father disappeared from her life long before humanity ever came into contact with the greater galactic community.

"So you've got nothing?"

The salarian smiled. "That's not what I said. It was difficult to track down, but there was something. It seems the left hand of the Alliance is unaware of what the right is doing."

She handed him a small optical storage disk.

"Make my life easier," Anderson said, taking it

from her and stuffing it into his pocket. "Just tell me what I'm going to find when I scan this thing."

"The day Kahlee Sanders graduated from your military training academy at Arcturus, an encrypted message was forwarded through classified Alliance channels to an individual on one of your colonies in the Skyllian Verge. It was subsequently purged seconds after it was received."

"How'd you get access to classified Alliance channels?" Anderson demanded.

The salarian laughed. "Your species has been transmitting data across the extranet for less than a decade. My species has been directing the primary espionage and intelligence operations for the Citadel Council for two thousand years."

"Point taken. You said the message was purged?"

"True. Deleted and scrubbed from the records. But nothing is ever truly gone once it hits the extranet. There are always echoes and remnants for people like me to track down. The extranet works on a—"

"I don't need the details," Anderson interrupted, holding up a hand to cut her off. "What did the message say?"

"It was brief. A single text file comprised of Kahlee Sanders's name, final grades, and her class standing. Very impressive. She could have a bright future in my field if she wanted to come work for—"

Anderson cut her off again, growing impatient. "This was all in her personnel file. I didn't pay you to get me her marks."

"You didn't pay me at all," she pointed out. "This is being billed directly to your superiors at the Alliance, remember? I doubt *you* could afford to hire me. That's why you came to me in the first place."

Anderson's hands involuntarily went up and rubbed his temples. "Right. That's not what I meant." Salarians tended to talk in circles, changing topics with every breath. It gave him a headache, and it always seemed to take twice as long as it should to get what you needed out of them. "I hope to God you have something more than this."

"The sender of the message was one of the instructors at the Academy. A man long since retired. Preliminary follow-up indicates he is not germane to the investigation—he was likely only acting on orders of the recipient, and likely knew nothing about why the information was being sent.

"Though I have no proof, I suspect the recipient is Kahlee Sanders's father. As a high-ranking Alliance officer, he would have had the means to systematically cover up their relationship, and do so in a way that would make it difficult to track. However, I was not able to determine why the father and daughter chose to alienate themselves from each—"

"Please," he begged, cutting her off one more time. "All I want is a name. Don't say anything else. Just tell me who received the message, and where I can find him."

She blinked again, and from the change in her expression Anderson thought he might have hurt her feelings. Mercifully, though, she did as he had asked.

"The message was sent to Rear Admiral Jon Grissom. He's on Elysium."

TEN

"This is a private club, batarian," growled the krogan security guard who stepped in Groto Ib-ba's way as he tried to enter the doors of the Sanctuary.

"Tonight I'm a member," the batarian mercenary replied, holding up his financial access card to the scanner and letting it deduct the four-hundred-credit cover charge directly from his bank account. The krogan didn't move, barring his way until the transaction was approved. He only took his eyes off Groto for an instant, to glance at the name and ID picture that flashed up on the screen. He was checking to see if the access card had been stolen. But the ID image was clearly that of the batarian standing before him; there was no mistaking the blue sun tattoo emblazoned on his forehead, just above his left inner eye.

It was clear from the krogan's expression he still didn't want to move aside and let Groto in. "The cover charge only grants entrance to the club," he noted. "Any services will be an additional fee. A significantly additional fee."

"I know how it works," Groto spat back. "I have money."

The krogan considered for a moment, hoping to

find some other way to keep him out. "There are no weapons permitted inside the club."

"I said I know how it works," Groto snarled. Still, the guard hesitated.

The batarian spread his arms out wide and held them in place. "Just search me and get it over with."

The krogan stepped back, beaten. "That won't be necessary." He tilted his head to the left, a batarian sign of respect. "My apologies, Mr. Ib-ba. Helanda at the counter in the back can attend to your needs."

Groto lowered his arms, a little surprised. It was amazing the kind of respect money could buy. If he had actually thought it was possible to get in without being searched he would have smuggled a pistol in under his belt. Or at least slipped a knife in his boot.

Instead he slowly tilted his head to the right in acknowledgment of the apology, playing the part of a man whose honor had been insulted. He boldly walked past the doorman and into the most exclusive whorehouse on Camala, trying to appear calm though his heart was racing.

Part of him had been afraid they would simply turn him away even if he paid the cover charge. It was obvious he didn't belong here; the Sanctuary was reserved for the rich and elite—those with fortunes, not soldiers of fortune. For the most part the cover fee kept men like Groto out. There were plenty of other places on Camala to buy companionship for the night, none of them nearly as expensive as the Sanctuary.

But the Blue Suns's new employer had paid a substantial fee for their exclusive services over the next few months, including a large bonus after the attack on the Sidon military base. Groto hadn't been directly involved in the attack, and he hadn't been in the warehouse when their employer had met up with Skarr. If he had, he'd know who was paying them, but he might also have been one of the unlucky mercs who ended up dead at Skarr's hands.

The Blue Suns paid every member an equal share anyway, so Groto hadn't missed out on anything but the chance of getting killed. And the mercs who'd been at the warehouse were still on the job: they'd been contracted as personal bodyguards for the anonymous moneyman. Groto, on the other hand, was free to go out and enjoy his share of the credits. And, for once in his life, he was going to experience a pleasure reserved for those far more wealthy and powerful than he.

He'd spent part of the bonus on new clothes, but even so he began to feel self-conscious as he crossed the room. He didn't fit in, and the clientele—most of them batarians—were regarding him with open suspicion and curiosity. Societal caste was an important part of batarian culture, and Groto was openly defying the conventional norms. But when he noticed that even the employees were looking at him with contempt, his embarrassment transformed into self-righteous rage. Who were they to look down on him? Nothing but servants and whores!

As he marched up to the counter in the back, passing several more krogan security personnel, he vowed he'd make somebody pay. Once he had his whore in a private room, he'd turn her scorn into fear and terror.

"Welcome to the Sanctuary, Mr. Ib-ba," cooed the

young batarian woman behind the counter. "My name is Helanda.

"I apologize for the incident at the door," she continued. "Odak sometimes takes his job too seriously. You have my personal assurance he will be properly respectful next time."

"Good. I expect better treatment in a place like this." There wasn't going to be a next time, but Groto wasn't going to tell her that.

"We have a wide variety of services available," Helanda explained, smoothly glossing over the doorman's indiscretion and moving on to the business at hand. "The Sanctuary aims to satisfy the desires of all our clientele, no matter how . . . esoteric. If you tell me what you are interested in, I will personally help you select an appropriate consort—or consorts—for the evening."

"I'm interested in you," he said, leaning forward on the counter, responding to the unspoken invitation.

"That is not my role here," she said curtly, taking a half step back, the lids of her inner eyes flicking quickly in distaste. He realized her charm was nothing but an act; a game she was playing with him. Her involuntary reaction exposed the truth: she felt the same revulsion he'd seen in the other employees.

From the corner of his eyes Groto noticed one of the krogan guards casually moving closer to them, and he decided now was not the time for retribution.

He forced a laugh, as if he found her stinging rejection amusing. "Actually, I'm interested in a human female."

"A *human* female?" Helanda asked, as if she wasn't sure she had heard him properly.

"I'm curious," he replied coldly.

"Very well, Mr. Ib-ba," she said, touching a button behind the counter that brought up a small screen in front of her. "I should advise you that there is a premium charged for all interspecies requests. The appropriate fees are listed beside each consort."

She spun the screen to face him. The display showed several prospects, along with the allotted price for each. Groto had to check himself to keep from choking in shock when he saw the amounts. Unlike the whorehouses he usually frequented, hourly rates weren't an option here. A full night at the Sanctuary was going to cost several hundred credits more than his entire bonus. For a brief second he considered turning around and just walking out, but if he did, the four hundred credits he'd paid at the door were gone for good.

"Her," he said, pointing at one of the pictures. There were less expensive options, but he was damned if he was going to let them bully him with their prices. He was never coming back here, so he was determined to get exactly what he wanted. Truthfully, he didn't know all that much about humans. But something about this individual appealed to him. She seemed fragile. Vulnerable.

"An excellent choice, Mr. Ib-ba. I will have someone escort you to your room for the evening. Your consort will be up shortly."

A few minutes later Groto was alone in one of the soundproofed private rooms, pacing back and forth and slamming his fist into his hand. He was thinking back on all the humiliations he had suffered since arriving at this place, working himself up into a fever, determined to take it out on the unfortunate human girl who was about to become his victim for the evening.

He wasn't physically attracted to humans, female or otherwise. But this night wasn't going to be about sex. Groto simply didn't like humans. They bred and spread like vermin, swarming out across the Verge, gobbling up colony worlds and forcing other species out—like the batarians. The humans he worked with in the Blue Suns knew how to handle themselves in a fight, but like all of their kind they were arrogant and self-important. Tonight he would take one of that proud species and make her suffer. He would humiliate, degrade, and punish her. He would break her!

There was a knock; soft and timid. He pulled open the door, reaching out to grab the woman's wrist and yank her into the room. But he froze when he saw a male turian standing there.

"Who are— *urk*."

His words were cut off as the turian punched him hard in the throat. Choking and gagging, Groto staggered back and fell onto the bed in the center of the room. The turian calmly stepped inside, closing the door behind him. Groto heard the lock click into place, sealing the pair of them in together.

Somehow scrambling to his feet, Groto struggled to catch his breath as he brought his fists up, waiting for the turian to move in and try to finish him off. After locking the door, however, the turian just stood there.

"Who are you?" Groto finally gasped.

"Saren" was the one-word reply.

Groto shook his head; he didn't recognize the name. "How'd you get past the guards?" he demanded.

"They didn't try to stop me," Saren replied, his voice relaxed. "I think they actually wanted me to come in here and take care of you."

"What . . . what do you mean?" Groto's voice was shaky; the unnatural calm of the turian was unsettling. He kept his hands up, poised in case the intruder made a move.

"Are you really that stupid? Don't you realize they knew exactly what you had planned for tonight? They knew what you were after the moment you asked for a human consort."

"What . . . what are you talking about?"

The turian took a single step forward. Groto scuttled two steps back, his fists raised and ready. He would have retreated further but he had reached the wall on the far end of the room—there was nowhere left to go.

"The Sanctuary does not allow its consorts to be harmed or injured," Saren explained calmly. As he spoke he began to slowly advance, one deliberate step at a time. "They were monitoring the room." *Step*. "The moment you laid a hand on that woman, an angry krogan would have burst in and ripped your head off." *Step*.

"I wasn't . . . I didn't even do anything!" the batarian protested, finally dropping his fists. He felt like a fool waving them around when the other man seemed so calm.

Step. "I convinced them to let me handle it instead," Saren continued, ignoring him. "They were concerned about bothering the other guests." *Step*. "Then I reminded them that the walls are completely soundproof." *Step*. "And you've already paid for the room." *Step*.

The turian was directly in front of him now, though he still appeared completely relaxed. Groto brought his fists up again. "Back up or I'll—"

He never had a chance to finish the sentence as Saren delivered a solid kick to his nether regions. Blinding bolts of furious pain shot up through Groto's bowels and stomach. He collapsed to the ground, the agony so great he could only whimper.

Saren grabbed him by the material of his newly purchased suit and yanked him back to his feet, then jabbed his thumb into one of Groto's inner eyes, rupturing the orb and blinding him with a single blow. The batarian fainted, lapsing into unconsciousness from the sudden shock and pain.

Seconds later he woke screaming as Saren broke his right elbow. Howling in agony, he curled up into a ball, rolling back and forth as his body experienced physical suffering beyond anything he had ever imagined.

"You disgust me," Saren whispered, kneeling down to grab Groto's left wrist. He extended the batarian's good arm, locking out the joints, and began to apply pressure. "You wanted to torture an innocent victim for your own pleasure. You sick bastard.

"Torture is only useful if it has a purpose," Saren added, though his words were drowned out by the crack of Groto's left elbow and the subsequent shrieks.

Saren stepped back from the convulsing man, letting the waves of pain rack his body. It took nearly a minute for shock to set in, numbing his mangled limbs to the point where Groto could finally speak.

"You'll pay for this," Groto wailed up at him from the ground, sobbing freely. Tears and mucus mixed with ocular fluid from his blind eye, dribbling down into his mouth and slurring his words into a blubbery parody of a threat. "Do you know who I am? I'm with the Blue Suns!"

"Why do you think I followed you here?"

A look of horror spread across Groto's face as he finally understood. "You're a Spectre," he mumbled. "Please," he begged, "tell me what you want. Anything. I'll give it to you."

"Information," Saren replied. "Tell me what you know about Sidon."

"We were hired to take out the base," the crippled man admitted.

"By who?"

"I don't know. I only dealt with a go-between. I never saw him, never heard a name."

Saren sighed and knelt down on the floor beside Groto. There were many exotic methods of interrogation, a million ways to inflict pain and punishment on a victim. But turians were a practical people, and he personally preferred the brutal effectiveness of simple, basic techniques. Grabbing the man's dangling left arm by the wrist, he took a firm grip on one of his fingers and began to bend it backwards.

"*No!*" the batarian screamed. "*No!* Please . . . it's the truth! That's all I know! You have to believe me!"

He stuck to the story even after three of the fingers on his hand were broken at the middle knuckle, convincing Saren he was telling the truth.

"How did you get inside the base?" Saren asked, changing his line of questioning.

"The man who hired us," Groto muttered, his voice raw and raspy from the fresh round of screaming that had torn up his throat. "He had someone on the inside."

"Give me a name."

"Please," he begged in high-pitched, mewling whine. "I don't know. I wasn't even there."

Saren grabbed another finger, and the words began to pour out.

"Wait! I don't know the inside man! But . . . but I can tell you other stuff. After the attack we brought in an outsider. A freelance bounty hunter. A big krogan named Skarr."

"Good," Saren said, releasing his hold on the uninjured digit. "Keep going."

"Something went wrong at Sidon. Someone survived the attack. A loose end. Skarr was hired to hunt her down. A human. She's on Elysium. I don't know her name."

"What else? Why were you hired to attack the base?"

"I don't know," Groto whispered fearfully. "We weren't given any details. The moneyman was afraid someone would talk. He didn't want . . . he didn't want the Spectres to find out."

Saren broke two more of his fingers just to be sure.

"Please," the batarian sobbed once he'd stopped screaming. "It's not me you want. There was a meeting at the warehouse with Skarr and the man who hired us. Talk to someone who was there."

The turian wasn't surprised his victim was offering up someone else. It was a common reaction in most subjects. Typically it was a sign the interrogation was nearing an end; once the subject realized they were running out of useful information to surrender, betraying their allies became their only chance of avoiding further torture.

"Where can I find someone from the warehouse?" the Spectre demanded.

"I . . . I don't know," Groto admitted, his voice trembling. "They're with the moneyman. He hired them on as his personal bodyguards."

"Guess I'm stuck with you then," Saren replied.

"That's all I know," the batarian protested weakly, his voice completely devoid of guile, subterfuge, or hope. "Even if you break every bone in my body, I can't tell you anything else."

"We'll see," Saren promised.

It was a long night for Saren. The batarian went into shock and passed out three more times during the interrogation. Each time it happened Saren would have to sit down and wait for him to regain consciousness—there was no point in torturing an unresponsive subject.

In the end, it turned out Groto had been telling the truth. Saren didn't get anything more out of him.

He'd suspected as much, but he had needed to be absolutely sure. There was too much at stake.

Someone had hired the Blue Suns. Someone with enough wealth and power to secure their exclusive loyalty. Someone who had taken extra precautions to make sure the Spectres wouldn't find out what was going on. Saren needed to know who had ordered the attack on Sidon and why. Billions of lives could be at stake, and he was more than willing to torture a single merc for hours on end if there was even the smallest chance he could learn something that might help him break the case.

Not that there weren't consequences to his actions. The soundproof room had amplified the piercing shrieks and keening wails of his victim. The screams had physically hurt Saren's ears, and now he had a pounding headache.

Next time, he thought as he rubbed his temples, *I'll bring earplugs.*

He had lifted the batarian up onto the bed partway through the interrogation; it was easier to work on him there than to constantly bend down to reach him on the floor. Now Groto was just lying motionless on his back, breathing softly in a deep sleep brought on by utter mental and physical exhaustion.

There wasn't much to go on, but Saren had a solid lead to follow. He knew Skarr by reputation, and he knew the bounty hunter was headed to Elysium. It shouldn't be hard to pick up his trail there.

First, though, he had to clean up this mess. Arresting Groto wasn't an option; it would draw attention and alert whoever had hired the Blue Suns that a

Spectre was on the case. It was easier—and safer—to just dispose of the body.

Saren gently placed a hand on either side of the batarian's head, then gave a savage twist at an awkward angle, breaking his elongated neck. A quick and painless death.

After all, he wasn't a monster.

ELEVEN

Anderson disembarked on Elysium with the three hundred other passengers who had booked a seat on the public-transport shuttle from the Citadel.

The landing port teemed with people. The densely packed crowd was a mix of every known species in the galaxy; some arriving, some leaving, most waiting in the long, winding lines to clear customs and border stations. Security had always been tight on Elysium, but with the attack on the nearby Sidon base things had been elevated to a level Anderson had never seen before.

Not that he disapproved. Ideally located near the nexus of several primary and secondary relays, Elysium was a major hub for travel and commerce that the Alliance could not afford to expose to possible terrorist attacks. The colony was only five years old, but already it was one of the busiest trade ports in the Verge. The population had exploded; recently passing one million, if you included all the various and varied resident aliens who accounted for nearly half the total inhabitants. Unfortunately, that also meant a disproportionately high number of visitors to Elysium were nonhuman, and subject to heightened screening procedures.

The extra security made arrivals and departures a long and cumbersome experience for most travelers. Even humans were subjected to major delays; the staff taken away to help process the alien visitors meant fewer people left behind to deal with the Alliance citizens.

Fortunately for Anderson, his military ID gave him the luxury of bypassing the long lines. The guard at the Alliance station scanned his thumbprint and studied his identification for a few seconds before saluting and waving him through.

Officially, Anderson wasn't here in any authorized capacity. He was just an Alliance marine taking shore leave, a believable enough cover story to avoid drawing any unwanted attention and hide the true purpose of his visit.

Jon Grissom was Kahlee Sanders's father. It was pretty obvious they were estranged, but there was still a good chance Grissom knew something that could help Anderson's investigation. Sidon was only a few hours away from Elysium. There were records of Sanders booking a passage here when she went UA. And even though it looked like Grissom hadn't communicated with his daughter in at least ten years, it was public knowledge that the Alliance's most recognizable soldier had taken early retirement and become a recluse on humanity's largest colony in the Verge.

Anderson still couldn't wrap his head around the idea that Sanders was a traitor. The pieces just didn't add up. But he knew she was involved somehow; her sudden disappearance had to be more than coincidence. Maybe she had gotten in over her head and panicked when things got out of control. He could imagine her arriving on Elysium: scared, alone, not knowing who to trust. Estranged or not, her father was the most likely person she'd turn to for help.

After checking his gear at the hotel, Anderson rented a car and drove out to the isolated estates on the outskirts of the city. It took him awhile to find Grissom's house; the addresses in the area were so inconspicuous as to be almost hidden. It was obvious the people who lived out here valued their privacy.

Exiting the vehicle, he began the long walk across the grounds of the estate toward the surprisingly small domicile located as far back from the road as possible. Anderson didn't understand Grissom's desire to withdraw from the public eye. He respected the man and his reputation, but he couldn't imagine any way to justify simply walking away like he did. A soldier didn't turn his back on the Alliance like that.

You're not here to pass judgment, he reminded himself as he reached the door. He rang the bell and waited, involuntarily standing at attention. *You're just here to find Kahlee Sanders.*

It took several minutes before he heard someone coming on the other side, grumbling as he approached. A moment later the door opened, revealing Rear Admiral Jon Grissom in all his glory.

The salute Anderson had been on the verge of snapping off by way of greeting died at his hip. The man before him wore nothing but a tattered housecoat and dirty boxers. His hair was long and uncombed and his face was partially hidden behind a three-day stubble of gray and black hairs. His eyes were hard and bitter, and his face seemed frozen in a scowl.

"What do you want?" he demanded.

"Sir," Anderson replied, "my name is Lieutenant Commander David And—"

Grissom cut him off. "I know who you are. We met back at Arcturus."

"That's right, sir," Anderson acknowledged, feeling a faint surge of pride at being recognized. "Before the First Contact War. I'm surprised you remember me."

"I'm retired, not senile." Despite the joke, there was nothing humorous in Grissom's tone.

There was an awkward pause as Anderson tried to reconcile his memories of the iconic figure of Grissom's past with the disheveled grouch now standing in front of him. It was Grissom who filled the silence.

"Look, kid, I'm retired. So go back and tell the brass that I'm not going to do any interviews or speeches or appearances just because one of our military bases got attacked. I'm done with that crap."

Anderson pounced, convinced the other man had already slipped up. "How do you know Sidon was attacked?"

Grissom glared at him like he was a fool. "It's all over the damn news vids."

"That's not why I'm here," Anderson said, trying to hide his embarrassment. "Can we talk inside?"

"No."

"Please, sir. It's a matter I'd rather not discuss out here in public."

Grissom held his ground, blocking the door so Anderson couldn't enter.

The lieutenant realized tact and diplomacy weren't going to be any use here. Time to be blunt. "Tell me about Kahlee Sanders, sir."

"Who?"

The old man was good. Anderson had been hoping to see some reaction at the name of his long-lost daughter, his only flesh and blood. But Grissom hadn't even flinched.

"Kahlee Sanders," Anderson repeated, his voice becoming noticeably louder. It was unlikely anyone would hear him—the neighbors were too far away. But he had to do something to get inside that door. "Your daughter. The soldier who went UA from Sidon mere hours before it was attacked. The woman we're looking at as a traitor to the Alliance."

Grissom's scowl became a grimace of pure hatred. "Shut up and get your ass in here," he muttered, stepping aside.

Once inside, Anderson followed his reluctant host into the small living room. Grissom settled into one of the three padded chairs, but the lieutenant remained standing, waiting for an invitation to do the same. After several seconds he realized the invitation wasn't forthcoming, and he took a seat on his own.

"How'd you find out about Kahlee?" Grissom finally asked, speaking as casually as if they were discussing the weather.

"There are no secrets in this day and age," Anderson replied. "We know she was last seen here on Elysium. I need to know if she came to talk to you."

"I haven't spoken to my daughter since before she

was a teenager," Grissom replied. "Her mother didn't think much of me as a husband or a father, and I couldn't really argue with her. I figured the best thing was to just get out of their lives.

"Hey," Grissom suddenly recalled, "last time we met you said you were engaged. A girl waiting for you back on Earth, right? You must be married by now. Congratulations."

He was trying to throw Anderson off balance. Grissom knew damn well how hard it was for an Alliance soldier to make a marriage work; his innocent question was meant to rattle his guest. He may have looked like a harmless, burned-out old man, but there was still plenty of fight left in him.

Anderson wasn't about to rise to the bait. "Sir, I need your help. Your daughter is suspected of being a traitor to the Alliance. Doesn't that mean anything to you?"

"Why should it?" he shot back. "I barely know her."

"I found out you two were related. Eventually somebody else is going to make that connection, too."

"What? You think I'm worried about my reputation?" he scoffed. "You think I'm going to help you because I don't want people to know the great Admiral Grissom had an illegitimate daughter who's accused of treason? Ha! You're the ones who care about crap like that. I really couldn't give a damn."

"That's not what I meant, sir," Anderson replied, refusing to be provoked. "I tracked Kahlee here. To you. That means someone else can track her here, too. I came to you because I want to help your daughter. But the next person who comes after her—and we both know there will be others—might be looking to harm her."

Grissom leaned forward slowly and placed his head in his hands, considering Anderson's words. Several long moments went by before he sat up straight again. His eyes were moist with tears.

"She's not a traitor," he whispered. "She didn't have anything to do with this."

"I believe you, sir," Anderson said, his voice sincere and sympathetic. "But not many others will. That's why I need to find her. Before something happens to her."

Grissom didn't say anything, but simply sat there chewing on his lower lip.

"I won't let anything bad happen to her," Anderson reassured him. "I give you my word on it."

"She came here," Grissom finally admitted, taking a deep breath. "She said she was in trouble. Something to do with Sidon. I didn't ask her any of the details. I guess . . . I guess I was afraid of what she might tell me."

He leaned forward and clasped his head in his hands again. "I was never there for her when she was growing up," he mumbled, sounding as if he was on the verge of tears. "I couldn't turn her away now. I owed her."

"I understand, Admiral," Anderson said, reaching forward to place a comforting hand on Grissom's shoulder. "But you have to tell me where she went."

Grissom looked up at him, his expression naked and vulnerable. "I gave her the name of a freighter captain down at the ports. Errhing. Captain of the

Gossamer. He helps people who want to disappear. She left last night."

"Where was she going?"

"I didn't ask. Errhing takes care of all the details. You need to talk to him."

"Where is he?"

"The *Gossamer* left this morning on a trade run out near the Terminus Systems. He won't be back for weeks."

"We don't have weeks, sir."

Grissom stood up, his posture a little straighter than it had been when Anderson first arrived, as if his muscles were trying to remember what it was like to stand proudly at attention. "Then I guess you'll just have to get your patrols out there and find him, soldier. He's the only one who can lead you to my daughter."

Anderson jumped crisply to his feet. "Don't worry, Admiral. I won't let anything happen to her."

He started to salute, but Grissom turned his head away.

"Don't," he muttered, ashamed. "I don't deserve that. Not anymore."

Anderson extended his hand instead. The older man hesitated a moment, then reached out and clasped it in a surprisingly firm grip.

"You're a better man than I ever was, Anderson. The Alliance is lucky to have you."

The lieutenant didn't know what to say, so he only nodded. Grissom took him firmly by the elbow and led him out of the living room to the front door.

"Remember your promise," he said as his parting words. "Don't let anything happen to my daughter."

*   *   *

Grissom watched the lieutenant leaving his home on the vid-screen for the security camera over his door, only turning away when the young man got into his vehicle and sped off. Then he made his way slowly to the back of the house and knocked once on the closed door of his bedroom.

A second later Kahlee opened it and asked, "Who was it?"

"Some Alliance snoop who figured out we were related. I sent him on a wild-goose chase. He'll spend the next two weeks out near the Terminus Systems chasing down an old friend of mine."

"Are you sure he bought it?" Kahlee asked.

"I gave him exactly what he wanted," Grissom said with a cynical smile, "the chance to help an old, broken-down hero remember something of who he used to be.

"But he's not the one we have to worry about," Grissom continued. "Things won't get tough until we run into someone involved in the attack on Sidon."

Kahlee reached out and grabbed his hand, pressing it firmly between her own palms. "Thank you," she said, staring up into her father's eyes. "I mean it."

He nodded, and shifted uncomfortably until she released her grip. "We'll wait a few more days," he said, turning away and leaving her to the privacy of her room, "then we'll figure out some way to get you off this planet."

A large, dark shadow crept quickly and quietly across the moonlit grounds of Grissom's estate, making its way toward the home.

Skarr could move silently when he had to, even in full body armor. It slowed him down, but he usually relied on strength rather than speed anyway.

There were no lights on inside the small house of the man Skarr now knew to be the father of his target. He'd been surprised when his batarian information broker had come up with the name of an Alliance hero, but it didn't really change the job. It just meant there'd be more fallout when he was done.

The krogan didn't know if Kahlee Sanders was inside, but even if she wasn't her father probably knew how to find her. Skarr was confident he could make the human talk . . . as long as he didn't accidentally kill him first. That's why he was traveling light, armed only with a pistol and his favorite knife.

He paused outside the only door, listening for signs of life. From his belt he pulled out his omnitool, using it to hack in and disable the security system and override the electronic lock. He slid the omnitool back into his belt, exchanging it for his pistol, and pushed the door open.

His eyes still adjusting to the darkness, he put one foot across the threshold. The shotgun blast took him square in the chest.

There was a blue flash as the reflexive system of kinetic barrier fields reacted to the impact, deflecting most of the rounds harmlessly away. A few tore through the kinetic barriers only to ricochet off the ablative plates of his body armor, or bury themselves into the thick padding underlay. A handful penetrated every layer of protection and tore into the flesh beneath.

The force of the blast lifted the krogan off his feet,

knocking the pistol from his grip and hurling him back out the door to land heavily on the ground.

Grissom jumped up from the chair where he'd been holding a nightly vigil ever since Kahlee had arrived and raised the gun for another shot. He'd recognized the blue flash as the intruder's kinetic barriers that absorbed most of the initial blow. But the point-blank hit would've drained the shields, and one more good shot should finish the job.

Lying on his back, Skarr yanked the knife from his belt and flung it end over end at his attacker. The blade sank deep into the muscle of Grissom's left bicep as he squeezed the shotgun's trigger again, knocking him back and throwing off his aim. Instead of blowing away the krogan's head, he left a scorching hole in the ground just beside him.

The shotgun's barrel slipped from Grissom's suddenly nerveless hand. Skarr was on his feet and back inside the house before the old man could use his one good arm to bring the weapon to bear again. Bellowing in anger, the krogan slapped the gun away with one massive fist, sending it skittering into the living room. He grabbed the human and flung him against the wall hard enough to crack the plaster.

The blade slipped from Grissom's arm as he slumped down to the floor, all the air knocked out of his lungs. The alien loomed above him, turning its head slightly so it could fix one of its cold, reptilian eyes on him. Grissom was no coward, but he felt fear grip his heart as he stared up into the dead, black pupil.

Then he heard a loud *crack, crack, crack*—the familiar retort of an Alliance Hahne-Kedar P15-25—

and the krogan staggered away. He'd been shot three times in the heavy hump of muscle and bone on his back, but he was still standing.

Lieutenant Anderson stood in the doorway, pistol drawn. He came into the room, firing the pistol a half dozen more times as the krogan turned to face him. He aimed low, looking to take out the legs. One of his shots found the exposed joint at the knee where the hard plates of body armor were connected by a flexible, but vulnerable, padded mesh.

Roaring in rage and agony the krogan crashed to the ground, clutching at his wounded joint.

"One move and the next shot goes right between your eyes," Anderson warned, taking a bead on the bony ridge running along the top of the krogan's skull.

Grissom was impressed. It wasn't easy to take a human in full body armor down with a pistol, never mind a krogan.

"I'm glad to see you here," he managed to gasp once the wind returned to his lungs.

"You didn't honestly expect me to be fooled by that little performance you gave the other day," Anderson replied, never taking his eyes or his weapon off the krogan in the corner. "I've been watching this place ever since I walked out your door."

Grissom struggled to his feet, his left arm still dangling uselessly, his right pressed against his heavily bleeding wound. A moan of pain escaped his lips.

"Your friend is hurt," the krogan growled.

Anderson wasn't distracted, even for an instant. "He's tough. He'll live."

The krogan was bleeding from the shot to his knee.

The armor on his chest was peppered with small holes, the padding beneath scorched and burned. Dark blood oozed from three of them. Anderson guessed at least one of the shots to the back had penetrated deep enough to do some damage as well. But he'd seen krogans take a hell of a lot more punishment than this and keep coming.

The alien on the ground was a wounded beast—angry, desperate, and unpredictable. He was panting, though whether from pain, exertion, or pure rage it was hard to say. His scarred, brutish face was a mask of intense concentration; his muscles were tensed as if he was gathering himself to make a move.

But if he tried anything Anderson would shoot him in the head from inside of three meters. Even a krogan couldn't survive that.

He heard a door open and footsteps come running down the hall. "Oh, God! You're hurt!" a woman screamed.

Anderson wasn't stupid enough to turn his head. But for a split second his eyes glanced in the direction of her voice. That was all the time the krogan needed.

He lashed out with a fist, sending a shock wave of rolling energy rumbling across the room. Anderson had never been hit with a biotic attack before, and he hadn't expected one from a krogan. In the split second it took him to realize what was happening, he'd been swept up in the vortex and thrown all the way into the living room, where he crashed to the ground. It felt like being in an artificial gravity chamber when somebody switched the polarity: an instantaneous, inescapable, and irresistible force.

He couldn't recover in time to grab his pistol from

where it had fallen, nor could he reach the shotgun laying only a few feet away. Somehow the krogan, despite his injuries, was already back on his feet and nearly on top of him, swinging his fist with enough power to cave in Anderson's skull. He ducked and slipped to the side, avoiding the punch. The follow-through landed square on the living room table; it disintegrated into splinters at the impact.

Everything had descended into chaos. Grissom was shouting at Kahlee to run, she was screaming at Anderson to grab one of the guns. The krogan was roaring in anger, flailing about the room, flinging and tossing the furniture like it was made of balsa wood while Anderson dodged and scrambled for his life, only able to avoid the killing blows because his opponent was still hobbled by his wounded knee.

From the corner of his eye he saw Kahlee rush forward into the fray, lunging in a desperate bid to get the shotgun. The krogan saw her, too, and wheeled on the young woman. He would have killed her right then if another bullet hadn't ripped through a seam in his armor at his hip, making him stagger off balance and misdirecting his blow.

Anderson whipped his head around to see a turian standing in the door where he had been mere minutes before, firing a pistol at the krogan. The lieutenant had no idea who he was or why he was here . . . he was just glad they had somebody else on their side.

Most of the shots ricocheted off the krogan's armor as the beast ducked down and tried to cover his head, the only exposed part of his body. He glanced back at the turian, then leaped through the living room window, smashing through the plate glass. The krogan landed on his shoulder on the grass outside and rolled to his feet in one smooth motion. He took off in a lumbering run, his gait awkward because of his injured leg, but moving far faster than Anderson would have believed possible for a creature of his size.

The turian stepped outside and fired a few shots into the darkness, then turned and came back into the house.

"Aren't you going after him?" Grissom asked their unknown ally. He was still sitting on the floor, but he'd used the belt of his bathrobe to tie a tourniquet around his upper arm, stemming the flow of blood from his wounded bicep.

"Not armed only with this," the turian responded, holding up his pistol. "Besides, only a fool faces a krogan biotic alone."

"I think what Admiral Grissom actually meant to say," Anderson said, coming over and extending his hand, "was thank you for saving us."

The turian stared down at the offered hand, but made no effort to extend his own. Embarrassed, the lieutenant pulled his hand back.

"I know why he's here," Grissom said through teeth gritted against the pain, nodding his head in Anderson's direction. "What's your story?"

"I've been tailing Skarr for two days," the turian replied. "Waiting for him to make a move."

"Tailing him?" Kahlee asked as she came over to check on her father's wound. "What for? Who are you?"

"My name is Saren. I'm a Spectre. And I want some answers."

TWELVE

Anderson and the Spectre sat in the kitchen, staring across the table at each other without speaking. The living room would have been more comfortable, but none of the chairs in there had survived the krogan's rampage.

Like all turians, Saren's face was covered by a mask of hard cartilage. But Saren's mask was the pale color of bone; it looked like a skull. He reminded Anderson of the old Earth paintings depicting the Grim Reaper, the embodiment of death itself.

Kahlee was in the back, tending to Grissom's wounds. The admiral had tried to protest, but he was weak from loss of blood and she'd managed to get him to lie down. She found a military field kit in his medicine chest with enough medigel to stabilize his condition, and now she was dressing his wound.

She'd wanted to take him to a hospital, or at least call an ambulance, but the Spectre had adamantly refused. "After you answer my questions" was all he'd say.

Anderson knew right then that he didn't like Saren. Anyone who would use the prolonged pain and suffering of a family member for leverage was a sadist and a bully.

"He's resting now," Kahlee said, emerging from the back. "I gave him a sedative."

She entered the kitchen and took a seat beside Anderson, instinctively aligning herself with one of her own kind. "Hurry up and ask your questions," she said tersely, "so I can get my father to a hospital."

"Cooperate and this will be over soon," Saren assured her, then added, "Tell me about the Sidon military base."

"It was wiped out in a terrorist attack," Anderson answered, jumping in before Kahlee could say anything incriminating.

The turian glared at him. "Don't play me for a fool, human. That krogan who nearly killed you all is a bounty hunter named Skarr. I've been following him for the past two days."

"What does that have to do with us?" Kahlee asked, her voice so innocent Anderson almost believed she really didn't know what was going on.

"He was hired by the man who ordered the attack on Sidon," Saren replied with a scowl. "They sent him to eliminate the only survivor from the base. You."

"Sounds like you know more about this than we do," Anderson countered.

The turian slammed his fist down on the table. "Why was the base attacked?! What were you working on there?"

"Prototype technology," Kahlee offered before Anderson could speak. "Experimental weapons for the Alliance military."

Saren tilted his head to the side, puzzled. "Experimental weapons technology? That's all?"

"What do you mean 'that's all'?" Anderson sputtered in disbelief, running with the lie Kahlee had so deftly handed him.

"That hardly seems like justification for attacking a heavily armed Alliance base," the turian replied.

"We're on the edge of a war in the Verge," Anderson insisted. "Everybody knows it's got to be us or the batarians. Why wouldn't they want to attack our primary weapons research base?"

"No," Saren said flatly. "There's something more. You're hiding something."

There was a long pause, and then the turian casually brought out his pistol and set it on the table.

"Perhaps you don't understand the full extent of Spectre authority," he said ominously. "I have the legal right to take any action I deem necessary during my investigations."

"You're going to kill us?" Kahlee exclaimed, her voice rising in shock and disbelief.

"I have two rules I follow," Saren explained. "The first is: never kill someone without a reason."

"And the second?" Anderson asked, suspicious.

"You can always find a reason to kill someone."

"Biotics," Kahlee blurted out. "We were trying to find a way to turn humans into biotics."

The turian considered her explanation for a moment then asked, "What were the results?"

"We were close," the young woman admitted, her voice getting softer. "We found a handful of human subjects with latent biotic abilities. Children, mostly. Far weaker than what we'd measured in other species, but with the amplification nodes and proper training we still hoped to see results.

"We just completed the implantation surgery on several of our most promising candidates a few weeks ago. None of them survived the raid."

"Do you know who ordered the attack?" he asked, changing tack.

Kahlee shook her head. "Batarians, probably. I was on leave when it happened."

"Why are they coming after you now?" Saren pressed.

"I don't know!" she shouted, banging her fist on the table in exasperation. "Maybe they think I can get the program up and running again. But they destroyed the files. Killed the test subjects. All our research is gone!"

She dropped her head down onto her arms, crying against the table. "And now everybody's dead," she mumbled between sobs. "All my friends. Dr. Qian. All of them . . . gone."

Anderson placed a comforting hand on her shoulder, while the turian just sat there watching impassively. After several seconds he pushed himself away from the table and stood up.

"I will find out who ordered the attack," he told them as he put his gun back into his belt and turned to go. "And why."

At the door he paused and turned back to them. "And if you're lying to me, I will find that out, too."

A moment later he was gone, disappearing into the night.

Kahlee was still sobbing. Anderson pulled her close, trying to offer her comfort. She'd done a good job with Saren, spinning lies with just enough strands of truth to make them hold together. But there was nothing false about her reaction now. The people at Sidon had been her friends, and they were all dead.

She pressed her head up against him, seeking solace in the closeness of a fellow human being. A few minutes later the tears stopped, and she gently pushed herself away from him.

"Sorry about that," she said, giving a nervous, rueful laugh and wiping her eyes.

"It's okay," Anderson replied. "You've been through a lot."

"What's going to happen now?" she asked. "Are you going to arrest me?"

"Not yet," he admitted. "I meant what I said to your father the other day. I don't believe you're a traitor. But I need you to tell me what's going on. And not the story you sold to that turian. I want the truth."

She nodded and sniffled. "I guess it's the least I can do after you risked your life for us. But can we take my dad to the hospital first?"

"Of course."

It turned out getting Grissom to the hospital wasn't going to be easy. He was a big man, and the sedative Kahlee had given him had made him groggy. He was nothing but dead weight. Uncooperative dead weight.

"Leave me alone," he grumbled as they struggled in vain to lug him out of bed and get him on his feet.

Kahlee stood on one side of the bed holding his uninjured arm. Anderson was on the other, awkwardly gripping him around the waist and back to avoid touching his wounded bicep. Each time they tried to pull Grissom to a sitting position, he simply flopped back down.

His daughter tried to reason with him, grunting each time they hoisted him up. "We have to . . . unh . . . get you . . . unh . . . to a hospital. Ungh!"

"Bleeding's stopped," he protested, his words thick and slurred from the sedative. "Just let me sleep."

"Let's try something else," Anderson said to Kahlee, standing up and coming around to her side. He sat down on the edge of the bed, facing away from the admiral as he pulled the older man's good arm up across his back and over his shoulder. With Kahlee's help he managed to stand, taking Grissom's not inconsiderable weight in a modified fireman's carry.

"Put me down, you bastard!" Grissom moaned.

"You were stabbed in the arm and thrown against a wall by a pissed-off krogan," Anderson said, taking an unsteady step toward the hall. "Someone needs to check you out."

"You stupid son of a bitch," Grissom mumbled. "They'll figure out Kahlee's hiding here."

Anderson hesitated, then staggered back a step and half sat, half fell onto the bed, letting Grissom slip back down onto it.

"Is he too heavy?" Kahlee asked, concerned for both of them.

"No," Anderson said, panting slightly from the exertion. "But he's right. We take him in and you're finished."

"What are you talking about?"

"The ports are already on increased alert because of the attack on Sidon. We bring an Alliance legend like Admiral Jon Grissom into a hospital with these kinds of injuries and security goes through the roof. There's no way in hell we'll be able to get you off the planet without being recognized.

"I believe you're innocent, Kahlee, but nobody else does. They'll arrest you on sight."

"So I'll just stay at the house," she said. "Nobody knows I'm here. Nobody even knows we're related."

"Yeah, right. Nobody but me, a Spectre, that krogan . . . We all figured it out, Kahlee. How long before somebody else makes the connection and comes snooping around? Before all this, nobody knew who you were; nobody bothered with you. Now you're a suspected traitor—your name and picture are on every news vid out there.

"Reporters will be digging into your past, trying to find out everything about you. Sooner or later someone's going to figure out the truth."

"So what can we do?"

It was Grissom who chimed in with the answer. "Get the hell off this planet," he muttered. "I know people who can sneak you past port security. Just need to call them in the morning."

With that, Grissom rolled over and began snoring, finally giving in to the sedatives. Anderson and Kahlee left the room and headed into the kitchen.

"Your father's a pretty smart man," Anderson said.

Kahlee nodded, but all she said was "You hungry? If we're stuck here until morning we might as well have something to eat."

They found some bread, cold cuts, and mustard in his fridge, along with thirty-six cans of beer. Tossing one over to Anderson, Kahlee said, "He's probably got something stronger hidden around here if you're interested."

"Beer's fine," Anderson replied, cracking it open and taking a swig. It was a local brew, one he'd never tried before. It had a strong bite; bitter, but no after-taste. "Should go good with the sandwich."

"Not much of a meal," she apologized once they were sitting at the table.

"It's fine," he answered. "Tastes a little odd with the cold bread, though. Who keeps their bread in the fridge?"

"My mother always did," she answered. "Guess that's the one thing my parents could agree on. Too bad you need more than that to make a marriage work."

They ate in silence after that, letting their minds wind down. When they were done Anderson collected both plates and took them over to the counter. He grabbed them each another beer from the fridge and came back to the table.

"Okay, Kahlee," he said, handing her the can. "I know it's been a long night. But now we have to talk. You up for this?"

She nodded.

"Take your time," he told her. "Just start at the beginning and work your way through. I need to know everything."

"We weren't working on biotic research at the base," she began softly, then smiled. "But I guess you already know that."

She has a pretty smile, Anderson thought. "A good cover story for that Spectre, though," he said aloud. "If he found out what was really going on . . ." he trailed off, remembering Ambassador Goyle's warnings about the Spectres.

Saren had saved their lives. He wondered if he really could have brought himself to murder the turian if it had been necessary to keep humanity's secret. And even if he tried, could he have succeeded?

"Let's just say that was quick thinking on your part," he finally told her.

Kahlee took the compliment in stride and continued with the story, her voice slowly growing in strength and confidence as she spoke. "Sidon was dedicated to one very specific task: the development and study of artificial intelligence. We knew it was risky, but we had rigid safety protocols to make sure nothing could go wrong.

"I started as a low-level systems analyst at the base two years ago, working directly under Dr. Qian, the man in charge of the project.

"People use the term 'genius' all the time," she said, making no attempt to hide her admiration. "But he really was one. His mind—his research, the way he thinks—it's on a level so far above the rest of us we can barely even grasp it. Like most of the people there, I just did whatever Dr. Qian told me to. Half the time I didn't even fully understand why I was doing it."

"Why weren't you at Sidon when it was attacked?" Anderson asked, gently nudging her toward the relevant part of her tale.

"A few months ago I noticed some changes in Dr. Qian's behavior. He was spending more and more time in the lab. He started working double shifts; he hardly slept. But he seemed to have this endless supply of desperate, frantic energy."

"Was he manic?"

"I don't think so. I never saw any sign of it before. But suddenly we were integrating all sorts of new hardware into the systems. Our research started going in totally different directions—we completely abandoned conventional practices and went with radical new theories. We were using prototype technology and designs unlike anything we'd ever seen before.

"At first, I just thought Dr. Qian had made some kind of breakthrough. Something that got him all fired up. In the beginning it was exhilarating. His excitement was infectious. But after a while I started to get suspicious."

"Suspicious?"

"It's hard to explain. Something about Dr. Qian was different. *Altered*. I worked with him for almost two years. This wasn't like him. There was definitely something wrong. He wasn't just working harder. He was obsessed. Like he was being . . . driven by some.

"And it felt like he was hiding something. Some secret he didn't want anyone else on the project to know about. Before, if he needed something from you he'd go into excruciating detail about why your work was important. He'd tell you how it interconnected with every other department on the project, even though I think he knew nobody else could really grasp the full complexity of what we were working on.

"The past few months were different. He stopped communicating with the team; he'd give orders but no explanations. It just wasn't like him. So I started digging into the data banks. I even hacked into Dr. Qian's restricted files to see what I could find out."

"You what?!" Anderson was shocked. "I can't believe you . . . how is that even possible?"

"Encryption and security algorithms are my specialty," she said with just a hint of pride. Then her voice became defensive. "Look, I know it was illegal. I know I broke the chain of command. But you weren't there. You can't understand how strange Dr. Qian was acting."

"What did you find out?"

"He hadn't just taken the project in a radical new direction. Our research was completely off the grid. All the new theories, the new hardware—it was all based on preparing our neural networks to link into some kind of alien artifact!"

"So what?" Anderson said with a shrug. "Pretty much every major advance we've made in the last two decades was based on Prothean artifacts. And it's not just us—galactic society wouldn't even exist if it wasn't for compatible alien technology. Every species in Citadel Space would still be stuck inside their own solar system."

"This is different," she insisted. "Take the mass relays. We only have a limited understanding of how they work. We know how to use them, but we don't understand enough to try and actually build one. At Sidon we were trying to create an artificial intelligence, possibly the most devastating weapon we could unleash on the galaxy. And Dr. Qian wanted to introduce an element to the research that was beyond even his comprehension."

Anderson nodded, recalling the infamous Manhattan Project of the early twentieth century from his history courses at the Academy. Desperate to create an atomic weapon, scientists on the project unwittingly exposed themselves to dangerous levels of radiation as a matter of course in their experiments. Two researchers actually died on the project, and many others were stricken with cancer or other long-term consequences from prolonged radiation poisoning.

"We weren't supposed to repeat the mistakes of the past," Kahlee said, making no effort to hide the disappointment in her voice. "I thought Dr. Qian was smarter than that."

"You were going to report him, weren't you?"

The young woman nodded slowly.

"You were doing the right thing, Kahlee," he said, noticing the uncertainty in her expression.

"It's hard to believe that when all my friends are dead."

Anderson could see she was suffering from a classic case of survivor guilt. But even though he felt sorry for her, he still needed more information.

"Kahlee . . . we still have to figure out who did this. And why."

"Maybe somebody wanted to stop Dr. Qian," she offered in a whisper. "Maybe my investigation tipped someone else off. Someone higher up. And they decided to shut the project down for good."

"You think someone in the Alliance did this?" Anderson was horrified.

"I don't know what to think!" she shouted. "All I know is I'm tired and scared and I just want this all to be over!"

For a second he thought she was going to start crying again, but she didn't. Instead, she stared right at him. "So are you still going to help me figure out who's behind this? Even if it turns out the Alliance is somehow involved?"

"I'm on your side," Anderson promised her. "I don't believe anyone in the Alliance was behind this. But if it turns out they were, I'll do my best to take them down."

"I believe you," she said after a moment. "So what now?"

She'd come clean with him. Now he had to do the same. "Alliance Command told me they think whoever attacked the base was after Dr. Qian. They think he might still be alive."

"But the vids are saying there were no survivors!"

"There's no way to be sure. Most of the bodies were vaporized at the scene."

"So why now?" Kahlee asked. "The project's been running for years."

"Maybe they just found out. Maybe Qian's new research tipped them off. Maybe there's some connection to that alien artifact he discovered."

"Or maybe I forced them to make a move."

Anderson wasn't about to let her go down that road. "This isn't your fault," he told her, leaning in and grabbing her hand tightly. "You didn't order the attack on Sidon. You didn't help anyone bypass base security." He took a breath, then spoke his next words slowly and emphatically. "Kahlee, you are not responsible for this."

He released her hand and sat back. "And I need you to help me figure out who was. We need to find

out if anybody else knew about this Prothean artifact."

"It wasn't Prothean," she corrected. "At least, not
according to Dr. Qian's notes."

"So what was it? Asari? Turian? Batarian?"

"No. Nothing like that. Qian didn't know what it
was, exactly. But it was old. He thought it might even
predate the Protheans."

"Predate the Protheans?" Anderson repeated, trying to make sure he'd heard her properly.

"That's what Qian thought," she said with a shrug.

"Where'd he find it? Where is it now?"

"I don't think it was ever at the base. Dr. Qian
wouldn't have brought it in until he was ready to integrate it into our project.

"And he could have found it anywhere," she admitted. "Every few months he'd leave the base for a
week or two. I always assumed he was giving some
kind of status report to his superiors at Alliance Command, but who knows where he went or what he was
up to."

"Somebody outside the base had to know about
this," Anderson pressed. "You said Dr. Qian changed,
took the research in a whole other direction. Was there
anyone not on the project who might have noticed
something out of the ordinary?"

"I can't think of . . . wait! The hardware for our
new research! It all came from the same supplier on
Camala!"

"Camala? Your supplier was batarian?"

"We never dealt with them directly," she explained,
speaking quickly. "Suspicious hardware purchases
anywhere in Citadel Space are red-flagged and re-

ported to the Council. Throughout the existence of the project we used hundreds of shell companies to place individual orders for each component; orders too small to attract attention on their own. Then we configured them at the base and integrated them into our existing hardware infrastructure.

"Dr. Qian wanted to avoid compatibility issues in the neural networks, so he made sure almost everything could be traced back to a single supplier: Dah'tan Manufacturing."

It made sense in a convoluted way, Anderson realized. Given the current political tension between batarians and humans, nobody would suspect that the primary supplier of a classified Alliance research project would be based on Camala.

"If somebody at the supplier noticed a pattern in the purchases," Kahlee continued, "they might have figured out what we were up to."

"As soon as Grissom gets us off this world," Anderson declared, "we're going to pay the Dah'tan facility a little visit."

THIRTEEN

Saren made his way through the darkness of Elysium's moonless night toward his waiting vehicle. He knew the humans back at the house were hiding something from him. There was more going on at Sidon then they had admitted.

As a Spectre, he had the legal right to forcibly extract information from anyone, even Alliance soldiers. But having that right and actually being able to use it were two different things.

Elysium was an Alliance world. He had no idea if one of Grissom's neighbors had called the authorities after the gunfight with Skarr. It wasn't likely—the house was well isolated from its neighbors. But Saren couldn't take that chance. If the local Alliance authorities arrived to find a turian brutally interrogating their fellow soldiers, his Spectre status wouldn't help him.

Besides, they weren't the ones he was after. The humans were insignificant to his real investigation. They probably knew something about why Skarr had been sent after them, but he doubted they had any real idea *who* had sent him.

The krogan was the key. Saren had no trouble following him to Elysium; he'd just have to pick up his trail again. The Verge was the untamed frontier of Citadel Space, but even out here it was nearly impossible to travel between worlds without drawing attention. Smaller ships were physically capable of landing almost anywhere on a habitable planet. But any destination world occupied by an established colony would instantly pick up any incoming vessels that didn't touch down at the spaceport. They'd have military personnel on the scene ready and waiting to arrest everyone on board . . . if they didn't simply blast the offending ship from the sky.

That meant Skarr would have to use the spaceports. And even if he found some way to sneak past border security, he wasn't hard to pick out of a crowd. As a Spectre, Saren had eyes and ears on virtually every world scattered across the Verge. Wherever the bounty hunter turned up next, one of his contacts would let him know.

He could issue an order to have Skarr arrested, but he doubted the krogan would let himself be taken alive. Having him die in a gun battle with local authorities wouldn't get Saren any closer to whoever was behind the attack on Sidon. No, the better thing to do was to simply find him and follow him, as he'd done on Elysium. Eventually the krogan would lead him right to his employer.

Edan Had'dah was once again spending the night inside the loathsome warehouse outside Hatre. Once again, he was sitting in the uncomfortable chair waiting for Skarr to arrive. And once again, he was accompanied by his personal guard: the same Blue Sun mercs who had been there for the first meeting with the krogan. The ones who'd survived, anyway.

But this time, Edan knew, he had the upper hand. Kahlee Sanders was not dead. He'd paid the bounty hunter good money to do a job, and Skarr had failed. This time, Edan swore, he would be the one to dictate the terms of their meeting.

The warehouse was full of large shipping crates and cargo containers. A small area had been cleared out in the back for Edan to conduct his business; from this position it was normally difficult to hear when someone arrived at the front door. But there was no mistaking the loud pounding when the krogan showed up.

"Make sure you take his weapons," Edan called out as a pair of batarian mercs went to fetch the new arrival. "All of them," their employer added, vividly remembering the knife Skarr had snuck in last time.

From the front came the sounds of a loud argument; though he couldn't quite hear the words he could clearly make out the bass tones of the krogan's deep rumble. A minute later one of the batarians came back alone.

"The krogan won't hand over his weapons," he said.

"What?" Edan asked, surprised.

"He won't hand over his weapons. And he's wearing full armor."

"I won't meet with him if he's armed," Edan vowed.

"That's what I told him," the merc responded, tilting his head to the left in a gesture of supplication.

"He just laughed. Said he was happy to walk away and consider your business arrangement over."

Edan cursed under his breath. The krogan had been paid in full up front. Normally a batarian would never agree to such terms, but exceptions had to be made for a man of Skarr's reputation.

"Let him keep his weapons," he finally relented. "Escort him back here."

"Is that wise?"

"Tell your men they are free to kill him this time if he tries anything. Make sure the bounty hunter hears you."

The merc smiled, anticipating a chance for revenge, and headed back to the front. When he returned the bounty hunter was with him, and he looked angry. Edan had never actually seen a krogan Battle Master in full armor before. It was a terrifying sight: like a living tank rolling toward him. It was all he could do not to take a step back.

Skarr's weapons weren't drawn, but a full arsenal was slotted into his armor: a pistol on either hip; a collapsible heavy-fire assault rifle and high-powered shotgun were slung across his back. His armor had several small holes in the chest, each one ringed with discolored blood. Dark stains ran down from the wounds, tainting the armor and serving as mute testimony to the battle he had fought on Elysium.

The Blue Suns watched him closely; nine assault rifles tracking him every step of the way. The krogan didn't seem to care; he only had eyes for the man who'd hired him. He bore down on him with long, heavy strides, the relentless *clump-clump-clump* of his boots the only sound in the warehouse. For a brief second Edan thought he wouldn't stop—he'd just keep walking, churning the batarian's smaller frame beneath his feet, grinding him into pulp. Instead, he pulled up less than a meter away, his breath coming in angry, rasping grunts.

"You failed," Edan said. He'd meant it to come out as a stinging accusation, but standing in the shadow of the massive killer before him took all the bravado from his voice.

"*You* didn't tell me I'd have to deal with a Spectre!" Skarr snarled back.

"A Spectre?" Edan said with surprise. "Are you certain?"

"I know a Spectre when I see one!" Skarr roared. "Especially this one. Turian bastard!"

The corners of Edan's mouth turned down in an expression of displeasure, but he didn't say anything. This was bad. He knew Skarr was talking about Saren; the turian was easily the most infamous Spectre in the Verge. He was known for three things: his ruthlessness, his loyalty to the Council, and his ability to get results.

"I make it a habit never to get involved in Spectre business," Skarr said, his voice dropping to a low growl. "You knew that when you hired me. You tricked me, batarian."

"My guards will fire on you if you try anything," Edan said quickly, sensing the implied threat. "You might kill me, but you'll never get out of here alive."

The krogan's big head rolled from side to side, glancing at the armed mercs and evaluating his chances. Realizing this was a battle even he couldn't win, he slowly took a step back from Edan.

"I guess we're in this together then," he snorted. "But you're going to have to double my fee."

Edan blinked in surprise. This was not how he expected the negotiations to go.

"You're not bargaining from a position of power," he pointed out. "You didn't complete the job. If anything, I should ask for a refund. Or I could just have my men eliminate you now."

Skarr barked out a loud laugh. "You're right. Sanders is still alive. She's probably talking to Saren right now, telling him everything she knows. How long until he figures out you were behind all this? How long until he shows up on Camala?"

The batarian didn't answer.

"Sooner or later that Spectre will track you down," the bounty hunter warned, pressing his point. "When he does, your only hope of staying alive is to have me on your side."

Edan brought his hands together, forming a five-fingered steeple as he considered the situation. The krogan was correct; he needed his help now more than ever. But he wasn't willing to admit total defeat.

"Very well," he conceded, "I'll double your pay. But in exchange you'll have to do something for me."

Skarr didn't say anything, but merely waited for the batarian to continue.

"I was never at Sidon," Edan explained. "Sanders has no knowledge of my identity. With the files at the base destroyed, there is only one connection left linking me to this crime: Dr. Qian's supplier here on Camala."

"Dah'tan Manufacturing," Skarr said after only a moment's hesitation, quickly putting the pieces together. Once again Edan was impressed at how quickly his mind worked. "Does Sanders know about the supplier?"

"I can't be sure," Edan admitted. "But if she mentions it, that's the first place the Spectre will go. I'm not willing to take that risk."

"So what do you need from me?"

"I ordered you to come back to this world so you could wipe out Dah'tan Manufacturing. Eliminate all the personnel, all the records. Burn it to the ground. Leave nothing behind. *Nothing*."

"You brought me back for that?" Skarr spat out. "Are you stupid? Saren's going to have his people watching for me. He's probably already on his way here to try and track me down. We attack Dah'tan and he'll be there inside an hour. You'd practically lead him straight to your supplier!"

"He might learn about Dah'tan from Sanders anyway," Edan countered. He refused to back down this time. He was tired of losing face to this brute. "You can get in, finish the job, and disappear before Saren ever arrives," he insisted. "By the time he gets to Dah'tan all the evidence will be destroyed and you can be long gone. There won't be anything left for him to find.

"You'll just have to work fast."

"That's how mistakes get made," the bounty hunter argued. "I don't like sloppy missions. Tell your men to go in without me."

"This is not open to negotiation!" Edan shouted, finally losing his temper. "I hired you to kill someone! You failed! I demand something for the money I'm paying you!"

Skarr shook his head in disbelief. "You know it was a mistake bringing me back here for this. I thought you were smart enough not to put your pride ahead of business."

"You thought wrong," Edan replied, no longer shouting. But his voice was cold as ice. It was more than simple pride; batarian culture placed tremendous value on social caste. He was a man of high standing; if he simply forgave the krogan for this failure it would be an admission that they were equals . . . something he was not about to do.

The krogan took another long look at the Blue Suns stationed around the warehouse, their guns still raised and ready and pointing right at him. "Dah'tan has heavy security," he finally said. "How are we even supposed to get inside?"

"I have some of their people on my payroll," Edan replied with just a hint of smugness. He'd finally managed to back Skarr into a corner. They were bargaining on his terms now.

"You really think these *hrakhors* are good enough to handle a job like this?" the bounty hunter asked, making one last attempt to get out of it.

"They were good enough to take out the Alliance soldiers at Sidon."

"They screwed that mission up," Skarr objected.

"That's why I'm sending you along this time" was Edan's smug reply.

Anderson flashed his military ID and slipped his thumb into the portable scanner held by the Alliance guard working the port authority entrance. The young man, who'd jumped to stand at attention as they'd approached, glanced down at the computer screen to confirm the readout.

"Sir," the guard replied with a curt nod, handing it back to him a moment later. The lieutenant did his best not to hold his breath as Kahlee placed her own thumb into the scanner and handed over her phony ID and the optical storage disk with the counterfeit authorization orders they'd purchased earlier that day.

The man who'd forged them had come to the house first thing in the morning, arriving less than ten minutes after Grissom's phone call. He was young—no older than twenty by Anderson's guess. He was dressed in shabby, wrinkled civvies and he had long, greasy black hair. His face was covered with a dark growth he was trying to pass off as a beard, and it looked like he hadn't showered in a week. The admiral didn't say who the man was or how he knew him.

"He's a professional," he told Anderson. "He works fast, and he won't rat you out."

When he first arrived, the kid had looked in surprise at the broken windows, the smashed furniture, and the burned hole in the lawn where the shotgun blast had narrowly missed decapitating the krogan. But he hadn't asked any questions. Not about that, anyway.

"What do you need?" was all he had said once he was inside, setting a nondescript case he had with him on the kitchen table.

"Something to get them into the restricted loading bays at the spaceport," Grissom had replied. "Plus a disguise and a new ID for Kahlee. They need to leave today."

"I gotta charge extra for a rush job," he warned.

Grissom just nodded. "I'll forward it like always."

The young man opened the case to reveal an array of unusual tools, gadgets, and exotic equipment Anderson couldn't even begin to guess the function of. Using a variety of these, it took him half an hour to produce an OSD with the appropriate authorizations. It took another twenty minutes to encode a new name and rank on Kahlee's Alliance ID—Corporal Suzanne Weathers.

"That's not going to work," Anderson warned. "They won't have any records for Corporal Weathers in their systems."

"They will twenty minutes after I leave here," the kid assured with a cocky grin. "I'll add Corporal Weathers to the system. Then I'll mirror all Kahlee's data and block system access to her file. When they scan her thumbprint it'll be Weathers who shows up on their screens, not Sanders."

"You have access to the Alliance data files?" Anderson asked in disbelief.

"Only the ones at the ports. Don't try to use this ID once you're off Elysium."

"I didn't think it was possible to infiltrate the Alliance systems," Anderson said, fishing for information.

"You sure I can trust this guy?" the kid asked Grissom.

Funny, Anderson thought. *I was wondering the same thing about you.*

"For today," Grissom replied. "Next time you see him you might want to turn around and walk in the other direction, though."

"The Alliance has solid security," the young man

admitted, speaking with a casual nonchalance as he worked. "Getting in is tough, but it's not impossible."

"What about the purges?" Kahlee asked. Anderson looked at her quizzically and she explained for his benefit. "Every ten hours the Alliance runs a full security sweep on their systems to track down and quarantine any new data coming into the system. It lets them identify fraudulent data and trace it back to the source."

"I plant a little self-regressive algorithm in the data before I upload it," the kid explained, bragging more than just a little. "Something I came up with myself. By the time they run the security sweep your data will be back online and all traces of Corporal Weathers or these phony authorizations will be long gone. They can't trace something that isn't there."

Kahlee nodded in appreciation, and the man gave her a wink and a leering smile that made Anderson's fist involuntarily clench. It wasn't jealousy. Not exactly. Kahlee was his responsibility now. It was only natural he'd instinctively want to protect her. But he had to be careful not to overreact.

Fortunately nobody had noticed; they were all focused on the young man and his work. "They might have a physical description of you, too," he warned Kahlee. "We better change your appearance, just in case."

He digitally altered the existing photo on Kahlee's ID, darkening and shortening her hair, changing the color of her eyes, and deepening the pigments of her skin. Then he had her pop a handful of pigment pills. Next he used shaded contact lenses, hair dye, and a pair of scissors to make Kahlee's physical appearance match her digital image. He seemed to enjoy it a little too much for Anderson's comfort, working the dye into her hair for several minutes and lingering a little too long over her locks before he cut them.

By the time he was finished with her hair Kahlee's skin had become almost as dark as Anderson's. The kid stood directly in front of Kahlee and held the ID up beside her face, comparing the image to the real thing. "Not bad," he said appreciatively, though it wasn't clear if he was talking about his work or Kahlee herself.

"Your skin will start to lighten up again by tomorrow," he told her, standing up and holding out the reinvented Alliance ID card. "So be careful. You won't match the pic anymore."

"Shouldn't matter," she said with a shrug. "Corporal Weathers won't even exist in the system by then anyway, right?"

He didn't answer, but gave her another sly wink and let his fingers rub suggestively against hers as she took the ID from him. Anderson had to restrain himself from punching the slimeball right in the face. *She's not your wife,* he thought to himself. *Helping her won't make up for eight years of ignoring Cynthia.*

When all was said and done, however, the lieutenant had to admit the kid's forgery was good. He had special training to recognize fraudulent documents, and even though he knew they were fakes he couldn't tell them from the real thing.

This was the true test, however: running her thumbprint through the scanners at the port authority.

"Here you go, Corporal Weathers," the guard said, handing the altered documentation back to Kahlee after glancing briefly at his screen to confirm her identity. "You need to head to bay thirty-two. Way down at the far end."

"Thank you," Kahlee said with a smile. The guard nodded, snapped a crisp salute off to Anderson, then sat down and went back to the paperwork on his desk as they turned and walked away.

"Take a look to see if he's still watching us," Anderson whispered once they were out of earshot. They were still heading in the direction of bay thirty-two, but of course that wasn't their real destination.

Kahlee glanced back, coyly peeking over her shoulder. If the guard was watching them he'd hopefully just think the young corporal found him attractive enough to sneak a second look. But he was completely focused on the screen at his desk, the model of efficiency as he rapidly typed away at the keyboard.

"All clear," Kahlee answered.

"This is it," Anderson said, turning sharply into the entrance of bay seventeen and pulling her with him.

There was an old cargo freighter in the bay, a loading sled, and a number of heavy shipping crates. At first glance there didn't seem to be anybody in the bay, and then a short, heavyset man stepped out from the other side of the ship.

"Any problems with the guard?" he asked.

Kahlee shook her head.

"You know why we're here?" Anderson asked, not even bothering to ask the man's name, which he knew would never be given.

"Grissom filled me in."

"How do you know my father?" Kahlee asked, curious.

He regarded her coldly for a second then said, "If he wanted you to know, he probably would've told you himself." Turning away he added, "We're scheduled to lift off in a couple hours. Follow me."

Most of the space inside the ship's hold was filled with cargo; there was barely enough room for the two of them to sit down, but they did the best they could. As soon as they were settled, the man sealed the door and they were plunged into complete darkness.

Kahlee was sitting right across from him, but with no light it was impossible for Anderson to even make out her silhouette. He could, however, feel the outside of her leg pressing up against his—there simply wasn't room for either of them to pull away. The closeness was unsettling; he hadn't been with a woman since he and Cynthia had separated.

"I'm not looking forward to the next six hours," he said, looking to distract his inappropriate thoughts with conversation. Even though he spoke softly his words seemed unnaturally loud in the blackness.

"I'm more worried about what we'll do once we reach Camala," Kahlee answered, a disembodied voice in the gloom. "Dah'tan's not just going to hand their files over to us."

"I'm still working on that," Anderson admitted. "I'm hoping I'll come up with a plan on the trip."

"We should have plenty of time to think," Kahlee answered. "There's not even enough room here to lay down and get some sleep."

After a few minutes she spoke again, changing topics without warning. "Before my mother died I promised her I'd never speak to my father again."

Anderson was momentarily caught off guard by the personal confession, but he recovered quickly. "I think she'd understand."

"It must have been a shock for you," she continued. "Seeing the most famous Alliance soldier in a state like that."

"I'm a little surprised," he admitted. "When I was in the Academy your father was always portrayed as the embodiment of everything the Alliance stood for: courage, determination, self-sacrifice, honor. Seems a little strange that he knows the kind of people who can sneak us off a world like this."

"Are you disappointed?" she asked. "Knowing the great Jon Grissom associates with forgers and smugglers?"

"Considering our situation, I'd be a hypocrite if I said yes," he joked. Kahlee didn't laugh.

"When you hear about someone for so long you assume you know something about them," he said in a more somber tone. "It's easy to confuse the reputation with the real person. It's only when you meet them that you realize you never really knew anything at all."

"Yeah," Kahlee said thoughtfully. And then they were silent for a long, long time.

FOURTEEN

Jella had worked in the personnel and accounting department of Dah'tan Manufacturing for four years. She was a good employee: organized, meticulous, and thorough—all valuable assets for anyone in her occupation. On her performance evaluations she routinely scored above average to excellent. But according to her official job description she was "support staff." She wasn't "essential" to the company. The hardware designers were at the top of the corporate hierarchy; their innovations brought in the customers. And the people who worked the plant floor actually created the product. All she did was balance the sales figures with the inventory supplies.

She was nothing but an afterthought to those in charge . . . and her pay reflected it. Jella worked as hard as anyone in the company, but she was paid a mere fraction of what the designers and manufacturers earned. It wasn't fair. Which was why she felt no guilt over stealing from the company.

It wasn't like she was selling critical corporate secrets. She never did anything large enough to draw attention; she was only siphoning off tiny drops from the overflowing corporate bucket. Sometimes she'd alter purchase orders or manipulate supply records. Occasionally she'd make sure inventory was left unsecured and unregistered in the warehouse overnight. The next morning it would be mysteriously missing; moved by someone on the warehouse staff who was in on the deal.

Jella had no idea who took the inventory away, just as she had no idea who was behind the thefts. That was how she liked it. Once or twice a month she'd receive an anonymous call at the office, she'd play her part, and within a few days payment would be credited to her private financial accounts.

Today was no different. Or so she tried to tell herself as she walked down the hall, attempting to appear casual and hoping nobody would notice her. But there was something strange about this request. She'd been asked to shut down one of the security cameras and disable the alarm codes on one of the entrances. Someone wanted to sneak into the building undetected . . . and they were doing it in the middle of the day.

It was a stupid risk. Even if they somehow got inside, they were sure to be noticed; Dah'tan had regular security teams patrolling the entire plant. And if they were caught, they might give up Jella as the one who'd let them in. But the offer had been too good to turn down—triple what she'd ever been paid for a job before. In the end, greed had won out over common sense.

She paused near one of the emergency exits, directly beneath the security camera trained on the door. Quickly glancing around to make sure nobody was watching, she reached up with the screwdriver she'd taken from a tool belt hanging in the utility closet and jammed it into the back of the camera, taking out the power cell.

It sparked, startling her. She let out a little scream and dropped the screwdriver, her fingers tingling slightly from the shock. Hastily, she bent down and picked it up from the carpet, looking around to see if anyone had noticed her sabotage. The hall was still empty.

She looked up at the camera and saw a thin ribbon of white smoke wisping out the back. The power light was dead. If anyone up in central security looked over at the monitor for this camera they would notice it was out. But the guards barely even glanced at the monitors during the day. Not with the patrols wandering the halls and the building filled with staff. Only a fool would try to break in during business hours.

Even if they did notice the outage, there were over a hundred security cameras in the facility. One seemed to malfunction every other week. The most anyone would do would be to put in a maintenance request to get it fixed before the end of the shift. Satisfied, Jella continued down the hall to the security door.

She typed in an employee code to disable the alarm and open the lock. She didn't use her own code, of course. One advantage of working in her department was that she had access to personnel files. She knew the building entry codes for half the people in the facility.

When the light on the door panel went from red to green, Jella's part was done. All she had to do was head back to her office and continue her work as if nothing was wrong.

But once she returned to her desk, the bad feeling she had about this particular job continued to grow, making her feel queasy. After about twenty minutes She'n'ya, the woman she shared the small office with, must have noticed something was wrong.

"Are you okay, Jella? You look a bit flushed."

Jella's stomach nearly lurched out of her throat at the sound of the other woman's voice. "I'm . . . I'm not feeling well," she replied, hoping she didn't sound as guilty as she felt. "I think I'm going to be sick," she added, jumping to her feet and running to the bathroom to throw up.

Jella was still in there ten minutes later when the shooting started.

The mission was simple and straightforward, but Skarr still didn't like it. It had taken a day for them to assemble everything he'd said he'd need for the assault: explosives, a strike team of thirty mercs, including himself, and three rovers for transportation.

For reasons of corporate security and customer confidentiality, Dah'tan Manufacturing was located on three acres of private property well beyond the outskirts of Hatre. Every kilometer of the drive out there ate away at Skarr, and also at the limited time they had to do the job. Somebody was sure to have noticed him at the spaceport; somebody who would report him to Saren. The Spectre was probably already on his way to Camala . . . and getting closer with every passing second.

The facility consisted of a single structure that

housed the warehouse, factory, and offices. The grounds were surrounded by a chain-link fence, with several signs that read "Private Property" and "No Admittance" in all the various batarian dialects common to Camala.

Not that this deterred Skarr and his mercs. The rovers simply drove right through the fence, flattening it as they bore down on the lonely building on the horizon. Half a kilometer away they parked the rovers and continued across the barren desert terrain on foot. Approaching the factory on the side opposite the warehouse loading bays to avoid detection, they reached the building without incident.

Skarr was relieved to find the security entrance at the back unlocked—Edan's source inside had come through. But they still had to work quickly if they wanted to get in and out before Saren showed up.

Corporate paranoia was as much a part of batarian culture as their rigid caste system, and Dah'tan was no different. Unwilling to trust anyone else with sensitive information, all records and archives were kept on site: destroying the facility would wipe out all evidence that could lead back to Edan.

Each rover carried ten mercs. Skarr left eight men outside with sniper rifles to cover the exits, a pair stationed on each side of the building. The others were broken into seven infiltration teams of three members each.

"The bombs will detonate in fifteen minutes," Skarr reminded them.

The infiltration teams scattered, heading off down the various branching corridors leading to all the different areas of the facility. Their objective was to plant a number of strategically placed explosives; enough to reduce the entire building to ash and rubble. Along the way they'd take out the security patrols and mow down any employees they ran across. Anyone who fled the building would be shot by the mercs waiting outside. And any survivors who managed to hide inside the building would be killed by the explosions or burned alive when the incendiary charges were detonated.

With the snipers posted outside and the infiltration teams making their way toward the heart of the complex, Skarr was left alone to complete a very specific task. Edan had given him the name, description, and office location of his contact inside Dah'tan. It was unlikely the young woman knew whom she was working for, but the batarian didn't want to leave any loose ends.

The krogan made his way quickly through the halls toward the admin offices near the front of the building. From somewhere far away he heard the sound of gunfire and batarian voices screaming—the massacre had begun.

Moments later sirens started ringing. Skarr rounded a corner and nearly ran into a pair of Dah'tan security guards rushing to respond to the alarm. The two batarians hesitated for a mere instant, caught off guard by the sight of a heavily armored krogan crashing through the halls. Skarr seized the opportunity and smashed the butt of his assault rifle into one guard's face, sending him reeling backwards. At the same time he threw his body into the second guard, his mass bowling the much smaller man over and sending them both tumbling to the floor. As they rolled together on the ground Skarr leveraged the barrel of his gun under his adversary's chin and pulled the trigger, removing most of everything above the neck.

The first guard was just getting to his feet, still dazed and bleeding from his mouth. He fired his own weapon, but his aim was erratic and he only managed to rip a line of holes in the wall above where Skarr and the corpse of his friend were sprawled across the floor. Skarr responded by firing down the corridor, shredding his enemy's ankles and calves.

The batarian screamed and fell forward, dropping his gun as he threw his arms out to break his fall. Another burst from Skarr finished him off an instant after he hit the ground.

Leaping to his feet, the bounty hunter lumbered down the hall toward the office of Edan's contact. The door was closed but he simply kicked it in, sending it flying off its hinges. A young batarian woman was crouching on the floor, only half-hidden behind her desk. She screamed when she saw the gore-covered krogan standing in the doorway.

"Good-bye, Jella," Skarr said.

"No! Please! I'm not—"

The rest of her words were cut off as he squeezed the trigger, drowned out by the hail of bullets that riddled her body and blew it across the floor to the back wall of the room.

Skarr glanced quickly at his watch. Seven more minutes until the explosives detonated. Part of him wanted to spend the time searching the halls for more victims, but he knew that wasn't an option. It was too easy to lose himself in the bloodlust of his ancient ancestors. Swept up in battle fury, he could easily lose track of time in a slaughter like this, and he had no intention of being inside the building when it blew.

He made his way quickly back to the exit, ignoring the sweet screams of pain and terror beckoning to him from every corridor he passed.

Jella did her best to block out the staccato bursts of gunfire and the horrific screams of her coworkers. She was hiding inside the bathroom air vent—a tight fit but she had managed to wedge herself in. In her mind she could picture the scene outside, and she had no intention of leaving her hiding place.

Time passed with agonizing slowness; the sounds of the attack seemed to go on for hours, though in reality it was only a few minutes. She heard voices outside the bathroom door and she tried to scooch herself back even farther into the air shaft.

The door flew open and a pair of batarians leaped in, their automatic weapons already firing. They sprayed the entire room with bullets, reducing the thin sheet metal of the stall doors to ribbons, shattering the ceramic toilets and sinks and bursting several of the water pipes in the walls.

Fortunately Jella's hiding place was high up on the wall above one of the stalls—she'd mounted one of the toilets and clambered up onto the dividers between the stalls to remove the air vent's cover. Then she'd slid in feet first and carefully pulled the cover back into place once she was safely hidden inside.

From her vantage point she had a perfect view of the carnage, though she closed her eyes and covered her ears with her palms to try and block out the deafening retorts of their weapons. Only when the gunfire finally ended did she dare to open her eyes again.

The men were taking a last look around the bathroom, splashing noisily through the water gushing from the broken pipes, spreading out across the floor like a miniature lake.

"Nobody here," one of them said with a shrug.

"Too bad," the other replied. "I was hoping we could catch one of the women and drag her off with us for a little fun."

"Forget it," the other said with a shake of his head. "That krogan would never go for it."

"Edan's the one paying us, not him," his partner spat back. Jella instantly knew who he was talking about: Edan Had'dah was one of the most wealthy, powerful, and infamous individuals on Camala.

"I dare you to say that to his face," the first man said with a laugh, even as he crouched down and attached something to the wall. A moment later he stood up. "Let's move. We need to be out of here in two minutes."

The men ran off down the hallway, their footsteps echoing in the distance. Jella crawled slowly forward from her hiding place, trying to see what they had placed on the wall. It was about the size of a lunch box, with wires running into it from all sides. Even though she had no military training or experience, it was obvious the device was some kind of bomb.

She paused for a moment, listening for more gunfire. Everything was silent except for a faint *beep-beep-beep* as the timer on the explosive counted down. Jella knocked the cover off the ventilation shaft and dropped down to the floor. She ran out of the bathroom, sprinting down the corridor toward the same security exit she had unlocked earlier, unwittingly allowing the slaughter to happen.

But she couldn't think about that now. Refusing to even glance at the bodies of her coworkers in the hallway, she reached the door and yanked it open. Two men from the warehouse lay just outside, each shot between the eyes.

Jella hesitated, expecting a similar fate. But whoever had killed the men was gone, clearing the surrounding area before the building detonated. As soon as her shell-shocked mind grasped the fact that she was still alive, the young woman put her head down and ran. She managed half a dozen steps before the explosion turned her world to fire, agony, and then darkness.

By the time Saren arrived at the Dah'tan Manufacturing facility, the place was in ruins. Emergency response crews had put out the fires, but the building was little more than a burned-out shell. The top two floors had collapsed and one of the walls had caved inwards, reducing the interior to a pile of scorched rubble. Rescue workers were busy picking through the debris. Looking at the scene it was obvious they weren't looking for survivors; they were collecting remains.

Several news crews were filming the wreckage from a respectful distance away, careful not to interfere with the emergency crews but anxious to get some dramatic footage for the vids.

Saren parked his vehicle beside them, got out, and marched toward the ruins.

"Hey!" one of the batarian emergency workers called out on seeing his approach, running over to intercept him. "You can't be here. This is a restricted area."

Saren glared at him and produced his identification.

"Sorry, sir," the batarian said, stopping short and tilting his head in deference. "I didn't know you were a Spectre."

"Any survivors?" Saren demanded.

"Only one," he replied. "A young woman. She was outside the building when it blew. The blast took her legs, and she has critical burns to ninety percent of her body.

"She's en route to the hospital now. It's a miracle she survived, but I don't think she's going to make it through the—"

"Take your crew and go," Saren said, cutting him off.

"What? We can't! We're still looking for survivors."

"There aren't anymore survivors. You're done here."

"What about the bodies? We can't just leave them like this."

"The bodies will still be here in the morning. Clear out. That's an order. And take the damn vid crews with you."

The batarian hesitated, then acquiesced with another tilt of his head and went to round up his crew. Five minutes later the rescue vehicles and media vans were pulling away, leaving Saren alone to search the wreckage for clues.

* * *

"My God," Kahlee gasped as their rover climbed over a rise and they caught their first glimpse of what had once been the Dah'tan Manufacturing plant. "The whole place is gone!"

It was almost dusk, but Camala's large orange sun still provided enough light for them to see the destruction clearly.

"Looks like somebody else got here first," Anderson noted with a grim frown.

"Where are the rescue crews?" Kahlee asked. "They have to know about this by now!"

"I don't know," Anderson admitted, grinding the rover to a stop. "Something's not right. Wait here."

Hopping out of the vehicle he approached the remains of the building on foot, pistol drawn, running in a quick crouch. He was less than twenty meters away when a single shot ricocheted off the ground just in front of him.

Anderson froze. He was completely exposed and in the open; the shooter could easily have killed him if that was the intent. The shot was meant as a warning.

"Drop your weapon and walk forward!" a voice called out from somewhere in the ruins up ahead. Anderson did as he was ordered, setting his pistol on the ground and continuing on unarmed.

A second later a familiar turian figure emerged from behind the debris he'd been using for cover, his rifle trained directly on Anderson's chest.

"What are you doing here?" the Spectre demanded.

"The same thing you are," Anderson said, trying to sound more confident than he felt. "Trying to find out who was behind the attack on Sidon."

Saren snorted in disgust, but didn't lower his weapon. "You lied to me, human." The way he said "human" made it sound like an insult.

Anderson didn't say anything. The Spectre had found his way to the Dah'tan plant; he was smart enough to put the pieces together.

"Artificial intelligence is a violation of Citadel Conventions," Saren continued when he didn't respond. "I *will* report this to the Council."

Again, Anderson remained silent. He had the impression Saren was still digging for information. Whatever the turian was looking for, Anderson wasn't going to be the one to accidentally give it to him.

"Who was behind the attack on Sidon?" Saren asked, his voice heavy with the implied threat as he brought the rifle sight up to his eye and took dead aim at the lieutenant's chest.

"I don't know," Anderson admitted, staying perfectly still.

Saren fired a shot into the ground at his feet.

He flinched, but didn't step back. "I said I don't know!" he shouted, letting his anger boil over. He was almost certain Saren meant to kill him, but he wasn't going to go down begging for his life. He wasn't going to let some turian thug intimidate him!

"Where is Sanders?" Saren barked, changing tactics.

"Somewhere safe," Anderson snapped back. There was no way in hell he was going to let this monster get anywhere close to Kahlee.

"She's lying to you," Saren told him. "She knows much more about this than she's told you. You should question her again."

"I'll run my investigation, you run yours."

"Maybe I should focus on finding her, then," he said, his voice dripping with menace. "If I do, my interrogation will uncover all her deepest secrets."

Anderson felt his muscles tense, but he refused to say anything more about Kahlee.

Realizing the human wasn't going to rise to the bait, the turian switched topics yet again. "How did you get here?"

"I'm done answering questions," Anderson said flatly. "If you're going to kill me, just do it."

The turian took a long look at the surrounding area, scanning the horizon in the fading light. He seemed to reach some kind of decision, then lowered his weapon.

"I am a Spectre, an agent of the Council," he declared, a timbre of nobility giving strength to his voice. "I am a servant of justice, sworn to protect and defend the galaxy. Killing you serves no purpose, human."

Again, the word was a thinly veiled insult.

Saren turned his back and walked away, heading toward the barely visible silhouette of a small rover in the distance. "Go ahead and pick through the rubble if it makes you feel better," he called back over his shoulder. "There's nothing left to find here."

Anderson didn't make a move until Saren climbed into his rover and sped off. Once the vehicle was out of sight, he turned and retrieved his pistol from the dirt. It was almost dark; there was no point in searching the debris now. And he actually believed what the turian had said about there being nothing left to find at Dah'tan.

Moving carefully through the deepening gloom of the night, it took him several minutes to make his way back to his own rover.

"What happened?" Kahlee asked as he climbed inside. "I thought I saw you talking to someone."

"Saren," he told her. "That turian Spectre."

"What's he doing here?" she asked, alarmed by the memory of their last encounter and the mere mention of his name.

"Looking for evidence," Anderson admitted.

"What did he say to you? What did he want?"

He briefly debated telling her a lie; something that would put her mind at ease. But she was a part of this, too. She deserved the truth. Or most of it, anyway.

"I think he was seriously considering killing me."

Kahlee gasped in horror.

"I can't be sure," he added quickly. "Maybe I'm wrong. Turians are hard to read."

"Don't give me that crap," she countered. "You wouldn't say something like that if you weren't sure. Tell me what happened."

"He was fishing for information," Anderson said. "He'd already figured out we were lying to him about what you were working on at the base."

"Dah'tan's not known for making biotic implants," Kahlee conceded.

"I didn't tell him anything. Once he realized I wasn't going to help his investigation he got this hard look in his eyes. That's when I thought he was going to kill me."

"But he didn't." Her words were half statement, half question.

"He took this slow look around, like he was trying to see if there was anyone else nearby. Then he just walked away."

"He wanted to know if you were out here alone!" she exclaimed, coming to the same conclusion he had already reached. "He couldn't kill you if there were any witnesses!"

Anderson nodded. "Legally a Spectre has the right to do whatever he wants. But the Council doesn't condone wanton murder. If he killed me and someone reported it, they'd step in."

"You really think the Council would take action if he killed a human?"

"Humanity has more political significance than any of those aliens want to admit," Anderson explained. "We've got enough ships and soldiers to make every other species think twice about crossing us. The Council needs to stay on our good side. If word got out that Spectres were killing Alliance officers without justification, they'd have to do something."

"So what happens now?"

"We head back to the city. I need to send a message to Ambassador Goyle in the next burst."

"Why?" Kahlee asked sharply. "What for?" The hint of alarm in her voice reminded him that she was still a fugitive on the run from the Alliance.

"Saren knows humanity's been conducting illegal AI research. He's going to report it to the Council. I have to warn her so she's ready for the political fallout."

"Of course," Kahlee replied, her voice a mixture of relief and embarrassment. "Sorry. I just thought . . ."

"I'm doing everything I can to help you," he told her, trying to hide how much her suspicion had hurt him. "But I need you to trust me."

She reached out and put her hand on top of his. "I'm not used to people looking out for me," she said by way of apology. "My mother was always working and my father . . . well, you know. Looking out for myself just became habit.

"But I know what you're risking to help me. Your career. Maybe your life. I'm grateful. And I do trust you . . . David."

Nobody ever called him David. Nobody but his mother and his wife. *Ex-wife,* he corrected. For a brief moment he was on the verge of telling Kahlee what Saren had said about focusing his investigation on her, but at the last second he bit his tongue.

He was attracted to Kahlee; he had already admitted that to himself. But he had to remember how much she'd already been through. She was vulnerable; alone and afraid. Telling her about Saren's threats would only exacerbate those feelings. And while it would probably make her more willing to accept him as her protector and draw them closer together, Anderson wasn't about to take advantage of a situation like that.

"Let's get moving," he said, gently pulling his hand out from under hers and turning the rover back toward the dim glow of the city in the distance.

FIFTEEN

Saren stood at the side of the hospital bed, looking down at the young batarian woman fighting for her life . . . though in her present condition it was difficult to tell what species she belonged to. Only the four orbs of her eyes gave her away—the only part of her anatomy not covered by the bandages that wrapped her from her head down to where her legs had been amputated just above the knee. Dozens of wires and tubes ran from her body to the nearby machinery keeping her alive: monitoring vital signs; circulating essential fluids; pumping in a steady stream of drugs, antibiotics, and medigel; even breathing for her.

Batarians were on the cutting edge of medical science, and the standard of care at their facilities was among the best in Citadel space. Under normal circumstances she would be receiving around-the-clock attention from the staff, but apart from the two of them the room was empty. Saren had sent the doctors and nurses out once they had updated him on her status, closing the door behind them.

"You can't do this!" the doctor in charge had protested. "She's too weak. She won't make it!" But in the end neither he nor any of the other staff had the courage or the will to defy a direct order from a Spectre.

Generally batarians were a hardy species, but even a krogan would have had difficulty surviving the trauma this patient had been through. Her missing legs were the most obvious injury, but Saren knew her burns were the most horrific. Under the bandages her skin would be all but melted away, exposing the seared flesh and charred tissue beneath. The biolab in the basement was growing skin grafts from samples of her own genetic material, but it would be at least a week before they were ready to begin reconstruction.

The explosion would have scarred her internal organs as well, the pressure from the blast forcing superheated air and noxious fumes down her throat and damaging them beyond repair. Only the host of incessantly beeping machines kept her alive, struggling to compensate for the failing systems of her body while cloned organs were being grown. However, like the skin grafts, it would be many days before they would be ready.

Rampant infection and massive heart failure brought on by traumatic shock were a constant threat while she was hooked onto the machines. And even if she survived another week, the strain of the numerous surgeries necessary to repair all the damage might be more than her ravaged body could endure.

She was resting peacefully right now; the doctors had put her into a light drug-induced coma to allow all of her energy to be focused on healing. If she responded to treatment, she would come out of the coma spontaneously in three or four days as her condition improved.

However, the fact that they were waiting to see if she regained consciousness before beginning work on prosthetic limbs to replace her legs told Saren everything he needed to know about the patient's condition. For all the miracles of medical science, organic life was still delicate and fragile, and it wasn't likely this woman was going to survive.

But Saren didn't need her to survive. She was a witness to what had happened at Dah'tan—the only living witness. They had identified her by cross-referencing genetic material with an employee data bank: she was a low-level worker in the accounting department. And all Saren wanted was to ask her one question.

He took the syringe the doctor had reluctantly prepared at his order and plunged it into one of the intravenous lines. It was highly unlikely this woman knew anything about the attack on Dah'tan, and even less likely she knew anything about Sidon. But everyone else on duty at the plant was dead, and Saren had a hunch her survival was more than just blind luck. Maybe she had some warning, some knowledge none of the others did that had almost enabled her to escape unscathed. It was a long shot, but one he was more than willing to take.

One of the machines began to beep loudly, responding to her rapidly quickening heart rate as the Spectre pushed the amphetamines into her system. Her body began to quiver, then tremble, then went rigid and stiff as she sat bolt upright. Her eyelids shot open, though the orbs beneath had been cooked blind by the fires. She tried to scream, but the only sound her charred throat and lungs could produce was a rasping wheeze, barely audible from behind her ventilator mask.

Still sitting up, her body went into seizure, rattling the tubes and the metal frame of her hospital bed as she thrashed uncontrollably. After several seconds she fell back, exhausted and spent, panting for breath, her blind eyes closed once more.

Saren leaned in close to her melted ears, speaking loudly so she could hear him. "Jella? Jella? Turn your head if you can hear me!" At first there was nothing, then her head moved feebly from one side to the other.

"I need to know who did this!" Saren shouted, trying to pierce her veil of pain and drugs. "I just want a name. Do you understand? Just tell me the name!"

He reached over and lifted her breathing mask so she could speak. Her lips moved, but nothing came out.

"Jella!" he shouted again. "Louder, Jella! Don't let the bastard get away with it! Who did this to you?"

Her words were barely more than a whisper, but Saren heard them clearly. "Edan. Edan Had'dah."

Satisfied, he replaced her breathing mask and pulled a second syringe from his pocket. This one would put her back into the coma, giving her at least a fighting chance for survival.

He hesitated before administering it. As a Spectre, he was familiar with the reputation of the man she'd identified. A ruthless businessman who operated on both sides of batarian law, Edan had always been careful not to involve himself in anything that would draw the attention of the Council or its agents. He had never shown any interest in artificial intelligence research before.

Saren's train of thought was momentarily broken by the sound of Jella coughing and gagging in her bed. Dark specks spattered the inside of the ventilator mask, blood and pus expelled from her lungs with each choking breath.

There was more to the raid on Sidon than batarian nationalism or antihuman terrorism, he realized. Edan didn't mix politics and business. And it wasn't just about money—Edan had plenty of other ways to make a profit that didn't incur the risk of Spectre involvement. There was something strange going on here. Something he wanted to investigate in more depth.

Jella's body began to convulse; the beeping of the machines became a single high-pitched whine as her stats dropped below critical levels. Saren stood motionless, watching as her numbers plummeted while he considered his next course of action.

Edan had built a magnificent mansion near the city of Ujon, Camala's capital. Saren doubted he'd find him there now. Edan was a careful, cautious man. Even if he was sure nobody knew about his connection to Sidon, he'd have gone into hiding the moment he learned someone survived the attack, just to be safe. He could be anywhere by now.

No, Saren corrected himself, ignoring the frantic beeping of the machines and the violent spasms still rocking Jella's body. *Edan wouldn't have risked trying to clear port security.* Not if there was even the slimmest chance someone already knew about his involvement. Which meant he was probably still hiding somewhere on Camala.

But there were plenty of places Edan could hide on this world. He controlled a number of mining and refinery operations; enormous plants spread across the entire surface of the planet. Most likely he was holed up at one of these. The problem was figuring out which one. There were literally hundreds of those facilities on Camala. It would take months to properly search them all. And Saren suspected he didn't have that kind of time.

Jella was still thrashing uncontrollably, trapped in the throes of her ravaged body's desperate struggle to survive. But she was growing weaker now, her strength ebbing away. Saren idly twirled the hypodermic that might save her between his fingers, still considering the problem of Edan as he waited for her to expire.

It had been obvious the humans didn't know who was behind the attacks, so Saren didn't see any reason to share this latest information with the Council. At least not yet. He'd tell them about the illegal AI research at Sidon, of course. It would cause serious trouble for the Alliance, and draw attention away from his own continuing investigation into Edan's involvement. But until he knew exactly why the batarian considered the rewards of this mission worth the incredible risk, he'd keep Edan's name out of the reports. Now all he had to do was figure out how to find him.

Two minutes later, Jella was finally still. The turian checked her body for any signs of life, confirming what the monitors already told him: she was gone.

Only now did he take the syringe and inject it into the IV, knowing it was too late to have any affect. Then he carefully placed the empty needle in plain view on a small table near the bed.

He walked slowly to the door, unlocked it, and turned the knob. Outside, the doctor in charge of Jella was waiting, pacing anxiously in the hall. He turned to face the turian as he emerged from the room.

"We heard the machines . . ." the doctor said, trailing off.

"You were right," Saren told him, his voice showing no hint of emotion. "Jella was too weak. She didn't make it."

Ambassador Goyle marched purposefully across the rolling green fields of the Presidium toward the Citadel Tower rising up in the distance, her brisk, compact strides at odds with the gentle serenity of her surroundings. The tranquil beauty of the simulated sunshine reflecting on the central lake did nothing to calm her mood. She'd received Anderson's warning less than an hour before she'd been given the summons to appear in front of the Council. The timing couldn't be coincidence; they knew about the AI research. And that meant there was going to be hell to pay.

She ran through various scenarios in her mind as she walked, planning what she would say when she faced them. Pleading lack of knowledge wasn't an option: Sidon was an officially recognized Alliance base. Even if they believed her false claims that she knew nothing about their research, there was no way to separate the base's illegal actions from humanity as a whole. It would only make it appear as if she was a figurehead with no real power.

Being contrite and apologetic was another tactic, but she doubted that would have any influence on the severity of the punishments the Council would levy against humanity and the Alliance. And, like feigning ignorance, it would come across as a sign of weakness.

By the time she reached the base of the Tower, she knew there was only one option. She had to go on the attack.

A scale model statue of a mass relay stood off to her left; a twenty-foot-tall replica of the Protheans' greatest technological achievement that welcomed visitors approaching the heart of the galaxy's most magnificent space station. It was a striking piece of art, but the ambassador was in no mood to stop and admire it.

She marched up to the guards standing at the Tower's only entrance, then waited impatiently while they confirmed her identity. She was pleased to note that one of the guards was human. The number of humans employed in critical positions throughout the Citadel seemed to grow every day; further evidence of how valuable her species had become to the galactic community in only a few short years. It strengthened her resolve as she entered the elevator that would rocket her up the outside of the Tower to the Council Chamber.

The elevator was transparent; as she shot heavenward she could see the whole of the Presidium stretched out beneath her. As she climbed even higher she could see beyond the edges of the Citadel's inner ring. In the distance were the flickering lights of the wards, extending out of sight along the Citadel's five arms.

The view was spectacular, but the ambassador did her best to ignore it. It was no accident that the grandeur of the Citadel was on full display here. Though they held no official power, the three individuals who made up the Council were for all intents and purposes the rulers of the civilized galaxy. The prospect of meeting them face-to-face was a humbling experience, even for someone as politically savvy as the Alliance's top ambassador. And she knew enough to understand that the long elevator ride to the apex of the Tower had been carefully crafted to make visitors feel awed and overwhelmed long before they ever got to meet the Council itself.

In less than a minute she was at the top, her stomach lurching slightly at the deceleration as the elevator slowed, then stopped. Or maybe it was just nerves. The doors opened and she stepped into the long hallway that served as an anteroom to the Council Chamber.

At the end of the hall was a broad staircase leading up, with wide passages branching off to either side at its foot. Six honor guards—two turians, two salarians, and two asari, a pair of each species represented on the Council—stood at attention along either wall. She passed them by without acknowledging their presence; they served no purpose beyond pomp and circumstance.

One step at a time she climbed the stairs. As she ascended, the walls fell away, revealing the glory of the Council Chamber. It resembled the Roman amphitheaters of ancient Earth, a large oval with seats for thousands of spectators lining each side. Built into the floor on either end were raised platforms hewn from the same virtually impervious material that made up the rest of the station. The stairs she was climbing right now would bring her to the top of one of these platforms: the Petitioner's Stage. From here she would look across the vast chamber to the opposite stage, where the Council would be seated to hear her case.

As the ambassador stepped out onto the Petitioner's Stage and approached the podium, she was relieved to see that none of the spectator seats were occupied. Although their decision would be made public, it was obvious the Council wanted to keep the exact nature of this meeting with the Alliance secret. That further strengthened her resolve: part of her had feared this would be nothing but a spectacle for public show, with no chance for her to defend the actions of humanity.

At the far end, the members of the Council were already seated. The asari councillor was in the center, directly across from Ambassador Goyle. To her left, Goyle's right, was the turian councillor. To the asari's right was the salarian representative. Above each of them was a five-meter-tall holographic projection of their head and shoulders, allowing petitioners to clearly see the reactions of each individual Council member despite the distance between the two stages.

"There is no need for pretense here," the turian said, beginning the proceedings with surprisingly little formality. "We have been informed by one of our agents, a Spectre, that humanity was conducting illegal AI research at one of its facilities in the Skyllian Verge."

"That facility was destroyed," Ambassador Goyle

reminded them, trying to play on their sympathies. "Dozens of human lives were lost in an unprovoked attack."

"That is not the purpose of this audience," the asari said, her voice cold despite the underlying lyrical quality that was common to the speech of all her people. "We are only here to talk about Sidon itself."

"Ambassador," the salarian chimed in, "surely you understand the dangers artificial intelligence represents to the galaxy as a whole?"

"The Alliance took every conceivable precaution with our research at Sidon," Goyle replied, refusing to apologize for what had happened.

"We have no way to know that but your word," the turian shot back. "And you've already proved how unreliable your species can be."

"This is not meant to be an attack upon your species," the asari said quickly, trying to smooth over the turian's remarks. "Humanity is a newcomer to the galactic community, and we have done all we can to welcome your species."

"Like when the turians conquered Shanxi in the First Contact War?"

"The Council intervened on humanity's behalf in that conflict," the salarian reminded her. "The turians were escalating their response; assembling their fleet. Millions of human lives would have been lost if not for our intercession."

"I was in full support of the Council's actions then," the turian made a point of noting. "Unlike some of my species, I bear no ill will toward humanity or the Alliance. But I also do not believe you should be given preferential treatment."

"When we invited humanity to become part of Citadel Space," the asari said, picking up the turian's train of thought without missing a beat, "you agreed to be bound by the laws and conventions of this Council."

"You only want to make an example of us because we're pushing the batarians out of the Verge," Goyle accused. "I know their embassy has threatened to secede from the Citadel if something isn't done."

"We heard their case," the salarian admitted. "But we did not take any action. The Verge is unclaimed territory, and it is the policy of the Council not to become involved in regional disputes unless they will have widespread impact throughout Citadel Space. We seek to preserve the autonomy of every species in all matters except those that threaten the galaxy as a whole."

"Like your research into artificial intelligence," the turian added.

The ambassador shook her head in exasperation. "You can't be naïve enough to think humanity is the only species investigating this!"

"It is not naïveté, but rather wisdom that leads us to think this," the asari countered.

"Your people were not here to see the fall of the quarians at the hands of the geth," the salarian reminded her. "The dangers of creating intelligent synthetic life, in any form, were never more clearly illustrated. Humanity simply doesn't understand that the risks are just too great."

"Risk?" Goyle struggled to keep from shouting while she continued to press the attack. "The only risk is burying your heads in the sand and hoping this all goes away!

"The geth are still out there," she continued. "Synthetic life is a reality. The creation of a true AI—maybe an entire race of them—is inevitable. They might even be out there somewhere already, just waiting to be discovered. If we don't study synthetic life now, in a controlled setting, how can we ever hope to stand against it?"

"We understand there are risks inherent to the creation of synthetic life," the asari remarked. "But we do not automatically assume that we will have no other choice but to come into conflict with them. That is a conceit of humanity."

"Other species embrace the underlying philosophy of mutual coexistence," the salarian explained, as if he were lecturing her. "We see strength in unity and cooperation. Humanity, however, seems to still believe competition is the key to prosperity. As a species, you are aggressive and antagonistic."

"Every species competes for power," the ambassador shot back. "The only reason you three are able to sit and pass judgment on the rest of the galaxy is because the Council races control the Council Fleet!"

"The Council races commit immeasurable resources in our efforts to ensure widespread galactic peace," the turian angrily declared. "Money, ships, and even millions of our own citizens are all freely given in the service of the greater good!"

"Often the rulings of the Council go against our own species," the salarian reminded her. "You know this from experience: the turians were forced to make heavy reparations to the Alliance after your First

Contact War, even though it could be argued that the conflict was as much humanity's fault as theirs."

"The connection between theoretical philosophy and practical actions is a fine one," the asari conceded. "We do not deny that individuals on their own, and cultures or species as a whole, will seek to expand their territory and influence. But we believe this is best accomplished with the understanding that there must be reciprocity: what you humans call give-and-take.

"This makes us willing to sacrifice for the sake of others," she concluded. "Can you honestly say the same about humanity?"

The ambassador didn't make any reply. As the top Alliance representative on the Citadel, she'd studied interstellar politics in great depth. She was intimately familiar with every ruling the Council had made in the last two centuries. And although there was an ever-so-subtle bias toward their own peoples in the overall pattern of the Council's decisions, everything they'd just said was fundamentally true. The asari, salarians, and even the turians had well-deserved reputations for selflessness and altruism on a galactic scale.

It was one of the things she still struggled with, this delicate balance the other races maintained between self-interest and the collective well-being of every species who swore allegiance to the Citadel. The integration and amalgamation of new alien cultures into the interstellar community was almost too easy; it seemed unnatural. She had a theory that it was somehow connected to the underlying Prothean technology that was common to every space-faring species. It gave them a point of similarity, something to build on. But then why hadn't humanity adapted as smoothly as everyone else?

"We didn't come here to argue politics," the ambassador finally said, avoiding the asari councillor's question. She suddenly felt exhausted. "What are you planning to do about Sidon?" There was no point dragging this out; there was nothing she could do to change the Council's mind anyway.

"There will have to be sanctions against humanity and the Alliance," the turian informed her. "This is a serious crime; the penalties must reflect that."

Maybe this is just part of the process of assimilating humanity into the interstellar community, Goyle thought wearily. *A gradual and inevitable evolution that will bring the Alliance into line with the rest of the species who answer to the Council.*

"As part of these sanctions, the Council will appoint a number of representatives to monitor Alliance activity throughout the Verge." The salarian was the one speaking now, going into the details of humanity's punishment.

Maybe we're just fundamentally different from most other species, Goyle thought, only half-listening to the judgment being handed down. *Maybe we don't fit in because there's something wrong with us.* There were a few other species, like the krogan, that were warlike and hostile at their core. In the end the krogans had suffered for it, incurring the wrath of the rest of the galaxy, decimating their numbers and leaving them a scattered, dying people. Was this to be humanity's fate as well?

"These appointed Council representatives will also conduct regular inspections of all Alliance facilities and colonies, including Earth, to ensure you are in compliance with the laws and regulations of the Citadel."

Maybe we are antagonistic.

Humanity was certainly aggressive. Not to mention assertive, determined, and relentless. But were these really flaws? The Alliance had spread farther and faster than any other species before them. By her estimations, the Alliance would have the power to rival the Council races themselves in twenty or thirty years. And suddenly it all made sense.

They're scared of us! The fatigue and weariness that had overwhelmed Ambassador Goyle only moments before vanished, swept away by that single stunning revelation. *They're actually scared of us!*

"No!" she said sharply, cutting off the salarian as he droned on with his list of demands.

"No?" he said, puzzled. "No what?"

"I do not accept these terms." She had almost made a terrible mistake. She had let these aliens manipulate her, twist her mind until she doubted herself and her people. But she wasn't about to grovel before them now. She wasn't about to apologize for humanity acting human.

"This is not a negotiation," the turian warned her.

"That's where you're wrong," she said with a fierce smile. Humanity had chosen her as their representative, their champion. It was her duty to defend the rights of every man, woman, and child on Earth and across Alliance space. They needed her now, and she would fight for them!

"Ambassador, perhaps you fail to understand the gravity of the situation," the asari suggested.

"You're the ones who don't understand" was Goyle's stern reply. "These sanctions you're proposing will cripple humanity. The Alliance will not allow this to happen. *I* won't allow this to happen."

"Do you really think humanity can defy the Council?" the turian asked, incredulous. "Do you honestly believe your people could triumph in a war against our combined forces?"

"No," Goyle freely admitted. "But we wouldn't go down easy. And I don't think you're willing to go to war over something like this. Not with us. The cost would be too high. Too many ships and lives lost in a conflict we all want to avoid.

"Not to mention the impact it would have on all the other species. We're the dominant force in the Skyllian Verge and the Attican Traverse. Alliance expansion drives the economies of those regions; Alliance ships and soldiers help maintain order out there."

From the expressions on their respective holographic projections the ambassador could see she'd hit a nerve. Eager to press her point, she kept speaking before any members of the Council could respond.

"Humanity is a major trade partner with half a dozen other species in Citadel Space, including each of your races. We make up over fifteen percent of the population here on the Citadel, and there are thousands of humans working in C-Sec and Citadel Control. We've been part of the galactic community for less than a decade and we're already too important— too essential—for you to simply force us out!"

She continued her tirade, still talking even as she

drew in a much needed breath; a technique she'd mastered early on in her political career.

"I'll admit we made a mistake. There should be some type of penalty. But humans take risks. We push the boundaries. That's who we are. Sometimes we're going to go too far, but that still doesn't give you the right to slap us down like overly strict parents!

"Humanity has a lot to learn about dealing with other species. But you have just as much to learn about dealing with us. And you better learn fast, because we humans are here to stay!"

When the ambassador finally stopped, a stunned silence fell over the Council Chamber. The three representatives of the galaxy's most powerful government looked at each other, then shut off their microphones and the holographic projectors to hold a brief conference in private. From the other side of the room it was impossible for Goyle to read their expressions or hear what they were saying without any amplifying technology, but it was clear there was a much heated debate.

The meeting lasted several minutes before they reached some kind of accord and switched their mikes and holographic projectors back on.

"What kind of penalties are you suggesting, Ambassador?" the asari councillor asked.

Goyle wasn't sure if the question was sincere, or if they were trying to lure her into some kind of trap. If she suggested something too light, they might just dismiss her and force humanity to accept the original terms, consequences be damned.

"Monetary fines, of course," she began, trying to determine the bare minimum they would consider acceptable. Although she wouldn't admit it, Goyle knew it was important to discourage other species from illegal AI research, as well. "We'll agree to sanctions, but they have to be specific: limited in scope, region, and duration. We'll oppose anything unilateral on principle alone. Our advancement as a society cannot afford to be hindered by overbearing restrictions. I can have a team of Alliance negotiators ready tomorrow to work out the details of something we *all* can live with."

"And what about the inspectors appointed to oversee Alliance operations?" the salarian asked.

He'd made it a question, a request instead of an order. That's when Goyle knew she had them. They weren't ready to dig in their heels over this, and it was clear she was.

"That's not going to happen. Like many species, humans are a sovereign people. We won't stand for foreign investigators peeking over our shoulders at every little thing we do."

The ambassador knew they'd probably increase the number of intelligence operatives monitoring human activity instead, but there was nothing she could do about that. Every species spied on everyone else—it was the nature of government, an integral cog in the political machine. And everyone knew the Council played the espionage and information-gathering game as well as anyone. But having to escalate Alliance counterintelligence activities was a damn sight better than granting unrestricted access to a team of officially appointed Citadel observers.

There was another long pause, though this time the

Council didn't bother to confer. In the end it was the asari who broke the silence.

"Then for now that is how we shall proceed. Negotiators from both sides will meet tomorrow. This meeting of the Council is adjourned."

Goyle gave a demure nod of her head, keeping her expression carefully neutral. She'd won a major victory; there was no benefit in gloating over it. But as she made her way back down the stairs of the Petitioner's Stage and headed toward the elevator that would take her back to the Presidium, a sly, self-satisfied smile crept across her lips.

SIXTEEN

The voice of the woman on the news vid never wavered or changed in tone as she reported the details of their latest lead story.

"In addition to the fine, the Alliance has agreed to voluntarily accept numerous trade sanctions as punishment for violation of the Citadel Conventions. The majority of these sanctions are in the fields of drive-core manufacturing and production of element zero. One economist warned energy prices back on Earth could jump by as much as twenty percent in the next—"

Anderson flicked the vid off with the remote.

"I thought it would be worse," Kahlee said.

"Goyle's a tough negotiator," Anderson explained. "But I still think we got lucky."

The two of them were sitting on the edge of a bed in a Hatre hotel room. Anderson was the one who had actually rented the room, charging it to the Alliance as part of his investigation. However, sharing a single room was nothing more than a necessity of their situation: he still hadn't mentioned Kahlee to anyone back at Alliance HQ, and it would have raised suspicions if he'd requested another suite . . . or even a double bed.

"So what happens now?" Kahlee asked. "Where do we go from here?"

Anderson shrugged. "Honestly, I don't know. Officially this has become Spectre business, but there's still too many loose ends for the Alliance to just walk away."

"Loose ends?"

"You, for one. We still don't have any real proof that you aren't a traitor. We need something to clear your name. And we still don't know who the real traitor was, or where they've taken Dr. Qian."

"Taken Dr. Qian? What do you mean?"

"The ambassador's convinced Dr. Qian is still alive and being held prisoner somewhere," Anderson explained. "She thinks he's the whole reason the base was attacked. According to her, somebody wanted his knowledge and expertise, and they were willing to kill to get it."

"That's crazy," Kahlee insisted. "What about the alien technology he found? That's the real reason for the attack!"

"Nobody else knows about that yet," Anderson reminded her. "Just me and you."

"I figured you would have passed that on," she said, dropping her eyes.

"I wouldn't do something like that without telling you first," Anderson assured her. "If I gave them that kind of information, they'd want to know where I found it. I'd have to tell them about you. I don't think we want to do that yet."

"You really are looking out for me," she whispered.

There was something strange about her subdued reaction, as if she was embarrassed or ashamed. "Kahlee? What's going on?"

The young woman got up off the bed and walked to the other side of the room. She paused, took a deep breath, then turned back to face him. "I have to tell you something," she said, her tone grim. "I've been thinking about this a lot. Ever since you told me about running into Saren back at Dah'tan."

He didn't say anything, but merely nodded at her to continue.

"When I first saw you at my father's place I didn't trust you. Even after you fought off that krogan I couldn't be sure if it was because you really believed me, or if you were just trying to win me over so I'd tell you how much I knew about Sidon."

Anderson almost opened his mouth to say she could trust him, then changed his mind. Better to let her work through this on her own.

"And then we went to Dah'tan and you ran into Saren and . . . I know what happened out there, David. Even what you didn't tell me."

"What are you talking about?" he protested. "I told you everything that happened!"

She shook her head. "Not everything. You said Saren thought about killing you, then changed his mind because he was afraid there might be witnesses. But you never bothered to tell him you came with someone else, did you?"

"I didn't have to. He figured it out on his own."

"But if he *hadn't* figured it out, he would've killed

you! You put your own life in danger rather than tell that Spectre I was nearby."

"You're reading too much into this," Anderson said, shifting uncomfortably. "I just never thought to say anything until after he was gone."

"You're a terrible liar, Lieutenant," she said with a faint smile. "Probably because you're a good person."

"And so are you," he assured her.

"No," she said with a shake of her head. "Not really. I'm not a good person. Which must be why I'm such a good liar."

"You've been lying to me?" In his head Anderson could hear the warning Saren had given him during their confrontation outside the ruins of Dah'tan. *She's lying to you. She knows much more about this than she's told you.*

"I know who the traitor at Sidon was. I have proof. And I know how we can find out who he's working with."

Anderson felt as if he'd been slapped across the face. He didn't know what hurt more: the fact that Kahlee had deceived him, or the fact that it was obvious to Saren long before he even had a clue.

"Please," she said, reading his pained expression. "You have to understand."

"I understand," he said softly. "You were just being smart. Careful." *And I was too blind and stupid to see what was really going on.*

The divorce must have hit him harder than he'd realized. He'd been so desperate and lonely that he'd imagined some special connection between him and Sanders, when all they really had in common was a connection to an attack on an Alliance base. Sacrificing everything to be a better soldier had cost him his marriage. Now that his divorce was final, he'd let his personal feelings interfere with a military assignment. Cynthia would have laughed at the irony.

"I was going to tell you," Kahlee insisted. "That first night. After you saved us from the krogan. Grissom warned me not to."

"But you told him."

"He's my father!"

A man you barely even know, Anderson thought, though he didn't say anything out loud. Logically he understood why she'd done it, but that didn't make it sting any less. She'd used him. She'd been playing him through the whole investigation, giving him little bits of information to keep him distracted so he wouldn't realize the truth: she had the answers he was looking for all along.

Anderson took a long, slow breath and brought his emotions under control. There was no point in dwelling on this; it was over. Done. Thinking about how Kahlee had manipulated him wouldn't get them any closer to completing the mission; it wouldn't help avenge those who lost their lives at Sidon.

"So who's the traitor?" he asked, his voice carefully neutral.

"Dr. Qian. Isn't it obvious?"

Anderson couldn't believe it. "You're saying one of the most respected and influential scientists in the Alliance betrayed and helped murder his own hand-picked team? Why?"

"I already told you! He was afraid they'd shut the project down. He must have known I was going to report him. The only way he could keep studying that alien technology he discovered was to destroy Sidon and pin the blame on me!"

"You really think he'd be willing to kill over this?" Anderson asked, still skeptical. "Over research?"

"I told you he was obsessed, remember? It had some hold on him. It changed him. He . . . he's not in his right mind."

She came over and dropped to one knee in front of him, her hands reaching out and clasping his.

"I know it's hard for you to believe me after everything I kept from you. But Qian was unstable. That's why I decided to report him," she explained.

"I knew I was taking a risk," she continued, "but I didn't realize how serious things were until I heard the base had been destroyed. That's when I saw how dangerous Dr. Qian had become, how far he'd go. I was terrified!"

Her actions were completely justifiable, but Anderson didn't want to hear it. Not right now. He stood up, pulling his hand from her grasp as he walked away to the far side of the room. He wanted to believe her, but the situation just seemed too implausible. Could a respected man of science and learning suddenly turn into the kind of monster that would slaughter his friends and coworkers over some piece of alien technology?

"You said you had proof?" he asked, turning back to face her.

She pulled out a small OSD and held it up. "I made backups of his personal files. In case I needed something to bargain with." She tossed the disk to him; he caught it gingerly, afraid of damaging it. "Turn that over to the Alliance. It'll prove I'm telling the truth."

"Why didn't you just give me this before?"

"I didn't know if Qian was acting alone. He has so much power and influence in the Alliance: admirals, generals, ambassadors, politicians; he knows them all. If I gave you that disk and you turned it over to someone working with him . . ." She didn't finish the thought. "That's why I didn't tell you, David. I had to be sure."

"Why now? What's changed?"

"You have people you trust in the Alliance. And I've finally decided I can trust you."

He slipped the disk into the breast pocket of his shirt and came back over to sit down beside her on the bed.

"You also said you knew a way to figure out who Qian was working with."

"All his personal files from Sidon are on that disk," she replied. "A lot of it is extra research notes. Stuff he kept to himself. I didn't have a chance to hack into everything before I ran. But I made sure I grabbed all the financial records. Decrypt it and trace all the transactions back to the source and they'll eventually lead to whoever funded this whole operation."

Anderson nodded appreciatively. "Just follow the money."

"Exactly."

They sat for a while in silence beside each other on the edge of the bed, neither one speaking, neither one pulling away. Anderson was the first to make a move . . . he stood up and went to grab his jacket.

"We need to get this data to Ambassador Goyle,"

he told her. "It'll clear your name and tell us who Qian's working with."

"Then what?" she asked, jumping up eagerly to grab her coat as well. "What do we do next?"

"Then I'm going after whoever attacked Sidon. But you won't be coming with me."

Kahlee stopped, one arm in the sleeve of her jacket. "What are you talking about?"

He was still hurt that she hadn't trusted him, but that wasn't why he was doing this. His wounded feelings were his problem, not hers. She had just done whatever was necessary to survive this whole mess, and he couldn't honestly blame her for any of it. It wasn't her fault that he'd let himself become emotionally involved. But now it was his responsibility to make sure it didn't happen again.

"That krogan is still looking for you. We have to make arrangements to get you off this planet. Get you somewhere you'll be safe."

"Wait a minute!" she protested angrily. "You can't just leave me behind! Those were my friends who died in that attack! I have a right to see this through to the end!"

"Things are going to get rough," he told her. "You're part of the Alliance, but we both know you're no soldier. If you tag along, all you'll do is slow me down or get in the way."

She glared at him, but clearly couldn't think of anything to say to refute his argument.

"You did your part," he added, patting the pocket with the OSD. "Your job's over now. But mine's just beginning."

* * *

"This is unacceptable!" Dr. Shu Qian shouted.

"These things take time," Edan Had'dah replied, hoping to placate him. He'd been dreading this meeting all morning.

"Time? Time for what? We aren't doing anything!"

"There's a Spectre here on Camala! We have to wait until he gives up and leaves."

"What if he doesn't give up?" Qian demanded, his voice rising in pitch.

"He will. With Dah'tan and Sidon both destroyed, there's nothing left to connect my name to this. Be patient and he will leave."

"You promised me a chance to continue my research!" Qian barked, realizing the topic of the Spectre wasn't going to give him enough opportunity to complain. "You never said I'd be stuck wasting my time in the bowels of some grimy refinery!"

The batarian rubbed the spot just above his inner eyes with a free hand, trying to hold the mounting headache at bay. Humans in general were trying: as a species he found them excessively loud, crude, and impolite. But dealing with Dr. Qian had become its own special brand of torment.

"Constructing the kind of facility you need is a difficult task," he reminded the scowling doctor. "It took you months to adapt the equipment on Sidon. This time we're starting from scratch."

"It wouldn't be such a problem if you hadn't destroyed my lab and wiped out our supplier!" Qian accused him.

Actually, it had been Qian's idea to destroy the Alliance base. As soon as he'd discovered Kahlee Sanders was gone, he'd contacted Edan and demanded his batarian partner take action. He'd even provided the blueprints and access codes for the base.

"We couldn't let that Spectre get his hands on Dah'tan's records," Edan explained for at least the tenth time. "Besides, there are other suppliers. Even now my people are working on building you a new lab. One far beyond the borders of Citadel Space, safe from the prying eyes of the Council. But we can't just acquire everything we need with one enormous purchase. Not without drawing unwanted attention."

"You've already drawn their attention!" the human snapped, circling back to the topic of the Spectre yet again.

Qian had been extremely agitated ever since the raid on Sidon, and with each passing day he seemed to grow more irritable, confrontational, and paranoid. At first Edan thought it might be guilt over betraying his fellow humans that was driving Qian's rapid mental deterioration. It didn't take him long to realize the true cause was something quite different.

Qian was obsessed with the alien artifact. It was all he cared about, all he thought about day and night. It seemed to cause the doctor actual physical pain whenever he wasn't working on unlocking its secrets.

"That Spectre's looking for us right now," the doctor warned him, his voice dropping down to a harsh whisper. "He's looking for *it*!"

There was no need to clarify what *it* was. However, there was almost no chance anyone would stumble across the artifact by accident. It was still out where one of Edan's deep-space exploration teams had discovered it, orbiting an uncharted world in a remote system near the Perseus Veil. The only people who knew its location were the two of them and the small team of surveyors and scientists that had first stumbled across it, and Edan had been careful to keep them on the surface of the uncharted world, completely isolated from all other contact.

Had he known how irrational the doctor would become, Edan might have done things differently. Actually, if truth be told, there was an argument to be made that Qian wasn't the only one acting irrationally. Before all this Edan had made a point of never dealing directly with humans. And for all the illegal activities he'd used to build his fortune and empire, he'd never done anything that would fall under the jurisdiction of the Spectres.

Yet almost from the moment he first traveled out to inspect the incredible discovery of his survey team, he'd made decisions that many who knew him would have considered wildly out of character. But that was only because they were unaware of the sheer magnitude of what he'd stumbled across.

"It's not safe out there," Qian continued, his voice becoming a pleading whine. "We should move it. Somewhere closer."

"Don't be stupid!" Edan snapped. "Something that size just can't be moved to another system! Not unless we bring in tow ships and crews. That close to the Veil we'd be sure to attract the notice of the geth! Can you imagine what would happen if it fell into their hands?"

Qian didn't have an answer for that, but it didn't shut him up. "So it stays out there," he said, his tone cynical and sarcastic. "While your so-called experts down on the planet fumble around trying to grasp what they have found and I'm stuck here doing nothing!"

There had been several scientists on the exploration team that had discovered the artifact; the whole purpose of the trip had been to seek out unclaimed Prothean technology in the hopes Edan's corporate empire could somehow profit from it. But none of them were specialists in the field of artificial intelligence, and Qian was right when he said it was beyond their abilities.

Edan had searched long and hard for someone with the knowledge and expertise to help him unlock the potential of what he had found. And after millions of credits spent on extensive—and very discreet—investigations, he'd been forced to accept the inescapable conclusion that the only suitable candidate was a human.

Swallowing his pride, he'd had his representatives carefully approach Qian. Slowly they'd drawn the doctor in deeper and deeper, appealing to his professional pride and scientific curiosity by revealing only the smallest, most tantalizing details of their find. The bizarre courtship had lasted over a year, culminating in Qian's visit to the system to see the artifact himself.

The effect had been exactly as Edan knew it would be. Qian understood what they had discovered. He realized this went beyond mere human or batarian interests. He recognized that this had the potential to fundamentally change the galaxy, and he'd thrown himself completely into his efforts to unleash that potential.

But on days like today, Edan still had to wonder if he'd made a mistake.

"Your people are idiots," Qian stated matter-of-factly. "You know they can't make any progress without me. They can barely even get basic readings and simple observational data off it without accidentally skewing the results."

The batarian sighed. "This is only temporary. Just until the Spectre backs off. Then you'll have everything you want: unlimited access to the artifact; a lab right on the surface of the world; all the resources and assistants you need."

Qian snorted. "Hmph! A lot of good that'll do. I need experts in the field. People smart enough to understand what we're doing. Like my team at Sidon."

"That team is dead!" Edan shouted, finally losing his temper. "You helped kill them, remember? We turned them into ashes and vapor!"

"Not all of them," Qian said with a smile. "Not Kahlee Sanders."

Edan was stunned into momentary silence.

"I know what she can do," Qian insisted. "I need her on the project. Without her, we'll be set back months. Maybe years."

"Should we send her a message right now?" Edan asked sarcastically. "I'm sure she'd be thrilled to join us if we just ask her."

"I didn't say we should ask her," Qian replied. "Just take her. We'll find some way to convince her to help us. I'm sure you have people who can be very persuasive. Just be sure they don't do anything to damage her cognitive abilities."

Edan nodded. Maybe the doctor wasn't as irrational as he thought. There was only one problem, though.

"And just how are we supposed to find her?"

"I don't know," Qian shrugged. "I'm sure you'll figure it out. Maybe send that krogan after her again."

SEVENTEEN

For the second time in as many weeks, Ambassador Goyle was making her way across the lush fields of the Presidium to meet with the Citadel Council. Last time she embarked upon this journey she had been summoned by the Council so they could chastise her for humanity's violations of the Citadel Code. This time, however, she was the one who had requested the audience.

As before, she passed the sparkling lake that was the centerpiece of the pastoral scene. Once again she passed the replica of the mass relay. But this time as she rode the elevator to the top of the Citadel Tower, she actually allowed herself to enjoy the view.

She had won a victory on her last visit here by defying the Council. But in her long career as a diplomat she knew shows of strength weren't the only way to get what you wanted. Throughout the known galaxy, the Alliance was developing a reputation for being aggressive and confrontational. Her actions last time had no doubt cemented that opinion in the minds of the councillors. Today, however, she intended to show them another side of humanity.

Reaching the top of the Tower, she stepped from the elevator, passed the ceremonial honor guards, and ascended the staircase to the Petitioner's Stage. A moment later the councillors emerged from somewhere behind the raised platform at the other end of the chamber and took their seats, moving with a staid and solemn precision.

Reading the body language of other species was difficult, but it was a skill the ambassador had worked hard to develop. She could tell from their stiff and formal manner that they expected this meeting to be as unpleasant as the last one. Inwardly she smiled. They wouldn't be expecting this. Catching them off guard would give her an advantage in the negotiations.

"Welcome, Ambasssador Goyle," the asari councillor greeted her once they were all seated and the holographic projections and audio amplifiers had been switched on.

"Thank you for agreeing to see me, Councillor," she answered.

"Despite some of the disagreements at our last audience, you are still a member of the Citadel," the turian said pointedly. "We would never consider denying your right to an audience, Ambassador."

Goyle understood the subtle implications in his words and tone. They held no grudges; they were above petty feuds. Completely fair and impartial. Agreeing to see her only proved the Council races were morally superior to humans, more civilized.

"What is the purpose of this audience?" the asari asked, in a much more neutral tone. Although she might feel as superior as the turian, Goyle felt she did a much better job of masking her true feelings.

"At our last meeting you said humanity needed to learn to embrace the concept of mutually beneficial coexistence," she said. "I am here today to demonstrate that your words did not fall on deaf ears."

"And how do you propose to do that, exactly?" the salarian asked.

"I have come with a gift for the Council."

"Do you think you can buy our favor, Ambassador?" the turian snapped.

His reaction was exactly what Goyle was hoping for. If she could make it appear as if they were the ones being difficult here, it was more likely they'd give in to her demands before all this was through.

"I meant no offense," she humbly apologized while secretly smiling inside. "This is not a bribe, but rather an offer freely given."

"Please continue," the asari invited. Of the three, she was the one Goyle found the hardest to read. Not coincidentally, she was also the one the ambassador was the least confident in manipulating.

"I realize humanity made a mistake at Sidon. One we deeply regret. In an effort to make amends, I'm here to offer the Council copies of all the classified research files from the base."

"This . . . is a very generous offer," the salarian said after a moment's hesitation. "May I ask why you are willing to share this information with us?"

"Perhaps our research will prove useful to the rest of the galaxy. Maybe it will bring us closer to peaceful relations with the geth."

"I thought all the files at the base were destroyed in the attack," the turian said suspiciously.

Goyle had anticipated this. They probably thought the files were fake, or at least purged of sensitive data or censored in some way. But they'd be able to tell if they were doctored, so after reviewing them the ambassador had decided to release them in full to the Council. There was nothing incriminating beyond what they already knew; if anything, the files clearly showed Qian had been operating outside the scope of his official mandate, removing some of the Alliance's culpability.

"Lieutenant Kahlee Sanders, a survivor of the raid, made copies of the files before Sidon was destroyed."

Now that Qian was working with the batarians, it only made sense to make his research available to leading experts of allied species. They would likely reciprocate by helping defend the Alliance if the batarians tried to use Qian's work to develop AI technology to use against humanity. Besides, the Alliance experts who had reviewed the files had assured her that virtually all of the research was still theoretical. It would be years, maybe decades, before any of it would lead to any practical applications.

And there was one more significant consideration.

"The files make mention of an unknown piece of alien technology discovered out beyond the borders of Citadel Space," Goyle informed them.

"What kind of technology?" the salarian wanted to know.

"We don't know," she admitted. "Obviously it has some connection to synthetic intelligence, but beyond that Qian was intentionally vague about the details.

From his notes, it is clear he believes it was far more advanced than anything developed by any current species."

"Is it Prothean?" the asari asked.

"Not according to Qian's notes. Again, we don't have many details. But there is some indication the doctor thought it could be used in connection with the geth."

"The geth?" the salarian asked quickly. "In what way?"

"It's not clear. Maybe he thinks it will enable him to communicate with them somehow. Maybe even control them. We just don't have enough information to know for sure. But we believe this technology poses a legitimate threat. Not just to the Alliance, but to the entire galaxy."

"And you believe whoever attacked Sidon now possesses this technology?" the salarian asked.

"Possibly," she said, somewhat hesitantly. "It doesn't appear it was ever actually at Sidon. Qian's notes are a bit . . . erratic."

"Are you saying he was mentally unbalanced?" the asari asked.

"There is some evidence of that, yes."

"Are we certain this technology even exists?" the salarian wanted to know. "Or are we chasing the delusions of a madman?"

"If it does exist," she warned them, "we can't take the risk of ignoring this."

"We need to find the people responsible for the attack," the turian agreed. "Before they unleash this on the galaxy!"

"You should begin with Edan Had'dah. A batarian

from Camala. Lieutenant David Anderson, the man we sent to investigate this matter, believes he was behind the attacks. Your own people can confirm this when we send you the files."

There was a brief pause and the holographs momentarily shut down as the councillors held a brief conference.

"We will forward this information to the Spectre investigating this matter," the salarian informed her once they were done.

"The Council is grateful to you for bringing this to our attention," the asari said.

"The Alliance has no wish to be at odds with the Council," Goyle explained. "We are still new to the galactic scene, but we are eager to show our willingness to cooperate and coexist with the other species of the Citadel."

She could see from their expressions that she had won them over to her side. Now it was time to strike.

"Kahlee Sanders, the researcher who escaped Sidon, is in hiding on Camala right now," she continued, moving without pausing from supplication to an appeal she knew they would grant. "We have reason to believe her life is in danger as long as she remains on that world.

"The Alliance would like to arrange for one of our ships to touch down on Camala somewhere outside the spaceports to pick her up and bring her to safety."

"That is a reasonable request," the turian said after a moment's consideration. "The Council can make arrangements with batarian authorities to permit this."

"There is one more request I would make of the

Council," Ambassador Goyle added, employing one of the most basic, yet most effective, tactics of negotiation: little yes, big yes. Getting someone to agree to a minor concession established a tone of agreement and cooperation. It made it more likely they would be receptive to larger issues.

"Lieutenant Anderson, the Alliance operative who brought Edan's involvement to light, is also on Camala."

"You wish to have him evacuated as well?" the salarian guessed.

"Actually, we would like him to accompany your Spectre when he goes after Edan Had'dah."

"Why?" the asari asked. Goyle couldn't tell if she was suspicious or merely curious.

"Several reasons," the ambassador admitted. "We think Dr. Qian may still be alive. If he is captured, we would like him to be extradited to the Alliance to stand trial for his role in the murder of our people at Sidon.

"And we see this as a learning opportunity for Lieutenant Anderson. The reputation of the Spectres is well known; they are representatives of the Council, the guardians of Citadel Space. Working with your agent will help the lieutenant better understand the methods Spectres employ to defend interstellar peace and stability."

She hesitated briefly before continuing, taking a moment to precisely form her next argument. This request had the potential to backfire, but it was the whole purpose of this audience. And it was likely the councillors were thinking it themselves already.

"We are also hoping your agent can evaluate Lieutenant Anderson's performance on the mission. If he does well, perhaps he can be considered as a candidate for the Spectres himself."

"Admitting someone to the Spectres is a long and involved process," the turian protested. "Individuals must prove themselves through years of exemplary military or law enforcement service before they can even be considered for the honor."

"Lieutenant Anderson has served in the Alliance military for nearly a decade," the ambassador assured them. "He has completed our N7 elite special operations program, and won numerous citations, medals, and honors of distinction in the line of duty. I can easily make his records available to the Council."

"Candidates must undergo a rigorous screening process," the salarian explained, raising another objection. "Background checks, psychological evaluations, and a prolonged period of mentorship and field training are typically involved."

"I am not asking that you admit him to the Spectres," the ambassador clarified. "Only that you allow him to accompany Saren on his mission, and judge him based on his performance to see if he has the potential."

"Your species is still new to the galaxy," the asari told her, finally addressing the issue they were all dancing around. Officially, Spectres could come from any species. But almost invariably they were only chosen from the Council races.

The bias was perfectly understandable: giving individuals of a species direct access to the Council, along with the authority to act outside the bounds of galactic law when necessary, attached a perceived importance to that individual's species. Allowing a human into the Spectres would send a message to the rest of the galaxy that the Council considered humans on a par with the turians, salarians, and asari. That wasn't far removed from the truth, which was exactly why Ambassador Goyle was pushing for this now.

"Many species have been part of the Citadel for centuries, yet have never had a Spectre drawn from their ranks," the asari continued. "Granting this request may cause resentment among them."

"Just as I'm sure there was resentment among them when the turians were added to the Council," Ambassador Goyle countered.

"Those were exceptional circumstances," the salarian interjected, offering up a defense on behalf of the turian councillor. "The turians were instrumental in ending the Krogan Rebellions. Billions of lives were saved."

And they had a fleet almost as large as the asari and salarians put together, Goyle silently added.

Out loud she said, "At our last meeting you told me humanity had to be willing to sacrifice for the sake of others. I could have bargained for this concession with the information from Sidon, but I chose to give that to you freely for the greater good. Now I am offering you the aid of one of the Alliance's top soldiers to end a threat we may have unwittingly helped create.

"All I ask in return is that you consider the lieutenant as a possible candidate for the Spectres."

There was no immediate response from the Council. The ambassador realized they were still leery of her because of her actions at the last meeting. But there was a time for brinksmanship and a time for acquiescence. She had to show them the Alliance was willing to work both sides of that fence.

"I make no demands here. I'm not asking you to promise or commit to anything. I believe this experience will benefit Lieutenant Anderson and the Alliance. I believe it will strengthen humanity's bond with the rest of the Citadel. And I truly believe it will give us a better understanding of the duties and responsibilities we owe to the greater galactic community.

"However, if you refuse this request I will willingly accept the wisdom of your decision."

She expected the Council to confer once again to discuss her proposal. However, to her surprise, the asari simply gave her a warm smile.

"You have made your point, Ambassador. We will grant your request."

"Thank you, Councillor," Goyle replied. She was caught off guard by the sudden acceptance, but she did her best not to reveal how much she had been taken aback.

"This meeting of the Council is adjourned," the asari said, and the Council rose from their seats and disappeared down the stairs of their platform.

Goyle turned and made the long walk down from the top of the Petitioner's Stage, frowning. She had studied every decision made by the Council in the last five centuries in detail. In every case they had acted unilaterally. If there was ever any dissension, they would debate the issue until a mutual accord could be reached.

So how was it possible for the asari councillor to decide on her own to grant this request?

As she reached the elevator and stepped inside, the explanation finally popped into her head. Somehow they had anticipated her request before she'd even broached the subject. They must have known where she was leading them, and discussed it during the brief conference after she had mentioned Edan Had'dah. They had already decided how they would respond long before she ever brought the subject up.

Ambassador Goyle had thought she was in control, driving the negotiations to manipulate the Council to her best advantage, like she had at the previous meeting. She'd caught them off guard last time, but this time they'd been ready for her. They were the ones who'd been in control, walking her through the script like actors in a play, knowing the final outcome all along. And only in the final moment of the scene had they tipped their hand, a subtle revelation of the truth they must have known she would pick up on.

Riding down in the elevator, Ambassador Goyle tried to take solace in the knowledge that she had gotten exactly what she'd wanted out of the meeting. But she wasn't used to being outmaneuvered, and she couldn't help wondering if she had made a mistake.

Why had the Council been so eager to grant her request? Did they really think humanity was ready for this? Or were they expecting Anderson to fail, then hoping to use that failure as an excuse to hold the Alliance back?

If nothing else, the experience had given her a whole new respect for the Council and their understanding of negotiations and diplomacy. She considered herself a student of politics, and now she was very aware she had just been schooled at the feet of the masters.

They'd sent her an unmistakable message: they knew how to play this game as well as she. Whatever advantage the Alliance might have had in dealing with the Council, it was gone. The next time she had to face them, the ambassador realized, she'd be constantly second-guessing herself. No matter how prepared or careful she was, in the back of her mind there'd be that lingering uncertainty: was she leading the negotiations, or being led?

And she had no doubt that this was exactly what the Council wanted.

EIGHTEEN

"We're almost there, Lieutenant Sanders," the driver told her, shouting to be heard above the engine of the six-wheeled armored personnel carrier as it bounced along the hard-packed desert sand outside Hatre. "Just a few more klicks to the rendezvous site."

In addition to the driver, five other Alliance marines rode in the APC with her; a security detail pulled together at the last minute to protect her until she was off world. She and the driver sat up front, the rest of the crew were huddled together in the back. Four of the marines had already been on Camala when the orders came, the other two had arrived from Elysium the previous night in response to the instructions issued from Alliance HQ.

Their vehicle was batarian, loaned to the Alliance by local authorities at the "request" of the Council. It was all part of the deal the ambassador had worked out to get her safely off Camala and back to Alliance territory.

The engine whined as they climbed one of the immense sand dunes that stretched across the landscape out beyond the horizon toward the setting sun. In another twenty minutes it would be dark, but by then she'd already be aboard the Alliance frigate coming to pick her up.

"I'm surprised the batarians agreed to this," the driver shouted again, making conversation. "They don't normally authorize landings outside the space-ports. Especially not for Alliance vessels."

She understood his curiosity. He knew something big was going on, but his orders were simply to drive her out to the pickup. He had no way of knowing about her connection to Sidon, and nobody had told him about the shady backroom deals Ambassador Goyle must have made with the Council to make this happen. Kahlee stayed silent: she sure as hell wasn't about to fill him in.

She wondered how much the Alliance had given up in exchange for this concession. What kind of bargain had they struck? Anderson probably had some idea, but he had barely said a dozen words to her in the two days following her admission in the hotel room.

Not that she blamed him. He'd trusted her and she'd used him, at least in his eyes. Kahlee knew all too well how much betrayal could sting. And now she was being whisked off to some unknown location for her protection, while Anderson was staying behind on Camala to try and hunt down Dr. Qian.

She thought a lot about trying to contact him again after all this was over. At first she'd been drawn to him out of need: she was scared and alone, and she had needed someone to cling to besides a gruff, prickly father whom she barely knew. But even though they'd only been together a few days, she got the sense that there was a chance they could have be-come more than just friends.

Unfortunately, she doubted he'd want anything more to do with her now. Not after how she'd hurt him. The realization that she'd probably never see him again hit her harder than she would have expected.

"Hang on, ma'am!" the driver suddenly called out, startling her from her maudlin thoughts as he wrenched the wheel and veered them sharply off course, nearly flipping the vehicle in the process. "We've got company!"

From his perch on a rocky outcropping several kilometers away, Saren could just make out, against the glare of the setting sun, the silhouette of the APC carrying First Lieutenant Kahlee Sanders.

When he'd received the mission update from the Citadel Council yesterday he'd gone through the full spectrum of emotions. He began with outrage. They were ordering him to work with a human! And all because the Council felt it necessary to reward the Alliance for sharing information about the investigation into Sidon. Information Saren had already managed to figure out on his own!

He knew Edan Had'dah was behind the attack. But because he'd kept that information from the Council, he had to pretend to be grateful to the Alliance for handing it over to him. Now he had to allow one of the humans to work with him as he completed the mission. And not just any human, but that damnable Lieutenant Anderson, who kept interfering with his investigation.

But as he'd continued reading the update, his anger gave way to curiosity. He'd known about the batarian's involvement, but not about the extraordinary alien technology referenced in the files recovered from Sidon. Though there were few details, it seemed as if the artifact could be a relic dating all the way back to the Prothean extinction.

Saren had always been intrigued by the sudden and unexplained disappearance of the Protheans. What kind of unimaginable string of events, what kind of catastrophic occurrence, could cause an empire that spanned the known galaxy to vanish in less than a century? Virtually all traces of the Protheans had been wiped out; only the mass relays and Citadel survived, the enduring legacy of a once great people.

Hundreds of explanations had been put forward, yet these were all nothing but theories and speculation. The truth about the Prothean extinction was still a mystery . . . and this ancient alien technology could be one of the keys to unraveling it.

From what he could piece together from Qian's research notes, he suspected they had found some type of ship or orbiting space station. One with AI capabilities to self-monitor and even repair all its vital systems without the need for organic caretakers like the keepers back on the Citadel.

Delving deeper, it seemed the doctor believed the discovery could one day be used to forge an alliance with the geth . . . or possibly even control them. The implications were staggering: a massive army of synthetics, billions of troops whose absolute loyalty could be assured if one could somehow understand and influence their AI thought processes.

Then, as he'd continued reading the file even further,

his curiosity had transformed into cold, calculating satisfaction. Once he had learned the name of his quarry, the hardest part of his mission became locating Edan. He was probably cowering like an insect, burrowed into an underground bunker beneath one of the countless refineries spread across a thousand square kilometers of rock and sand. Ferreting him out was going to be a long, grueling, time-consuming process.

Or it would have been if he hadn't received the mission update from the Council. Included in the transmission were the details of the plan to evacuate Lieutenant Sanders from the world. Saren knew that Skarr was still on Camala; he'd had no reports of the big krogan being sighted at the spaceports. He was probably holed up with Edan.

And Edan had hired Skarr to kill the young woman. Saren knew enough about batarian culture to realize Edan wouldn't want to lose face by hiring someone who failed in their appointed task. If the opportunity presented itself, he'd send Skarr after Sanders again.

Saren had done his best to make sure that opportunity had presented itself. He knew Edan had spies in every level of government across Camala, and particularly at the spaceports. All he'd done was make sure the Council's request for an unscheduled Alliance landing in the desert was logged in the official government records.

The unusual request was sure to attract someone's attention. Inevitably it would be reported up through the chain of underlings and lackeys to Edan himself, and Saren was confident the batarian was smart enough to figure out who the Alliance was coming to pick up.

The only flaw in the plan was that it was almost too obvious. If Edan suspected it was a trap, he wouldn't send anyone in response to the message.

Still watching the Alliance-driven APC through his long-range binoculars, Saren saw the vehicle swerve and nearly spin out as the driver began taking evasive action. Scanning the nearby dunes he picked up the dust trails of four other vehicles closing in; small, quick rovers with mounted guns converging on the slower APC from all sides.

Edan had taken the bait.

"Goddamn!" one of the marines in the back shouted as a shell launched from one of the pursuing rovers exploded close enough to rock the APC's suspension.

The driver was doing his frantic best to avoid the shells being lobbed at them by the enemy, sending the APC careening haphazardly over dunes and into small valleys to keep the other vehicles from getting a lock on their position. True to its name, the APC was heavily armored. Still, it was only a transport vehicle; it wasn't intended for combat. They had no mounted guns, and the thick plating on the body and undercarriage was intended to protect the occupants from sniper fire and land mines. Against antitank weapons like those mounted on the pursuing rovers, the only purpose the armor served was to slow them down.

In the back, one of the marines was shouting into the radio, trying to warn the incoming Alliance frigate of their situation.

"Mayday! Mayday! We are taking fire. The landing zone is hot! I repeat, the landing zone is hot!"

"We got at least four of these bastards on our tail!" the driver shouted back to him as the vehicle lurched and bounced over an outcropping of small rocks and boulders.

"Four enemy rovers on site!" the radioman shouted. "*Iwo Jima,* are you reading?"

"This is the *Iwo Jima,*" a voice crackled back. "We read you, ground team. We're still fourteen minutes out. Hold on!"

The radio operator slammed his fist against the heavily armored side of the vehicle in frustration. "We'll never last that long!"

"You gotta outrun them!" another one of the men yelled up to the front.

"What the hell do you think I'm doing!?" the driver snapped back at him.

They flew over the top of another dune as a shell exploded just behind them, propelling the vehicle through the air for a full ten meters before it crashed heavily back down to the ground. The high-impact shock absorbers took most of the blow, but even though Kahlee was securely belted in, the force of the landing still caused her to whack her head on the ceiling. The impact drove her teeth into her tongue hard enough to make her taste blood.

The men in the back fared much worse. Crammed into the vehicle, none of them were wearing safety belts. They were thrown from their seats, smashed against the roof, then hurled back down to the floor in a jumble of colliding elbows, knees, and skulls.

Cries of surprise and grunts of pain were followed by a string of curse words directed at the driver.

He ignored them, instead muttering, "They're too fast. We'll never outrun them," though Kahlee wasn't sure if he was talking to her or himself. His eyes were wide and wild, and she wondered how much longer he could keep it together.

"You're doing great," Kahlee reassured him. "Just keep us alive for a few more minutes. You can do it!"

The driver didn't respond but only hunched forward, bringing himself closer to the wheel. Without warning he pulled a hard 180-degree turn, hoping to surprise the enemy with the desperate and erratic maneuver. The momentum of the APC spun them out of control, nearly causing them to roll. For a split second the vehicle teetered precariously, balancing over the wheels along one side before slamming back down with another hard jolt.

With all six wheels back on the ground, the driver slammed his foot onto the accelerator and they took off again, spewing a plume of pebbles, dust, and sand out behind them. From her seat in the front Kahlee could now see the enemy clearly. Two of their vehicles were spread wide, trying to outrace the APC and cut them off. The other two had originally fallen in behind them, firing at them with their mounted cannons as they steadily gained on their prey. With the sudden change of direction, however, the Alliance soldiers were now heading directly toward their former pursuers.

"You bastards ever play chicken!?" the driver screamed, never taking his foot off the gas as he steered the slower but much heavier APC head-on into one of the lightly armored rovers.

Strapped securely into her seat, Kahlee had no chance to stop what was about to happen. The distance between the vehicles was gobbled up in an instant, and all she could do was brace for impact. At the last second the smaller rover tried to veer off, but it was too late and the collision was unavoidable. The blunted nose of the APC slammed into the front left side of the oncoming rover as it tried to peel away from the crash, a glancing blow instead of a direct hit. But at a combined speed of nearly 200 km/h, a glancing blow was more than enough.

The enemy rover practically disintegrated. The force of the impact blew the frame apart. The axles snapped and the tires flew off. The doors sheared loose. Unidentifiable chunks of metal rent asunder and went flying and skipping across the sand. The fuel tank ruptured, sparked, and exploded, engulfing what was left of the rover's body in flames, reducing it to a molten slagheap. The driver, who had died in the first millisecond of the collision, was consumed by the great ball of tumbling fire that finally rolled to a stop hundreds of meters later.

The other occupants had all been thrown free on impact, their bodies sent whirling and skipping across the ground at over 100 km/h. Limbs cracked and shattered, necks and spines snapped, skulls were caved in. Huge chunks of flesh were ripped from the bones of the corpses as they skidded across the sharp pebbles and abrasive sand.

The sturdier APC held together on impact, though the entire front crumpled in like an accordion. Deflecting off the enemy rover, it flipped and rolled half a dozen times before coming to rest upside down. Kahlee was barely conscious. Stunned by the impact and disoriented by the blood rushing to her head, she felt someone fumbling at her seat belt. Instinctively she tried to fight them off, then heard a human voice shouting at her to calm down.

She tried to concentrate. The vehicle wasn't moving anymore, but her world continued to spin. The driver was still belted in beside her. The steering wheel had snapped off and the jagged end of the steering column had been driven back into his chest, impaling him. His dead eyes were open wide; the glassy pupils fixed in a frozen stare that seemed directed accusingly at her.

She realized she must have blacked out for a few seconds. One of the marines from the back was outside the vehicle now, reaching in through the shattered window to try and unbuckle her seat belt. She stopped fighting against him and instead reached out with her hands, pressing them firmly against the inverted roof so she wouldn't fall and hit her head the instant she was loose.

A second later the buckle detached. She managed to keep her head from slamming to the ground, though she did bang one of her knees painfully on the mangled dashboard as she fell. Strong hands seized her arms and pulled her to freedom through the gaping hole that had once been filled with tempered glass.

Now that she was upright, the excess of blood rushed away from Kahlee's head, allowing her world to slowly come back into focus. Miraculously, the marines in the back of the APC had all survived. The five of them and Kahlee were now huddled in the shadow of their overturned vehicle, temporarily using it for cover.

She could hear the sound of gunfire. It wasn't the heavy *thunk-thunk-thunk* of antitank weapons, but rather the sharp *rat-tat-tat* she recognized as bursts from an assault rifle. She could hear the metal pings as bullets ricocheted off the armor-plated rover that hid them from enemy sight.

Kahlee didn't even have a pistol on her, but the marines had recovered their weapons from the crash. Unfortunately, they were pinned down by a steady stream of enemy rounds, unable to use them. Given the constant barrage of enemy bullets, even a split second of exposure to try and return fire was too great a risk.

"Why aren't they using their cannons?" Kahlee shouted, her voice almost drowned out by the sounds of the battle.

"They must want to take us alive!" one of the marines replied, giving her a look that made it clear they all knew the enemy was only concerned with the survival of one specific person.

"They're trying to flank us!" another marine shouted, pointing off at the horizon.

One of the rovers had sped off in the distance, so far away it was barely visible. It was circling around behind them in a wide, looping arc, well beyond the range of the marines' automatic weapons.

Kahlee's attention was pulled away from the rover by a deafening roar from above; the unmistakable sound of a space vessel's drive-core engines burning in the atmosphere. Turning her attention upward, she saw a small ship swooping down from the sky.

"It's the *Iwo Jima*!" one of the marines cried out.

The ship was moving fast, diving straight for the lone rover trying to flank them. Less than fifty meters from the ground it pulled up sharply and opened fire. A single, well-targeted blast from the ship's GARDIAN defense lasers turned the rover into scrap metal.

The *Iwo Jima* banked and changed direction, its trajectory bringing it straight toward the two surviving rovers as the marines let loose with spontaneous, exultant cheers. The cavalry had arrived!

Skarr had seen the frigate approaching long before it fired the lethal volley that took out the first of the Blue Sun rovers. Its arrival was an inconvenient, but not unanticipated, event.

Moving with a quick but calm sense of purpose, he leaped out of his own rover and started shouting orders. Following his commands, the mercs quickly unloaded and assembled the portable mass accelerator cannon they'd stashed in the back of the vehicle.

While the Alliance frigate fired its lasers on the defenseless rovers, Skarr was arming the weapon; loading an ammo packet filled with hundreds of small explosive rounds. As the frigate banked toward them in a long, sweeping arc, he adjusted the aim and locked in on his target. And when he heard the cheers from the marines hiding behind the overturned APC, he fired.

The GARDIAN laser systems of the *Iwo Jima*, programmed to target and destroy incoming missiles, were overwhelmed by the sheer number of hypervelocity rounds fired at point-blank range. Normally the deadly projectiles would have deflected harmlessly off the ship's kinetic barriers. But in order for a space-faring vessel to touch down on a planet's surface and pick up a shore party, the barriers had to be shut down. As Skarr had suspected, the *Iwo Jima* hadn't had time to reactive them yet.

Hundreds of tiny explosive shells impacted the ship's exterior, shearing fist-sized holes in the hull as they detonated. The personnel on board were shredded by the sudden storm of burning shrapnel ricocheting around the interior of the vessel. The *Iwo Jima* veered out of control and crushed into the ground, disintegrating in a fiery explosion. Huge chunks of shrapnel rained down all around them, sending the mercs scampering and diving for cover. Skarr ignored the melted chunks of metal falling from the sky, instead slinging his assault rifle over one shoulder and marching out toward the overturned APC.

He headed straight at it, knowing the Alliance soldiers on the other side wouldn't be able to see him coming. The vehicle providing them with cover was also obscuring their view of what was directly in front of them.

As he approached the APC, the mercs behind him split out to the sides, triangulating their positions so they could keep firing around him. They kept a steady stream of deadly high-velocity rounds trained on the vehicle, keeping the marines pinned down behind it.

Ignoring the constant gunfire, the krogan stopped less than ten meters away from the APC. Every muscle in his body tensed as he began to focus his biotic abilities. The reaction triggered an automatic biofeedback response in the amplification modules surgically implanted throughout his nervous system. He began to gather dark energy, drawing it in and trapping it the way a black hole traps light. It took almost ten full seconds for the power to build to maximum capacity. Then Skarr thrust forward with a fist, hurling it toward his target.

The overturned APC launched into the air, flying over the heads of the stunned Alliance marines to land a dozen meters behind them. They were caught off guard, completely surprised and totally exposed by the unexpected maneuver. Nothing in their training had prepared them for this. Uncertain how to react, they simply froze: a small group huddled together, crouching in the sand.

They would have been gunned down right then were it not for the fact that their enemy was just as surprised as they. The mercs had stopped shooting, watching in utter amazement as the krogan biotic had simply hurled the four-ton APC out of the way.

"Throw down your weapons!" Skarr growled.

The marines complied, knowing the battle was lost. They slowly stood up and raised their hands above their head, letting their assault rifles fall to the ground. Knowing she had no other choice, Kahlee did the same.

The krogan stepped forward and seized her by the upper arm, squeezing so hard she let out a cry of pain. One of the marines made half a move to help her, then pulled himself back. She was glad—he couldn't help her; no sense getting himself killed.

While the mercs kept their weapons trained on their prisoners, Skarr half dragged, half carried Kahlee over to one of the vehicles. He threw her into the back, then climbed in beside her.

"Kill them," he said to his men, nodding in the direction of the Alliance marines.

The sharp retorts of gunfire drowned out Kahlee's screams.

Saren watched the entire scene unfold through his binoculars, never moving from his carefully chosen position. He was surprised when Skarr didn't kill Sanders, instead taking her prisoner. Obviously her connection to all this was more than he'd first realized. But it didn't really change anything.

The mercs climbed into their vehicles and sped off into the dusk, switching on their lights to guide them through the gloom.

Saren leaped down from his vantage point and ran over to the small scout rover he had parked nearby. The vehicle had been specially modified for stealth missions at night: the headlamps were equipped with dimming covers to disperse the illumination and angle it down toward the ground, creating a faint glow that would be enough to navigate by but was barely visible from more than a kilometer away.

In contrast, the high-powered beams of the other vehicles blazed like beacons in the darkness of the desert night. He'd easily be able to spot them from as far as ten kilometers out.

All he had to do was follow them, and they'd lead him right to wherever Edan was hiding.

NINETEEN

Anderson couldn't help but feel nervous about this meeting. Even though the Council had officially approved the ambassador's request, he was still haunted by the memory of his last meeting with Saren. For several long moments he'd been absolutely convinced the turian was going to leave him for dead outside the ruins of Dah'tan. When Ambassador Goyle had revealed that Saren might have a general hatred of the Alliance, he wasn't the least bit surprised.

"Personal information on Spectres is sealed," she told him, "but our intel dug up something interesting. Seems he lost his brother during the First Contact War."

The lieutenant knew there were more than a few turians who were still bitter about the conflict, especially those who had lost family members. And he suspected Saren was the type who didn't just carry a grudge, but fed it constantly. It may have started as a desire to avenge his brother, but after eight years it would have grown into something much darker: a twisted, festering loathing for all humanity.

As much as he wanted to catch those responsible

for what had happened at Sidon, he wasn't looking forward to working with Saren on this mission. He had a bad feeling about all this; just like the one he'd gotten when the *Hastings* had first responded to Sidon's distress call. But he'd been given his orders, and he intended to follow them.

The fact that the turian was over an hour late didn't make him feel any better. In the interests of trying to smooth things over, Anderson had let him pick the time and place of the meeting. He'd chosen midday at a small, dingy bar in a run-down neighborhood on the edges of Hatre. The kind of establishment where the customers made a point of ignoring neighboring conversations. Nobody here wanted to know what anybody else was up to.

Not that there was much chance of anyone over-hearing them, anyway. The place was practically de-serted this afternoon—probably the reason the turian had chosen this time of day. It made sense, but as Anderson sat alone at a table in the corner nursing his drink he couldn't help but wonder what kind of game Saren was playing.

Why wasn't he here? Was this some kind of setup? Or maybe a ploy to get him out of the way while the Spectre continued his investigation?

Twenty minutes later, he'd just made up his mind to leave when the door opened and the man he'd been waiting for stepped through. The bartender and the only other customer in the place besides Anderson glanced up as he entered, then looked away as Saren crossed the room with quick, angry steps.

"You're late," Anderson said as the turian sat

down. He wasn't expecting an apology, but he felt he was at least owed an explanation.

"I was working" was the curt reply.

The turian looked haggard, as if he hadn't slept all night. Anderson had contacted him early yesterday afternoon, right after he'd turned Kahlee over to the security team that was to help get her off world. He wondered if Saren had been working the case non-stop since then. Trying to finish everything off before he was forced to join up with his unwanted human partner.

"We're in this together now," Anderson reminded him.

"I received the Council's message," Saren replied, his voice heavy with contempt. "I intend to honor their wishes."

"Glad to hear it," Anderson replied coldly. "Last time we met I thought you were going to kill me." There was no point in holding anything back; he wanted to know exactly where he stood with the Spectre. "Do I have to spend the rest of this mission looking over my shoulder?"

"I never kill someone without a reason," Saren reminded him.

"I thought you could always find a reason to kill someone," the lieutenant countered.

"But now I have a very good reason to keep you alive," Saren assured him. "If you die, the Alliance will be crying out for my head. And the Council just might be inclined to give it to them. At the very least they'd revoke my Spectre status.

"Truthfully, I couldn't care less whether you live or

die, human," the Spectre continued. From his tone they might have been discussing the weather. "But I don't intend to do anything that will put my career at risk."

Unless you're sure you can get away with it, Anderson thought. Out loud he asked, "You got the files we sent?"

Saren nodded.

"So what do we do next? How do we find Edan?"

"I've already found him" was the smug reply.

"How?" Anderson asked, surprised.

"I'm a Spectre. It's my job."

Realizing no explanation was forthcoming, Anderson let the matter drop. "Where is he?"

"In a bunker at an eezo refinery," Saren replied. He tossed a set of architectural blueprints down on the table. "These are the schematics."

Anderson almost asked where he'd gotten them, then bit his tongue. By law all eezo refineries were required to undergo a semiannual inspection. The layout of each plant needed to be available to the inspectors; it would have been an easy matter for someone with the authority of a Spectre to get his hands on them.

"I scouted out the exterior," Saren continued. "It's surrounded by a civilian work camp; the defenses are minimal. If we wait until nightfall, we should be able to get inside the perimeter without alerting anyone."

"Then what? We just sneak in and kill Edan?"

"I'd prefer to take him alive. For interrogation."

Something in the way he said *interrogation* made Anderson shiver. He already knew Saren had a cruel streak; it wasn't hard to imagine that he actually enjoyed torturing prisoners as part of his job.

The turian must have seen his reaction. "You don't like me, do you?"

There was no point in lying to him. Saren wouldn't have believed him anyway.

"I don't like you. It's clear that you're not my biggest fan, either. But I respect what you do. You're a Spectre, and I think you're damn good at your job. I'm hoping I can learn something from you."

"And I'm just hoping you don't screw this mission up for me," Saren replied.

Anderson refused to rise to the bait. "You said we should infiltrate the refinery after dark. What do we do until then?"

"I need some rest," the turian stated flatly, confirming Anderson's suspicions that he'd been up all night. "The refinery's about two hours outside the city. If we leave two hours after sundown, we'll get there at midnight. That should give us enough time to get in and out before it gets light."

The turian pushed his chair away from the table; obviously he felt the meeting was over. "Meet me back here at sixteen hundred," he said before turning and walking away.

Anderson waited until he was gone, tossed a few credits down on the table to cover his drink, then got up and left. Camala used the galactic standard twenty-hour clock and it still wasn't even 12:00 yet. There was no way he was spending the next four hours in this dive.

Besides, he hadn't spoken to Ambassador Goyle since yesterday morning. Now might be a good time to check back in and see how Kahlee was doing. Strictly for the sake of the mission, of course.

*   *   *

"Is this line secure, Lieutenant?" Ambassador Goyle asked him.

"As secure as we're going to get on a batarian world," Anderson told her.

He was speaking to her via real-time video conference. Real-time communication from a colony in the Verge back to the Citadel was an incredibly complex and expensive process, but Anderson figured the Alliance could afford it.

"I met with Saren. Looks like he's willing to let me tag along."

There was a split second of lag as the signal was encrypted and packaged in a top-priority burst, then transmitted to a comm buoy orbiting Camala, and subsequently relayed across the extranet to the ambassador's terminal on the Citadel before finally being decoded. The delay was barely noticeable, but it did cause a slight hitch in the ambassador's image on his monitor.

"What else did he tell you, Lieutenant?" There was something gravely serious in the ambassador's expression.

"Is something wrong, ma'am?"

She didn't answer right away, choosing her words carefully. "As you know, we dispatched the *Iwo Jima* to pick Sanders up yesterday. When they arrived, the ground team was under attack."

"What happened?" Anderson asked, already knowing the answer.

"The *Iwo Jima* went in to help, then dropped out of contact. By the time we convinced the local authorities to send out a rescue team to the sight, it was too late. The marines sent to accompany Sanders were all dead. The *Iwo Jima* was destroyed. Nobody aboard survived."

"What about Lieutenant Sanders?" he asked, noticing the ambassador had left her conspicuously absent from the list of casualties.

"No sign of her. We think she may be a prisoner. Obviously we suspect Edan and Dr. Qian were behind the attack."

"How'd they find out about the pickup?" Anderson demanded angrily.

"The request for clearance for the out-of-port landing was entered into Hatre's main transport system data banks," the ambassador told him. "Someone must have seen the information there and relayed it to Edan."

"Who leaked it?" he wanted to know, remembering Kahlee's fears that someone in the Alliance brass might be working with Qian.

"There's no way to know. We can't even be sure it was intentional. It might have been an accident. A mistake."

"With all due respect, ma'am, we both know that's a load of crap."

"This doesn't change your mission, Lieutenant," she warned him. "You're still going after Qian."

"What about Lieutenant Sanders?"

The ambassador sighed. "We believe she's still alive. Hopefully, if you find Qian, you'll find her."

"Anything else, ma'am?" he asked, a little more curtly than he'd intended. He was still shaken by the news that someone had betrayed Kahlee again. And while he didn't suspect the ambassador, she had made all the arrangements for the pickup. He couldn't help blaming her at least a little for allowing this to happen.

"Saren's going to be evaluating you on this mission," the ambassador reminded him, shrewdly refocusing him back to his true priorities. "Do well and it could go a long way to proving to the Council that humanity deserves to have someone in the Spectre ranks.

"I shouldn't have to tell you what that could mean for the Alliance," she added.

"Understood, Ambassador," he replied, subdued. He knew she was right; he had to put his personal feelings aside for the sake of the mission.

"We're all counting on you, Lieutenant," she added just before signing off. "Don't let us down."

Saren wasn't late for their second meeting. In fact, he was already there, waiting at the same table when Anderson arrived. The bar was busier in the evening, but it was still far from crowded.

The lieutenant marched toward the turian and sat down across from him. He didn't waste any time with a greeting, but simply blurted out, "Did you see any sign of Kahlee Sanders when you were scouting out Edan's hiding place?"

"She is no longer a concern of mine," Saren told him. "Or yours. Stay focused on Edan and Qian."

"That's not an answer," Anderson pressed. "Did you see her or not?"

"I'm not going to let one human life get in the way of this mission!" Saren hissed at him. Something in his tone flipped a switch in the lieutenant's brain; the light came on and he suddenly understood.

"You're the one who leaked the pickup! That's how you found Edan. You used Kahlee as bait, then followed his people back to the refinery and scouted it out last night. That's why you were late this morning!"

"It was the only way!" Saren fired back. "It would've taken months to find Edan. Months we might not have! I don't have to explain myself to you. I saw an opportunity, so I took it!"

"You son of a bitch!" Anderson shouted, leaping across the table to grab him by the throat. But the turian was too quick for him. He jumped back beyond Anderson's grasp, then leaped in and seized Anderson's outstretched arms by the wrists, yanking him off balance.

As the lieutenant tumbled forward, Saren let go of one wrist and twisted hard on the other one, bending Anderson's arm up and behind his back. The turian used the human's own momentum against him to slam him to the ground. Still keeping Anderson's arm bent behind him, the turian dropped his knee between the lieutenant's shoulders, pinning him to the floor.

Anderson struggled for a few seconds, but he couldn't get free. He felt Saren applying pressure to his arm, and he went still before the turian decided to break it. The rest of the people in the bar had jumped up from their seats when the action started, but once they saw that the human was effectively helpless, they simply sat back down and resumed drinking.

"This is what it means to be a Spectre," Saren whispered, still atop him. He had leaned in so close that Anderson felt his hot breath in his ear and on the back of his neck. "Sacrificing one life for the sake of millions. Qian's research is a threat to every species in Citadel space. I saw a chance to stop him at the cost of a few dozen lives. The math is simple, human . . . but few people are able to do it right."

"I get it," Anderson said, trying to keep his voice calm. "So let me up."

"Try this again and I will kill you," the Spectre warned before releasing him. Anderson had no doubt he meant it. Besides, fighting with Saren in this bar didn't accomplish anything. If he really wanted to help Kahlee he had to be smart instead of impulsive.

He stood up and stared at the turian for a long moment. Despite being immobilized, the only thing hurting was his pride. So Anderson simply brushed himself off, then went and sat down at the table again. Realizing the human intended to hold his anger in check, the turian joined him.

"They didn't find Kahlee's body at the scene," Anderson said, resuming the conversation where they had left off. He'd need to come up with a plan to help Kahlee, but he didn't even know where she was being held. As much as it galled him, he needed to get the turian back on his side. "Were you there? Did you see what happened?"

"Your ground team was attacked by Skarr and the Blue Sun mercenaries," Saren told him. "When all hope was lost your soldiers tried to surrender, but the Blue Suns gunned them down."

"What about Kahlee? Is she still alive?"

"She was," Saren admitted. "They took her inside the refinery. I assume they must need her for some purpose."

"If they know we're coming, they might still kill her," Anderson said.

"That means nothing to me."

It took every ounce of military discipline the lieutenant had not to attempt to attack him again, but somehow he managed to stay in his seat.

"She means something to me," he said, straining to keep his voice even. "I want to make you a deal."

The turian shrugged, a truly universal gesture of indifference. "What kind of deal?"

"You don't want me here. You're only doing this at the order of the Council. You take me to Edan's hideout and give me a chance to rescue Kahlee, and I promise to stay out of your way for the rest of the mission."

"What do you mean by 'a chance to rescue Kahlee'?" the turian asked suspiciously.

"If they know we've found them, they'll probably kill her. So when we get to the refinery you let me go in first. Give me thirty minutes to find Kahlee before you go in after Qian and Edan."

"What if somebody sees you?" the turian asked. "There's security at the refinery. Not to mention Edan's mercs. You set off the alarms, and they'll all be on guard. That makes my job harder."

"No," Anderson argued. "It makes your job easier. I'll be a distraction; I'll draw them off. They'll be so concerned with me they won't even notice you sneaking in from the other side."

"If you get into trouble, I won't come to help you," Saren warned.

"I wouldn't expect you to."

Saren considered the offer for a full minute before nodding his head in agreement. "Thirty minutes. Not one second more."

TWENTY

Neither one of the men spoke during the long drive through the desert night. Saren was behind the wheel, staring straight ahead through the windshield of the rover while Anderson studied the blueprints of the refinery. He'd been hoping to see something that might give him some clue as to where Kahlee was being held, but there were simply too many places they could have converted into a makeshift prison for her. Instead, he focused on trying to memorize the general layout so he could find his way around quickly once he was inside.

After an hour they could see a dim glow in the distance; the refinery lights shining in the darkness. The facility ran two day shifts and two night shifts of nearly two hundred workers each; the eezo production continued around the clock. To accommodate such enormous labor requirements, the refineries offered free room and board to employees and their families in the surrounding work camps: prefab buildings assembled in an ever-widening circle around the chain-link fence protecting the refinery itself.

They were only a few hundred meters from the

edges of the work camp when Saren stopped the rover. "We walk from here."

Anderson made a mental note of where the vehicle was parked; he'd have to find his way back here through the dark after he found Kahlee. If he got lost, he doubted Saren would bother to come looking for him.

He grabbed his pistol, but hesitated before taking his assault rifle. The pistol had a silencer on it, but the assault rifle was loud—one burst from that and the whole place would know he was there. Plus, it was a lot easier to pick your targets carefully with a pistol than an automatic weapon.

"You'll need that," Saren advised him, noticing his indecision.

"Most of the people in that plant are just ordinary workers," Anderson replied. "They won't even be armed."

"Edan's working with the Blue Sun mercenaries. You'll run into plenty of them in there, too."

"That's not what I meant. I'm a little concerned about accidentally shooting innocent civilians."

Saren gave a harsh, bitter laugh. "You still don't get it, do you, human?

"Most of the workers in these camps own firearms. This refinery represents their livelihood. They aren't soldiers, but once the alarms go off they will try to protect it."

"We're not here to destroy the plant," Anderson objected. "All we have to do is grab Qian, Edan, and Kahlee and get out."

"They don't know that. When they hear sirens and bullets, they'll think the plant is under some kind of terrorist attack. You won't be able to pick and choose your targets when half of them are running around in a blind panic and the other half are firing guns at you.

"If you want to make it through this mission alive," Saren added, "you better be willing to shoot civilians if they get in your way. Because they'll be more than willing to shoot at you."

"Necessity is one thing. But how can you be so cold about killing innocent people?" he asked in disbelief.

"Practice. Lots of practice."

Anderson shook his head and took the assault rifle, though he promised himself he wouldn't use it unless absolutely necessary. He folded it down and snapped it into the armor slot on his back, just above the belt. Then he slapped the pistol into the slot on his hip, where he could easily grab it if necessary.

"We'll split up," Saren told him. "I'll head east, you go around the other way."

"You promised me a thirty-minute head start before you go in," Anderson reminded him in a hard voice.

"You'll have your thirty minutes, human. But if you're not here at the rover when I get back, I'm leaving you behind."

Anderson quickly made his way through the darkness to the edges of the work camp. Although it was the middle of the night, the place was buzzing with activity. Because of the staggered shifts at the refinery, there were always people who were recently getting off work or just about to start. The camp was like a small city. Over a thousand families made their homes here—husbands, wives, and even children were

milling about the streets, nodding greetings to one another and going about their daily lives.

With so many people around it was an easy matter
for Anderson to simply blend in with the crowd. He'd
thrown on a long, loose-fitting overcoat to cover his
body armor and conceal his weapons. And while
most of the employees of the refinery were batarians,
there were enough other species, including humans,
in the crowd that he didn't draw undo attention.

He hustled through the camp, pushing his way
through the crowd, occasionally nodding a greeting
as he passed some of his fellow humans. He walked
with long, quick strides, maintaining a brisk pace as
he worked his way toward the fence surrounding the
secured grounds of the refinery. He knew time was
slipping away, but breaking into a run was sure to attract notice.

After five minutes he had cleared the camp. The
buildings housing the workers formed an evenly dis-
tributed ring around the entire refinery, but nobody
wanted to live butted right up against the metal security fence. The inner edge of the camp stopped a good
hundred meters away from it, leaving a wide tract of
empty and unlit land occupied only by a few scattered
public lavatories.

Anderson kept his pace at a brisk walk until he was
far enough away from the lights to avoid being seen.
Anyone who had happened to spot him disappearing
into the darkness would have assumed he was headed
to the bathrooms, and not given him a second thought.

Safely out of sight, he slipped on a pair of night-
vision goggles, then broke into a run until he reached
the fence. Using a pair of wire clippers he cut a hole

large enough for him to fit through. He ditched the long coat before crawling through—it would only get in the way. Once on the other side, he pulled out his pistol, hoping he wouldn't have to use it.

From here on in the mission became more difficult. He was in a restricted area now. There were small security squads patrolling the grounds inside the perimeter of the fence; if they saw him they'd either shoot him or set off the alarm. Avoiding them wouldn't be too difficult, however; he'd see the glow of their flashlights on the ground long before they were close enough to spot him.

Cautiously making his way across the grounds, he approached a corner of the refinery. The complex was enormous—a main central building nearly four stories high held the primary processing plant. A number of smaller two-story structures had been built on every side to house storage, shipping, administration, and maintenance—Anderson's destination.

When he reached the maintenance annex he headed around to the small fire door in the back corner. It was locked, but only by a simple mechanical bolt, not one of the far more expensive electronic security systems. A refinery plant in the middle of the desert was typically concerned with limiting casual theft; they weren't built with the purpose of preventing infiltration operations.

Anderson placed a small glob of sticky explosives on the lock, stepped back, and fired the pistol at the putty. It exploded with a sharp bang and a bright flash, blowing the door open. He waited to see if there was any reaction to the noise, but hearing none he pushed open the door and stepped in.

He found himself standing by the employee lockers. The room was empty; it was the middle of the shift and the employees were all out on repair calls. In one corner was a large laundry basket on wheels, filled with soiled mechanics' coveralls. He rummaged around until he found a pair that fit over his body armor, then slipped it on. He had to remove his pistol and assault rifle—he didn't want to be fumbling beneath the coveralls to grab them if needed. He stuffed the pistol into the deep hip pocket of the coveralls. He didn't unfold the assault rifle, but wrapped it in a large towel he found in the laundry.

The disguise was far from perfect, but it would allow him to explore the plant without attracting too much attention. Seen quickly from a distance, most people would just assume he was one of the maintenance crew headed to a job and ignore him.

He rolled up the sleeve of the coveralls and glanced at his watch. Fifteen minutes gone. He'd have to hurry if he wanted to find Kahlee and get her out before Saren started his misson.

Waiting on the outskirts of the work camp, Saren glanced at his watch. Fifteen minutes had passed. Anderson was no doubt somewhere deep inside the refinery by now—too far in to turn back.

Stashing his weapons beneath a long coat in much the same way Anderson had done when he'd wanted to pass unnoticed through the camp, the turian stood up and marched toward the buildings.

He'd waited long enough. It was time for his own mission to begin.

*   *   *

Anderson navigated through the numerous halls, passing from the maintenance building into the main refinery. His heart began to pound when he saw his first employee heading his way. But the batarian woman only glanced at him for a second, then looked away and continued on past without saying a word.

He passed several more employees as he made his way up and down the halls, but none of them paid him any attention, either. He was beginning to grow frustrated—he didn't have time to search the entire facility. He'd assumed they'd be keeping Kahlee on the lower floors, but he was still going to need some luck if he wanted to locate her in time.

And then he saw it: a sign saying "No Admittance" beside a stairwell leading down to what he remembered from the blueprints was a small equipment storage room. The sign was so clean it almost sparkled; obviously it had only been placed there in the last few days.

He hurried down the stairs. At the bottom were two heavyset batarians, each marked with Blue Sun tattoos on their cheeks. They looked bored, slouched down in chairs on either side of a heavy steel door, their assault rifles propped up against the wall beside them. Neither of the guards was wearing body armor—understandable, given the nature of their assignment. They'd probably been sitting here all day, and body armor was hot and heavy. Wearing it for more than a few hours at a time was incredibly uncomfortable.

The guards had already seen him, so Anderson just kept on walking straight toward them. Hopefully they'd been warned to be on the lookout for a turian

Spectre. If that was the case, a human in maintenance coveralls wouldn't seem like much of a threat.

When he reached the small landing at the bottom of the stairs one of the mercs stood up and stepped forward, grabbing his assault rifle and pointing it at Anderson's chest. The lieutenant froze. He was less than five meters away; at this close range there was no possible way he'd survive if the merc pulled the trigger.

"What's that?" the guard asked, pointing the barrel of his gun to indicate the towel-wrapped assault rifle Anderson was carrying tucked under his arm.

"Just some tools. Gotta keep them dry."

"Put the package down."

Anderson did as he was told, setting the assault rifle on the floor carefully to make sure the towel didn't slip and reveal what was concealed beneath.

Now that Anderson was no longer carrying anything that might be a weapon, the guard seemed to relax, lowering his own rifle.

"What's the matter, human?" he demanded. "Can't you read batarian?" This drew a guffaw from his partner, still slouched in his chair.

"I need something from the equipment room," Anderson replied.

"Not this one. Turn around."

"I have an authorization slip here," Anderson said, fumbling around in his pocket as if trying to dig it out. The batarian was watching him with an expression of bored annoyance, totally oblivious as Anderson wrapped his hand around the handle of his pistol and slipped his finger over the trigger.

The roomy pocket of the coverall allowed him to

tilt the barrel of the pistol up just enough to bring it in line with the guard's midsection. He fired twice, the bullets shredding through the fabric of the coveralls and lodging themselves in the merc's stomach.

The batarian dropped his rifle in surprise, stumbling back and instinctively clutching at the holes in his gut. He hit the wall and slowly slid down to the floor, blood seeping out and welling up from the fingers he had pressed over the wounds.

His partner looked up in confusion; because of the silencer the pistol's shots had been muffled to a faint *zip-zip* that he probably hadn't even heard. It took him a second to realize what had happened. With an expression of dawning horror he went for his own weapon. Anderson whipped the pistol out of his pocket and fired two shots point-blank into the second guard's chest. He slouched down to the side, fell off the chair, and was still.

Anderson whipped the pistol back toward the first guard, still sitting motionless on the floor with his back to the wall. "Please," the mercenary begged, finally figuring out who Anderson was with. "Skarr's the one who gave the order to execute those Alliance soldiers. I didn't even want to kill them."

"But you did," Anderson answered, then fired a single shot right between the batarian's eyes.

He stripped off the coveralls, snapped the pistol back onto his hip and unwrapped the assault rifle, unfolding it so it was ready to go. Then he kicked open the door.

TWENTY-ONE

Like Anderson before him, Saren entered the refinery through an emergency door in one of the refinery's small, two-story annexes. But while the lieutenant had gone through the maintenance building on the westernmost side of the refinery, Saren entered through the shipping warehouse on the east. And unlike his human counterpart, he didn't bother with a disguise.

A pair of dockworkers saw him come in, their faces registering surprise and then fear at the sight of an armored turian carrying a heavy assault rifle. A quick burst from Saren's weapon ended their lives before they had a chance to cry out for help.

The Spectre moved quickly through the warehouse and into the main building. Again, unlike Anderson, he knew exactly where he was going. He made his way down to the lowest levels of the refinery, where deposits of rock and ore rich in element zero were melted down and the bulk impurities skimmed off the boiling surface. The molten liquid was then piped to an enormous centrifuge to separate out the precious eezo. He killed three more employees along the way.

He knew he was getting close to his destination when he passed signs on the wall reading "Restricted

Access." He rounded a corner and yanked open a door with "Authorized Personnel Only" painted across it. A wall of hot, hazy air rolled out, stinging his eyes and lungs. Inside, half a dozen engineers were scattered on walkways built around and above the colossal melting vats and the massive generator core used to heat them. They were monitoring the refining process, keeping an eye on the equipment to ensure it operated at peak efficiency and didn't experience a potentially deadly malfunction.

The employees were wearing headsets to protect their ears from the constant rumble of the turbines feeding the generator. One of them saw Saren and tried to shout out a warning. His words were swallowed up by the thunder of the turbines, as were the sounds of gunfire as the turian mowed them all down.

The slaughter lasted less than a minute; the Spectre was nothing if not brutally efficient. As soon as the last engineer died, tumbling from the catwalk into the vat of molten ore twenty meters below, Saren began the next phase of his plan.

There were too many hiding places here inside the refinery. Too many places Edan could bunker down behind a wall of armed mercs. Saren needed something to flush him out. A few strategically placed explosive charges would trigger a catastrophic series of explosions in the refinery core, setting off a general evacuation alarm for the entire facility.

Saren finished rigging the last of the munitions, then headed for the upper levels. He wanted to be well out of the blast radius when the charges detonated.

* * *

Kahlee was hungry, thirsty, and tired. But above all else she was scared. The krogan had told her Qian would be coming to see her in a few days, but that was all he'd said. Then he'd dragged her into a storage room and locked her inside the small, dark closet at the back. She hadn't seen or spoken to anybody since.

She was smart enough to understand what they were doing. She didn't know what Qian wanted, but it was obvious they were trying to break her will before the meeting. They'd left her for almost a full day in the cramped closet, in complete darkness with no food or water. There wasn't even a bucket so she could go to the bathroom; she'd had to relieve herself in the corner.

After two or three days of this Qian would come to her with his offer. If she accepted, they'd feed her and give her something to drink. If she refused, they'd throw her back into the makeshift cell and come for her again in another three days.

If she refused them a second time, things would most likely get really nasty. Instead of starvation and mental abuse, they'd move on to actual physical torture. Kahlee had no intention of helping Dr. Qian in any way, but she was terrified of what was to come. Worst of all was the knowledge that in the end they'd win anyway. It might take days, maybe even weeks, but eventually the endless torture and abuse would break her and they'd get whatever they wanted.

During the first few hours of her imprisonment she'd sought some way to free herself, only to realize it was hopeless. She had fumbled in the darkness with the door of the closet, but it was locked from the outside and the interior handle had been removed. Plus, even if she did get out of the closet there were almost certainly guards waiting on the other side.

She couldn't even escape by killing herself. Not that she was at that point yet, but the room she was in was completely empty: no pipes to hang herself from, nothing to use to cut or wound herself. She briefly considered the option of slamming her head over and over into the wall, but she would only succeed in knocking herself out and inflicting a lot of unnecessary pain—something she suspected there was already more than enough of in her future.

The situation was hopeless, but Kahlee hadn't given in to total despair quite yet. And then she heard a noise; a sound sweeter than the singing of angels. The sound of salvation: automatic gunfire on the other side of the door.

Anderson kicked open the door that the two mercs had been guarding. Beyond it was a large storage room. All the equipment inside had been dragged out; it was empty except for a small table and several chairs. Four more batarian Blue Suns were sitting around the table playing some type of card game. And standing off alone in the corner was Skarr. Like the men outside, none of them were wearing body armor.

The krogan was his first target—a stream of bullets hit the krogan square in the chest. Skarr's arms flew up and out as he was blown backwards, sending his gun sailing across the room. He struck the wall behind him, spun off it, and fell facedown on the floor, bleeding from too many wounds to count.

The mercs reacted to the sudden attack by flipping the table and scattering. Seeing Kahlee wasn't in the room, Anderson simply sprayed the entire place with bullets. He took the whole lot of them out before they ever had a chance to fire back. It wasn't a fair or honorable fight; it was a massacre. Considering the victims, Anderson didn't even feel bad.

After the shooting stopped, he noticed a small door in the back wall. It probably just led into a closet, but it was reinforced with metal plating and sealed with a heavy lock.

"Kahlee?" he shouted, running over to bang on the door. "Kahlee, are you in there? Can you hear me?"

From the other side he heard her muffled voice calling back to him. "David? David! Please, get me out of here!"

He tried the lock, but it wouldn't budge. He briefly considered blowing it off, like he had with the maintenance building door earlier, but he was worried the blast might injure Kahlee.

"Hold on," he shouted to her. "I need to find the key."

He took a quick glance around the room, his eyes coming to rest on the krogan's body lying crumpled in the corner. A thick pool of blood crawled out from beneath him, spreading rapidly across the floor. If anyone in this room had a key, Anderson knew, it would be Skarr.

He ran over to the body, set his gun on the floor, and grabbed the krogan's far shoulder with both hands, grunting at the effort necessary to roll him over onto his back. The krogan's chest was a bubbling mess of blood and gore; at least a dozen bullets had ripped through his torso. His clothing was soaked and sticky with the warm, dark fluid.

Grimacing slightly, Anderson reached out to dig through his pockets. Skarr's eyes snapped open and the krogan's hand shot out and grabbed him around the throat. With a roar the beast stood up, lifting the lieutenant off the ground with one arm. The other dangled bloody and useless at his side.

Impossible! Anderson thought, struggling like a helpless child as the krogan's grip slowly crushed the life from him. *Nobody can survive those kinds of injuries. Not even a krogan!*

Skarr must have seen the shock in his eyes. "You humans have a lot to learn about my people," he growled, bits of bloody froth bubbling up from his lips as he spoke. "A pity you won't live to tell them."

Anderson kicked and flailed, but the krogan held him at arm's length and his limbs were too short to reach his opponents body. Instead, he pounded down with his fists on Skarr's massive forearm. His efforts did nothing but elicit a gurgling laugh from the krogan.

"You should be glad," the bounty hunter told him. "You will have an easy death. Not like the female."

Suddenly the room was rocked by a massive explosion from somewhere deep inside the refinery. Huge cracks appeared in the finish of the walls and several ceiling tiles fell to the floor. The ground beneath their feet buckled and heaved, throwing Skarr off balance. Anderson thrashed his body in that instant and managed to break free of the krogan's grip, falling to the floor and gasping for breath.

Skarr staggered and stumbled, trying to stay upright. But his balance was hampered by his dead and useless arm, and he was weakened by the loss of blood. He fell heavily to the ground, only a few meters away from where Anderson had dropped his assault rifle.

Now free of the krogan's grip, Anderson whipped out his pistol and fired. But he didn't aim at the krogan. If a burst from an assault rifle hadn't stopped Skarr, a single shot from a pistol would barely slow him down. Instead, Anderson aimed at the weapon laying beside the krogan, hitting it square and sending it skittering across the floor and just out of the bounty hunter's reach.

Alarms started going off throughout the building; no doubt a response to the explosion. But Anderson had more immediate concerns. Armed only with the pistol, he knew he'd need a direct shot to the head to finish Skarr off. But the krogan leaped up and lunged toward him before he had a chance to take proper aim.

The bullet caught the krogan in his already paralyzed shoulder, but he just kept coming. Anderson dove to the side and rolled out of the way as his enemy howled in rage, narrowly avoiding being trampled to death.

But now Skarr was between him and the door, blocking any chance of escape. Anderson backed into the corner and raised his weapon again. But he was a fraction of a second too slow, and the krogan hit him with a quick biotic push that knocked the pistol from his hand and nearly broke his wrist.

Knowing the human was no match for him unarmed, the krogan slowly advanced. Anderson tried to feint and dodge, hoping he'd have a chance to make a grab for one of the weapons on the ground. But the krogan was cunning, and even with the injuries and blood loss he was quick enough to cut off the room, slowly working the lieutenant into a corner from which there was no escape.

The impact of the explosion sent Kahlee reeling through the darkness to slam face first into an unseen wall, knocking out one of her teeth and breaking her nose. She dropped to the floor and brought her hands up to her mangled face, tasting the blood flowing down her chin.

And then she noticed a small sliver of light coming from the edge of the door. The explosion must have jarred it off its hinges. Ignoring the pain of her injuries, she jumped up and backed away until she felt the wall behind her. Then she took three hard steps and threw herself shoulder first into the door.

The damage to the frame must have been extensive, because the door gave way on her first attempt, sending her sprawling into the room beyond. She hit the ground hard, landing on the same shoulder she'd used to knock open the door. A jolt of pain shot through her arm as the shoulder popped out of the socket. She sat up, shielding her eyes from the sudden brightness of the room after all the hours she'd spent in absolute darkness.

"Kahlee!" she heard Anderson scream. "Grab the gun! Shoot him!"

Squinting in the light, half blind, she fumbled around on the ground and wrapped her hands around the barrel of an assault rifle. She pulled it in and grabbed the handle as an enormous shadow suddenly loomed above her.

Acting on instinct, she pointed and pulled the trigger. She was rewarded with the unmistakable sound of a krogan roaring in pain, and the immense shadow fell away.

Blinking desperately to restore her vision, she was just able to make out the form of Skarr stumbling away from her, clutching at his stomach and looking at her in rage and disbelief.

And then Anderson stepped into view right beside him. He jammed the nose of his pistol against the side of the krogan's skull and fired. Kahlee turned away an instant too late—the sight of Skarr's brains being blown out through the far side of his head and splattering across the wall was one that would probably haunt her nightmares for the rest of her life.

And then David was there, crouching on the ground beside her.

"Are you okay?" he asked. "Can you walk?"

She nodded. "I think I dislocated my shoulder."

He thought for a second, then said, "I'm sorry for this, Kahlee." She was about to ask him *for what* when he grabbed her by the wrist and collarbone, yanking hard on her arm. She screamed in agony, nearly passing out as the shoulder popped back into place.

David was there to catch her so she didn't fall over.

"You bastard," she mumbled, flexing her fingers to try and work the numbness out of them. "Thank you," she added a second later.

He helped her to her feet, and it was only then that

she noticed all the other dead bodies in the room. Anderson didn't say anything, but simply handed her one of the dead men's assault rifles, then grabbed his own weapon.

"We better take these," he told her, remembering Saren's grim advice about shooting civilians. "Let's just pray we don't have to use them."

TWENTY-TWO

The explosion in the refinery core had exactly the impact Saren was hoping for. Panic and chaos descended over the plant. The alarms had sent people fleeing for the exits, frantic to get away from the destruction. But while everyone else was running out, Saren was working his way farther in, moving against the flow of the crowd. Most of the people ignored him, concentrating only on their own desperate flight.

He had to act quickly. The detonation he'd set off had only been the first in a chain reaction that would cause the vats of molten ore to overheat. When they erupted, all the machinery in the processing core would ignite in flames. The turbines and generators would overload, triggering a series of explosions that would reduce the entire plant to burning rubble.

Scanning the crowd Saren at last saw what he was looking for: a small group of Blue Sun mercs, heavily armed and moving together as a single unit. Like Saren, they were heading deeper into the plant.

All he had to do was follow them.

"What are we waiting for?" Qian screamed, almost hysterical. He held up a small metal case and waved it frantically in Edan's face. Inside was a flash drive containing all the data they had gathered on the project. "We have everything we need right here. Let's go!"

"Not yet," the batarian said, trying to remain calm despite the claxon's ringing so loudly he could barely hear himself think. "Wait for our escorts to arrive." He knew the explosion in the core was more than just a coincidence, and he wasn't about to go running out into a trap. Not without his bodyguards.

"What about them?" Qian shouted, pointing at the two mercs standing nervously just outside the door of the room in which he had been holed up ever since the attack on Sidon.

"They're not enough," Edan replied. "I'm not taking any chances. We wait for the rest of—"

His words were cut off by the sound of gunfire from the other room, mingling with the alarms and shouts from his guards. This was followed by a second of silence, and then an unfamiliar figure appeared at the door.

"Your escort isn't going to make it," the armored turian said.

Even though he'd never met the man before, Edan instantly recognized him. "I know you," he said. "The Spectre. Saren."

"You did this!" Qian screamed, pointing a shaking finger at Saren. "This is your fault!"

"Are you going to kill us now?" Edan asked. Surprisingly, he wasn't afraid. It was as if he'd known this moment was coming all along. And now that his death was upon him he felt only a strange sense of calm.

But the turian didn't kill them. Instead, he asked a question. "What were you working on at Sidon?"

"Nothing!" Qian shouted, clutching the metal case to his chest. "It's ours!"

Edan recognized the look in Saren's eye. He'd made his entire fortune off that look: hunger, desire, the lust to possess.

"You know," he whispered, realizing the truth. "Not everything. But just enough so that you want to know more." A faint smile creased his lips. There was a chance he might still get out of this alive.

"Shut up!" Qian screamed at him. "He'll take it from us!"

"I don't think so," Edan replied, speaking more to Saren than the raving scientist. "We have something he wants. He needs to keep us alive."

"Not both of you," Saren warned.

Something in his tone pierced the veil of Qian's madness. "You need me," he insisted in a rare moment of lucidity. "You need my research. My expertise." He was speaking quickly, desperate and scared. However, it wasn't clear if he was more frightened of death, or of losing out on the chance to continue his obsessive research. "Without me you'll never understand it. Never figure out how to unlock its power. I'm essential to the project!"

Saren raised his pistol and pointed it straight at the babbling human, then he turned his head toward Edan.

"Is this true?" he asked the batarian.

Edan shrugged. "We have copies of all his research, and I have my own team studying the artifact. Qian is brilliant but he's become . . . erratic. I think the time has come for him to be replaced."

No sooner were the words out of his mouth than Saren fired. Qian went rigid and toppled over backwards, a single bullet hole in his forehead. The metal case fell from his hands and clattered to the floor, the flash drive inside well-protected from the impact by the padded interior.

"And what about you?" the Spectre asked, aiming the pistol at the batarian.

When he'd thought there was no hope of survival Edan had been calm, resigned to his fate. Now that he saw a chance to escape with his life, the gun pointed in his direction filled him with a cold fear.

"I know where it is," he said. "How will you find it without my help?"

Saren nodded his head in the direction of the metal case. "There's probably something in there that'll tell me what I need to know."

"I . . . I have resources," Edan stammered, scrambling to find another argument capable of staying the executioner's hand. "People. Power. Money. The cost of the project is astronomical. If you kill me, how will you fund it?"

"You aren't the only one with wealth and influence," the turian reminded him. "I can find another moneyman without even leaving the Verge."

"Think of how much time and effort I've put into this!" Edan blurted out. "Kill me and you'll have to start from scratch!"

Saren stayed silent, but he did tilt his head slightly to the side as if considering what the batarian had said.

"You have no idea what this thing is capable of," Edan continued, pressing his point. "It's like nothing the galaxy has ever seen before. Even with Qian's files you won't find anybody who can just step in and resume work on the project.

"I've been involved from the beginning. I have a fundamental understanding of what we're dealing with. Nobody else in the galaxy can offer you that."

From the expression on the turian's face it was obvious he was buying into Edan's argument.

"If you kill me, you don't just lose my financial backing, you lose my experience. You might find someone else to fund the project, but that will take time. If you kill me, you'll be starting over from the beginning.

"You're not going to throw away three years of my groundwork just so you can have the satisfaction of shooting me."

"I don't mind waiting a few extra years," Saren replied as he squeezed the trigger. "I'm a very patient man."

Kahlee and Anderson were still inside the main building of the refinery when the second explosion came. The blast originated near the processing core's vats of molten ore; a geyser of fiery liquid erupted from the heart of the facility, shooting up three hundred meters into the sky. The glowing pillar mushroomed, spreading out to illuminate the night before collapsing to rain red hot death down over everything within a half-kilometer radius.

"Keep moving!" Anderson shouted, straining to be heard above the shrieking alarms. The plant was already structurally weakened by the first two explosions, and more were sure to follow. "We have to get outside before this place caves in on us!"

He led the way, one hand clutching the assault rifle, the other clenching Kahlee's wrist as he dragged the weakened young woman along with him. They emerged from the plant, racing for the perimeter fence, the lieutenant frantically scanning the area around them for any signs of pursuit.

"My God!" Kahlee gasped, pulling up short and forcing Anderson to do the same. He glanced back and saw her staring out into the distance. He turned to follow her gaze, then whispered a small prayer of his own.

The entire work camp was ablaze. Shielded by the roof and walls of the refinery, the two humans had been protected from the deluge of molten ore. Those outside the plant—the men, women, and children in the work camps—were not so lucky. Every building seemed to be on fire; a fierce orange wall of flames ringing them in.

"We'll never get through that," Kahlee moaned, collapsing to the ground, overwhelmed with exhaustion and fatigue.

Another explosion shook the facility. Glancing back Anderson saw the plant was on fire now, too. By the light of the flames he could see dark vapors crawling out from the windows—toxic chemical clouds released by the destruction.

"Don't give up!" Anderson shouted, grabbing her by the shoulders and hauling her to her feet. "We can make it!"

Kahlee only shook her head. He could see it in her

eyes; after everything she'd already been through since the destruction of Sidon, this was finally too much for her. She didn't have anything left; she'd finally given in to despair.

"I can't. I'm too tired," she said, slumping back down. "Just leave me."

He couldn't carry her the rest of the way; they had too far to go. And with her draped over his back he was afraid he wouldn't be able to move fast enough to get through the flame-engulfed work camp without them both burning to death.

Kahlee hadn't enlisted to serve on the battlefront. She was a scientist, a thinker. But all of humanity's soldiers went through the same basic training—before they became part of the Alliance they had to endure months of grueling physical ordeals. They were taught to push themselves to their limits and beyond. And when their bodies threatened to simply keel over from fatigue and exhaustion, they had to find a way to keep going. They had to break through the mental barriers holding them back and push further than they ever imagined was possible.

It was a right of passage, a bond shared by every man and woman in the Systems Alliance Military. It united them and gave them strength; transformed them into living symbols—flesh and blood manifestations of the indomitable human spirit.

Anderson knew he had to tap into that now. "Damn it, Sanders!" he shouted at her. "Don't you dare quit on me now! Your unit is moving out, so get up off your ass and get your feet moving! That's an order!"

Like a good soldier, Kahlee responded to his commands. Somehow she got back to her feet, still clutching her weapon. She broke into a slow, lumbering run—her will forcing her body to do what her mind told her it couldn't. Anderson watched her for a second to make sure she wouldn't topple over, then fell into step behind her, matching Kahlee's pace as they raced toward the smoke, screams, and flames coming from the buildings in front of them.

The work camp had become Hell itself. The roaring of the flames rose up from the conflagration to mingle with shrieks of pain and keening cries of terror and loss. The horrible cacophony was punctuated by the occasional earsplitting thunder of another detonation from somewhere inside the plant.

Greasy black clouds rolled across the rooftops and down to the ground as the fire leaped from building to building, devouring the entire camp, one structure at time. The heat was like a living thing, clutching and grabbing at their limbs, scraping searing claws across their skin as they ran past. Acrid smoke stung their eyes and crawled down their lungs, choking them with each breath. The sickly stench of burning flesh was everywhere.

Bodies lay strewn about the streets, many of them children. Some were victims of the molten ore that had rained down, charred husks lying in bubbling puddles of their own melted flesh. Others had succumbed to the smoke or flames, their corpses curling up into the fetal position as muscles and sinew shriveled and burned. Still others had been trampled by the stampede of those trying to escape, their limbs broken and bent at grotesque, unnatural angles; their faces smashed to a bloody pulp beneath the heedless feet of their neighbors.

For all the combat Anderson had endured, for all the battles he'd fought, for all the atrocities of war he'd witnessed firsthand, nothing had prepared the lieutenant for the horrors he saw during the remainder of their flight from the refinery. But there was nothing they could do for the victims; no aid they could offer. All they could do was put their heads down, crouch low, and keep running.

Kahlee stumbled and fell several times during their desperate flight, only to push valiantly on each time Anderson hauled her back to her feet. And by some miracle they made it through Hell alive . . . arriving just in time to see Saren tossing a small metal case into the back of the rover.

The turian looked at them in surprise, and in the glow from the fires of the burning camp behind them, Anderson was convinced he saw the Spectre scowl. He didn't say anything as he climbed into the vehicle, and for a second Anderson thought Saren was going to drive away and just leave them there.

"Get in!" the turian shouted.

Maybe it was the sight of the automatic assault rifles they both still carried. Maybe he was afraid someone would find out if he abandoned them. Anderson didn't really care; he was just glad the Spectre waited.

He helped Kahlee up into the vehicle, then scrambled in beside her. "Where's Edan?" he asked as the engine roared to life.

"Dead."

"What about Dr. Qian?" Kahlee wanted to know.

"Him, too."

Saren slammed the rover into gear, the wheels kicking up small bits of sand and gravel as they took off. Anderson slumped back against his seat. All thoughts of the small metal case slipped from his mind as he surrendered to utter exhaustion.

The rover sped away into the night, leaving the grim scene of death and destruction farther and farther behind them.

EPILOGUE

Anderson stepped out from the offices of the Alliance embassy on the Citadel and into the simulated sunshine of the Presidium. He made his way down the stairs and out onto the green grass fields.

Kahlee was waiting for him down by the lake's edge. She sat on the grass, barefoot so she could dip her toes. He came over and sat down heavily beside her, yanking off his own shoes and plunging his feet into the cool, refreshing water.

"Ahhh, that feels good."

"That was a long meeting," Kahlee said.

"I was afraid you might get bored waiting for me."

"Nothing else to do," she teased. "I already had my meeting with the ambassador. Besides, I figured I'd stick around." In a more serious voice she added, "I owe you that much at least."

"You don't owe me anything," he replied, and they lapsed into a comfortable silence.

It was four days since they'd fled the refinery on Camala. The first night had been spent at the medical facility near the spaceports. They were treated for smoke inhalation and possible exposure to toxins released into the air during the explosions, and Kahlee was given intravenous fluids to fight off the dehydration she'd suffered during her imprisonment.

The next morning they'd been met by a contingent of Alliance representatives: soldiers to provide protection and intel officials to gather their statements. They'd been whisked onto a waiting frigate and taken to the Citadel to deliver their reports and individual accounts to the powers-that-be in person: three days of meetings, hearings, and inquiries to determine what had happened . . . and who was at fault.

Anderson suspected the high-level political fallout would continue for months, maybe years. But with the end of this final meeting in the ambassador's office, it was officially over for him. For both of them.

This was the first chance they'd had to be alone since that hellish night. He wanted to reach his arm around her shoulder and pull her close, but he wasn't sure how she'd react. He wanted to say something, but he couldn't figure out what to say. So they just sat there, side by side on the edge of the lake, not speaking.

It was Kahlee who finally broke the silence. "What did the ambassador say?"

"About what I expected," he said with a sigh. "The Council rejected me as a candidate for the Spectres."

"Because Saren screwed you," she said, disgusted.

"His report doesn't paint a very flattering portrait of me. He says I ignored the true goal of the mission. Claims I blew his cover by tipping off the mercs inside the base by going in too soon. He even manages to blame me for the explosion."

"But it's all lies!" Kahlee said, throwing her hands up in exasperation.

"With just enough truth mixed in to sell it," he noted. "Besides, he's a Spectre. One of their top agents. Who are they going to believe?"

"Or maybe the Council's just looking for an excuse to keep humans out of the Spectres. Holding the Alliance back again."

"Maybe. But that's Goyle's problem now."

"And the alien technology he discovered?" Kahlee demanded.

"The Council had its own experts study the files from Sidon," Anderson explained. "It's all theory and conjecture. They don't believe there ever was any alien technology."

"What about all the research he had us doing?" she protested. "What was he trying to accomplish?"

Anderson shrugged. "They say Qian was unstable. They think he conned Edan with wild claims and false promises based on his own psychotic delusions. And they think he was just dragging the entire Sidon project deeper and deeper into his own private madness."

"What did the ambassador say about you?" Kahlee asked after a moment's hesitation, her voice growing softer.

"She wasn't too happy at first," he admitted. "I didn't get into the Spectres, and this mission left a hell of a political mess for her to clean up."

"What about all the civilians who died in the explosion? The Alliance isn't trying to pin that on you, are they?" There was no mistaking the concern in her voice, and Anderson regretted not putting his arm around her earlier.

"No. Goyle's not looking for a scapegoat. The

Council sealed all the records associated with Saren's involvement. Officially they're calling it an industrial accident.

"Once the ambassador calmed down I think she realized the mission wasn't a complete failure. We found out what really happened at Sidon, and the men responsible are dead. I think she's giving me some credit for that."

"So this won't hurt your military career?"

"Probably not. But it won't help, either."

"I'm glad," she said, reaching out to put a hand on his shoulder. "I know how much being a soldier means to you."

He reached up gently and placed a hand on the back of her head, pulling her in slightly as he leaned toward her. Their lips brushed for the faintest of instants before she pulled back.

"No, David," she whispered. "We can't do this. I'm sorry."

"What's wrong?" he asked, puzzled.

"They offered me a new posting at my meeting this morning. They want me to join the research team on another project. Even promoted me."

"That's great, Kahlee!" he exclaimed, genuinely excited for her. "Where will you be stationed?"

She gave him a wan smile. "It's classified."

The smile on his face fell away. "Oh."

"Don't worry," she told him, trying to make light of the situation. "We're not studying anything illegal this time."

He didn't answer, trying to digest the situation.

"We can make this work," he declared suddenly.

"There's something special between us. We owe it to ourselves to give this a chance."

"With me on a top-secret project and you always out on patrol?" She shook her head. "We'd just be kidding ourselves."

Even though it hurt to admit it, he knew she was right.

"You're a good man, David," she said, trying to make the rejection less painful. "But even if I wasn't going away I don't think we could ever be more than just friends. The military's always going to come first in your life. We both know that."

He nodded, but couldn't bring himself to look her in the eye. "When are you shipping out?"

"Tonight," she said. "I need to go get ready. I just wanted the chance to see you one last time. To thank you for . . . for everything."

Kahlee stood up and brushed herself off, then leaned in and gave him a quick kiss on the cheek. "Good-bye, soldier."

He didn't watch her walk away, but instead stared out over the lake for a long, long time.

In the privacy of his small one-man craft, Saren had been studying the data on the flash drive inside Qian's metal case for hours. His suspicions had been correct: the alien technology was a vessel of some sort. It was called *Sovereign;* a magnificent relic from the time of the Prothean extinction; an enormous warship of tremendous power.

But it was much more than a mere ship. Its systems, processes, and technology were so advanced that they dwarfed every accomplishment of the Citadel species.

Its grandeur and complexity rivaled the greatest creations of the Protheans—the mass relays and the Citadel. It may have even surpassed them. And if Saren could learn and understand how it worked, he could seize all that power for himself.

He'd spent his entire life preparing for a moment like this. Everything he'd ever done—his military service, his career with the Spectres—was only a prelude to this revelation. Now he had found his true purpose; destiny had led him here.

How else to explain how perfectly everything had worked out for him? Anderson had been rejected by the Spectres. The Alliance had been politically humiliated. The Council was convinced the artifact didn't even exist. And the only men who could have exposed him were now dead.

Their deaths didn't come without a cost, however. Qian may have been losing his grip on reality, but just from looking at his notes it was obvious he was brilliant, a true genius. Saren understood the fundamental theories and principles of AI technology, but it was clear the human's research was far beyond anything he could ever hope to grasp. He'd need to find someone equally brilliant to head up the study of *Sovereign;* it might take him years to locate a suitable replacement.

But he didn't regret killing Qian. The doctor was in too deep. The notes on the flash drive showed a steady progression into dementia, a deteriorating mental state directly linked to incidents of exposure to *Sovereign.* There must have been some kind of field generated by the vessel; some kind of radiation or emission. Something that had destroyed and corrupted Qian's mind when he went to study it in person.

It had affected Edan, too, though the transformation was more subtle. The batarian had begun acting differently from the moment he first visited the site of the artifact: consorting with humans, risking the wrath of the Spectres. Edan probably hadn't even been aware of the changes, though looking back it was obvious to Saren.

He had to be careful. Avoid unnecessary exposure until he knew exactly what caused the mental deterioration. He'd work through intermediaries, like Edan's research team out near the Perseus Veil.

Saren planned to contact them soon enough. Cut off from all external communications they probably had no idea what had happened to their former employer. If they were willing to work for him once they found out—and if they had shown any progress in their research—he might not have to eliminate them. At least not until the inevitable alterations to their minds and personalities began to affect their work.

There was another problem to consider, as well. The ship was just beyond the borders of the Perseus Veil, right on the edges of geth space. Eventually he'd have to deal with them . . . though if everything went as planned, he might be able to use *Sovereign* to bend the geth to his purpose.

The dangers were great, but the potential rewards were worth the risk. He'd just be cautious. Patient. He'd move slowly. It might take years. Maybe decades. But the secrets of the alien vessel, all its power, would one day be his to command.

Once he unleashed that power, everything would

be forever changed. Never again would the turians be forced to bow before the will of the Council, as they had when they'd been commanded to make reparations for the First Contact War. At long last there would be a reckoning for the Alliance. Humanity would learn its place, along with every other species that paid homage to the Citadel.

And *Sovereign* was the key to it all.

<u>COYOTE</u>

Allen Steele

Embark on an incredible journey of courage, ambition and discovery.

Forty-six light years from Earth, six moons orbit a gas giant three times the mass of Jupiter. Each has been designated a name from the animal demigods of Native American mythology: Dog, Hawk, Eagle, Coyote, Snake and Goat.

Only the fourth moon, Coyote, is likely to sustain life. The crew setting out on Mankind's greatest adventure know that the success of the mission will depend on how well they adapt to their new home. There will be no going back.

But Coyote is also known as the trickster.

SHADOW WARRIOR

Chris Bunch

The epic space adventure trilogy in one blistering volume
from the master of military SF.

The Great War is over. The last pockets of resistance long
eliminated. For many, the alien Al'ar are now little more than
a memory. But there is one man who cannot forget: Joshua
Wolfe. Friend, prisoner, then betrayer and executioner of the
Al'ar. To humans he is a hero, a legend.

To the aliens he is the Shadow Warrior, master of the arts of
killing. And his story has only just begun . . .

THE VATTA'S WAR SERIES

Elizabeth Moon

An explosive military SF adventure

Kylara Vatta was a military cadet destined for great things, until
an act of kindness incurred the Academy's wrath and ended her
career. Instead of the expected disgrace, her trader family gave
her captaincy of a small ship, to sell for scrap. But in typical
flagrant disregard of others, she saw the opportunity to make a
profit and save the ship.

Several upgrades later, she is determined to retain her
independence in the cut-throat world of interplanetary trading.
But a complex political situation becomes increasingly
dangerous, and she becomes far more involved with the military
than she planned in her new career.

She must keep her wits, and trade on every bit of her hard-won
experience, or she – and her family – could
lose everything.

For high-octane action read:

TRADING IN DANGER
MOVING TARGET
ENGAGING THE ENEMY
COMMAND DECISION
VICTORY CONDITIONS

DARK SPACE

Book One of The Sentients of Orion

Marianne de Pierres

While drifting in space, lost, due to navigational failure, a mineral scout discovers an Entity so powerful and alien, it can only be described with one word: God.

On the arid mining planet of Araldis, Baronessa Mira Fedor finds herself on the run from the authorities, her life in tatters and her future stolen. Araldis itself buckles under the onslaught of a ruthlessly executed invasion.

None of this is coincidence. The more Mira discovers about her planet's elite and the forces arrayed against them, the more things seem to point to a single guiding intelligence: nothing that has happened to her or her world is an accident.

Mira Fedor has stumbled into a galaxy-sized intrigue. But will she live long enough to tell anyone . . . ?